A MONTH IN PROVENCE

GILLIAN HARVEY

Boldwood

First published in Great Britain in 2023 by Boldwood Books Ltd.

Copyright © Gillian Harvey, 2023

Cover Design by Alice Moore Design

Cover Photography: Shutterstock

A CIP catalogue record for this book is available from the British Library.

Paperback ISBN 978-1-80426-983-1

Large Print ISBN 978-1-80426-982-4

Hardback ISBN 978-1-80426-984-8

Ebook ISBN 978-1-80426-981-7

Kindle ISBN 978-1-80426-980-0

Audio CD ISBN 978-1-80426-989-3

MP3 CD ISBN 978-1-80426-988-6

Digital audio download ISBN 978-1-80426-986-2

Boldwood Books Ltd
23 Bowerdean Street
London SW6 3TN
www.boldwoodbooks.com

In memory of Katherine Harvey
1957–2023
A shining light

whatever it was worth, to turn this place around. And she hoped she hadn't bitten off more than she could chew.

Placing the phone on the table, she got up causing a creak from either her hip or the bed and walked to the antique chest of drawers where a tiny powder-blue kettle and a sweet porcelain cup and saucer had been placed on a tray for her use. A basket next to the cup contained individually wrapped spiced biscuits and a few pieces of dark chocolate, each foil clad square marked with what she assumed must be the name of a local patisserie. Maybe the owner wasn't so bad after all.

'Well, Steve,' she said to nobody as the kettle shuddered into life. 'I wonder what you'd make of all this.'

1

Nicky uncurled her hand and let the heavy bag fall to the floor, sending up a puff of dust. Her fingers were bruised from lugging it up the two flights of stairs. But she was here. She was actually *here*!

The euphoria of making it this far suddenly turned to fatigue and she sank down onto the bed, pulling out her mobile to let Jenny know she'd made it.

'Well, I'm in Provence!' she said, the moment Jenny answered.

'And?'

'And what?'

'And,' said her friend patiently. 'What is it like? Think you can work with it?'

Nicky could feel her breath, hot and sticky on the mouthpiece. She looked around the enormous room – the wood panels, scattered with knots, tiny holes; bold, floral wallpaper that had faded over the years; the webs of ancient spiders that formed ghostlike nets in the corners. A bluebottle banged itself repeatedly against the window and she walked over, mobile still clamped to her ear, and flung it wide.

After a few failed attempts, the fly managed to free itself, and soared off into the bright sky.

She imagined herself, too, embracing this opportunity – learning how to soar. *I could be just like you*, she thought to herself watching the black dot speed towards the horizon.

Had she seriously just adopted a bluebottle as her role model?

'I mean, yeah. Hopefully...' She ran her hand along the windowsill then regretted it. 'It's a beautiful house – although it definitely needs a dust.'

'Ah dust, schmust. Nothing that a flick over with a wet rag won't cure.'

'I'll take your word for it.'

'And four-poster beds though?'

'Yep.' Looking at the enormous bed and imagining herself sinking into it, Nicky felt a little out of place. 'Look, it's a big job. And I'm going to do my best. But... I hope I don't mess it up.'

'Don't be ridiculous.' Her friend barked out a laugh. 'Nicky, you are the most capable woman I know. Most people – well, they'd have fallen apart after... well, after everything that happened. But you worked your socks off to support those girls. And now look! You've got two daughters standing on their own two feet. Chloe has her own start-up for God's sake, and when she's not popping out adorable grandchildren, Amy runs bloody marathons in her spare time... I'm willing to bet there's nothing you can't do if you put your mind to it.'

'Nothing I can't do?'

'Nothing.'

'Except maybe the splits?' Nicky thought back to a rather intense yoga class they'd attended recently.

'Ah, the splits are overrated. Only really sought out by yoga teachers and perverted men on Tinder. So 1980s.'

'You're right,' Nicky said, feeling herself begin to smile. 'I've got this... at least... I think.'

'Well, I *know*!' There was a smile in Jenny's voice too. 'And I'm not just saying it. I wouldn't have suggested you if I didn't think you were up to the job. This is your second chance, Nicky. Your time to shine. And don't you think you've earned it?'

'Thanks.' Nicky smiled. 'Well, I guess we'll both have to hope you're right.' After hanging up, she studied her faint reflection in the small window; the ghost of her head and torso superimposed over the French countryside, with its patchwork of greens, browns and in the distance – a riot of sunflower yellow. Yesterday, St Albans Today, Provence. Tomorrow, the world, she thought to herself.

Maybe, just maybe, this was going to be brilliant.

She was itching to see the rest of the place, figure out exactl what she'd let herself in for, but frustratingly the owner, Rober hadn't been here to welcome her when she'd arrived. Instead, neighbour brandishing a key had opened up for her and given h directions to her room. 'Monsieur Robert, he says 'e is sorry,' th elderly neighbour had told her sadly, 'but 'e will be 'ere soon, huh

It wasn't quite the welcome she'd expected. 'I bet,' she'd said herself, dragging her suitcase up two wooden flights of sta towards the attic, 'Alex Polizzi doesn't have to deal with this sort thing.'

When she'd first stepped into the stone building she'd o previously viewed on screen, Nicky had felt a little wobble. T B&B was described on the information sheet she'd been given a 'beautiful *chambre d'hôte* in the heart of sun-drenched Proven And perhaps once it had been. But clearly the description had b penned by someone with poor eyesight, or had been copied fro brochure written a decade ago.

She'd have to use all her long-dormant design prowess,

2

When Jenny had phoned her two weeks ago to arrange a coffee and cake meet-up, Nicky hadn't expected anything more than a caffeine hit and an hour's conversation about Jenny's husband, Jacob and his apparent inability to either put the toilet seat down or hit the target when using it.

But she'd known, almost as soon as she'd arrived, that something was up. First of all, because the habitually late Jenny had arrived before her. And secondly because she had hardly been able to see her friend behind the two enormous cream-topped hot chocolates and pile of muffins she'd garnished the table with.

'What's up?' she asked warily, eyeing the goodies stacked between them.

'I need to ask you an enormous favour,' Jenny said, flicking her blonde hair over her shoulder. As always, her hair obediently settled against her back as smoothly as if it had been trained.

'Oh God – what have you done now?' Nicky pulled up a chair and fixed her friend with a mock stare as she gathered her own, messier, red hair into a ponytail. 'No, don't tell me. You've dented

Jacob's precious MG? No, wait, you've joined some sort of cult and need me to break you out of it?'

'What makes you assume I've done anything?' Jenny replied, coquettishly, batting her eyelashes.

Nicky gave her a look. 'The eyelashes don't work on me, remember?' she said.

'Oh yes, I forgot. You've raised two girls,' Jenny joked. 'But anyway, this time, for once, you're wrong. Perhaps I shouldn't have called it a favour. Let's rephrase. I would like to offer you the opportunity of a lifetime.'

'Why does that make me feel even more nervous?' Nicky asked, with a grin, pulling a chunk off one of the muffins and popping it into her mouth.

Jenny smiled. 'It's actually... Well, it's quite exciting really.'

'Go on...' Nicky leaned forward, her hand resting on the handle of her cup.

'Well, you know the project I'm working on right now...'

'You mean, the *Save Me I've Bought a Business on The Continent and I Have No Idea What to Do With it Show*?'

'I think you'll find it's called *The Great B&B Rescue*,' her friend had corrected, with mock-hurt. 'Much more catchy, don't you think?'

'Ah yes, the show where you're transforming Brit-run B&Bs across Europe.'

'Well, just in France for starters. But if the format works – sky's the limit.'

'Hmm... well. Let's just say,' Nicky said, spooning some cream into her mouth, 'that you *might* have mentioned it, oh, once or twice.'

The show was to be – as Jenny had put it herself – the pinnacle of her career. Ten failing hotels sprinkled across France would be given a complete makeover by business experts.

her upper lip and wiped it away. 'I've got no experience. Nobody knows who I am... I've never... I've... I've...'

'No, listen. Hear me out. It's being presented by the gorgeous Ryan Camberwell, and there's loads of different properties featured. All with different experts. Some well-known, some... well, less well-known. You'd get assigned a property and your job would just be to go over, turn your nose up at the carpets, advise them to charge more and cut costs, that sort of thing. You'd get a budget to make some decorative changes – spruce it all up. Help them to get things back off the ground.'

'But...'

'It's your dream job!'

'Well, maybe once. But you know... I haven't...' She trailed off. Jenny knew only too well how her aspirations had changed and why.

Jenny leaned forward, her eyes suddenly earnest. 'Exactly! It's the kind of opportunity you used to dream of.'

'Well,' Nicky said, feeling sweat prickle across her forehead. 'Well, yes. But...'

'And don't give me any rubbish about being too old,' Jenny added, making a face. 'You're hardly the typical grandmother.'

'I wasn't,' Nicky said, 'going to say anything about being old.' She was, in any case, at forty-nine, only two years older than Jenny, despite having recently welcomed her first grandbaby.

'Good. Didn't think you were ready for the beige mac and trolley combo.'

'No.'

'Or curlers.'

'I do actually,' Nicky grinned, 'have some curlers. But think more Instagram influencer than blue rinse silver surfer.'

'Glad to hear it.'

'But, I mean, the internet is packed with design gurus and business experts – why not one of them?'

'Come on,' Jenny said, rolling her eyes. 'Yes, I could have found someone on social media. And you know, they would have something you haven't.'

'Exactly.' Although she'd been saying it herself, Nicky felt a little pang of disappointment at hearing her failings repeated back to her. 'Experience. Acumen.'

'No. *Self-belief*. Bloody hell, girl, you've got a degree in interior design and business experience in spades. I'm not taking no for an answer. People are *full* of hot air these days online. They talk themselves into a CEO job with three GCSEs and a handful of magic beans. But they don't have the goods. They just talk the talk. But you...'

'Me?'

'Yes! Girl, if I hadn't had you to help me with my new kitchen, I'd have ended up with those ghastly laminate cupboards I was obsessed with at the time.'

'Well, yeah. Maybe...'

'No doubt about it, honey. Come on, where's that budding interior designer spirit?'

'I think those dreams were abandoned a decade ago,' Nicky said, thinking about the folder stuffed with vision boards up in the attic. The faded dreams. 'My budding days are over. More of a dead-head situation here.'

'Ah, don't be daft,' Jenny said. 'You've been on pause is all. Anyway, dead-heading makes way for new growth, so my green-fingered friends tell me.'

Nicky snorted. 'Come on, really?'

'Just add a drop of fertiliser and – poof!'

'And the fertiliser is...?'

'You're looking at her!' Jenny said triumphantly.

It was hard not to laugh. 'You've literally just likened yourself to horse shit,' Nicky said. 'You must really want me for this job.'

'Of course I do.'

'But my skills – what's left of them. I'm not sure they'll cut the mustard.'

'Honey,' her friend said. 'You are the real deal. Cut the mustard? You *are* the mustard.'

'I am?'

'You are.'

'And that's... good?! I mean, mustard? Is that really... something to aspire to?'

'Yes! Just think of it! Get this right and you could become the next Laurence Llewelyn-Bowen.'

'Not sure that's a compliment?'

'OK, well someone sexier then. St Albans's answer to Kelly Hoppen. Less beard and more killer heels.'

They laughed. Nicky took a sip of hot chocolate to buy a moment's thinking time. 'So,' she said at last. 'If I do this favour...'

'You mean, take this opportunity.'

'OK, yes *opportunity*. Say I take it. When does it start? How long do I have to prepare?' She'd need to do some research, watch old property selling shows, generate some idea of what she should be doing.

Jenny seemed suddenly interested in the icing on one of the muffins. 'Just... well, it actually starts in a couple of days.'

'What? A couple of days? Are you actually *mad*? I have a job... a...'

'I know.' Jenny's hand crept across the table like a jewelled assassin and clasped Nicky's firmly. 'But I need someone I trust... someone I know has the goods... a friend.' Her eyes, blue and kohl-edged, stared into Nicky's.

'I don't...'

'And you know, I also thought, well, it's about bloody time you did something for *you*,' her friend added, in a more forthright tone.

'What?'

'Well, you've been amazing. I mean, seriously amazing. If I had my way, we'd make a documentary all about you and how strong you've been since Steve. I mean, I'd have lost the plot entirely! You? You're a total inspiration!'

'Thanks. I think...?'

'But don't you think it's your turn now?'

Nicky sighed. 'Look, it does sound amazing,' she said, lifting her slightly cooled hot chocolate and taking a sip. But two days – I just can't... and how long for?'

'A month.'

'A month! Well, then. I can't just let my employer down like...'

'I've already sorted that,' Jenny interrupted excitedly.

'What?'

Jenny's smile faded a little. 'Well, I spoke to your boss... we'd pay for a temp, of course. You're only part-time so it's quite afford-able. And...' Jenny's voice trailed off under Nicky's gaze.

'Pretty presumptuous of you.' She raised an eyebrow.

'You know me! Never one for holding back. And you know, you deserve this, Nicky, you really do.'

They looked at each other for a moment.

'What if I mess it up entirely?' Nicky said quietly.

'You won't.'

'What if I get camera shy and can't say anything?'

'You won't. Anyway, Ryan Camberwell is hosting, he'll pep you up.'

Nicky paused, cup resting against her bottom lip. What *did* she have to lose? Her job would be waiting when she got back. She'd probably be able to handle giving a little advice to a small business. The cameras would be... well, it would take some getting used to.

But Jenny was right – before Steve... she'd had dreams. Maybe not of TV stardom, but certainly of success. Instead, she'd watched as her best friend had risen the ranks in various TV companies, and she'd raised the girls alone on part-time wages. And it had been fine. It had been the Right Thing to do. But maybe it was time to try something else.

'OK... I'll do it!' She'd found it hard to believe the words had come out of her mouth.

'Yes!' Jenny had said, triumphantly peeling the paper case off her second muffin. 'And thank God.'

'Thank God?'

'Yep. Because I already told them you'd agreed.'

3

When he turned around at the top of the aisle and they locked eyes, they both had to fight the giggles. It had seemed ridiculous – her in a white dress, him in a suit his dad had forced him to hire. If it had been up to them, they'd have had a quick wedding in the town hall, a pub lunch to follow. But once Steve's mum had got involved, there were no holds barred. 'If you're going to do it,' she'd said. 'You're doing it right.'

And in Steve's mum's eyes, doing it right had meant the whole kaboodle. Church, dress, bridesmaids, flowers, confetti, photos and a slap-up 'breakfast' in a posh hotel.

They'd only been twenty-four – babies really. But they'd known. They'd known from the word go.

Nicky shook her head and tried to get her mind back to the present. Sipping her coffee, she was just wondering whether it would be OK for her to explore the seemingly empty building or whether she ought to stay holed up in her room until the owner decided to make an appearance, when the front door slammed. She jumped: a splash of black coffee landing squarely in the middle of her white top and scalding her in the process.

'Shit,' she said, getting to her feet and grabbing the nearest item – a pair of knickers from her open case – and dabbing at the hot stain.

Before she had time to react further or change, footsteps thundered up the stairs and there was a knock on the door. She opened it tentatively to find a dark-haired man dressed in a pair of khaki trousers and an old Def Leppard T-shirt. He fixed his brown eyes on her but his expression was hard to read.

'Nicky?' he asked, holding out a hand for a shake. His mouth twitched slightly, but didn't quite form a smile.

'That's me,' she replied, putting out her hand instinctively, before realising she was brandishing her underwear at him. She quickly threw the lingerie on the bed then shook his hand. 'And you're Robert?' she asked, her face feeling hot.

'Yes,' he said, his eyes looking over her shoulder at the slightly damp pair of lacy knickers she'd sent flying across the room. His brow furrowed.

'Oh,' she said. 'That was... I was just... they're wet. I mean, not with... it was coffee I spilled.' She gestured to her blouse and the enormous brown stain that had developed there. She gave a little, nervous laugh.

'Yes, of course,' he said, nodding as if it was customary to spill a drink and mop it up with knickers on arrival at a French *Chambre d'Hôte*. His face remained impassive, despite the laugh. A dog that looked like a lab cross with black and white fur appeared at his side, tongue lolling and gave a single bark. Robert grabbed his collar. 'Buster,' he said, 'not now!' He rubbed the dog's head affectionately.

'Don't worry,' Nicky said. 'These things happen.'

'Sorry?' he said, confused. 'You mean dogs barking?'

'No! Being late. These things happen.'

'Oh. Right.'

She was about to add that she was a human disaster zone herself, then remembered why she was here and stopped herself just in time. In this manifestation of her life she was Nicky Green – Transformation Guru.

'Anyway, look,' he continued, 'how about I make a proper cup of coffee downstairs. Then I'll give you the tour. See what you make of the place?'

'Sounds good,' she said. 'I'll just...' She gestured to her blouse.

He nodded and turned towards the stairs, Buster trotting obediently at his heels.

She shut the door and pulled off her blouse, laying it over a chair to be washed later. Then she grabbed a blue T-shirt out of her case and pulled it over her head. She took a quick look in the mirror: shoulder-length red hair pulled into a messy ponytail, her favourite jeans – she'd do. Then she left the room and made her way down the stairs, trying to find exactly where he'd disappeared to.

The building was three storeys high, her room in part of a converted attic. Despite the fact it was a little down-at-heel, it retained a kind of faded grandeur – plaster mouldings, ceiling roses, the kind of wallpaper that had probably been expensive in its day. She could definitely see its charms. At least its potential charms.

On the way down, she passed several doors marked with the words *Chambre* as well as one marked *Privé* with its door slightly ajar. She had to resist the urge to peep inside – presumably this was Robert's room. The hallways were light and bright, despite their slightly dated appearance and she supposed the right customer might describe the look as 'shabby chic' or 'rustic charm'.

She paused at the end of the corridor at a large window which looked out over the back of the property. There was a small terrace with a table, bathed in sunlight, and – beyond – a garden that, despite being overgrown and with walled-in mismatched stone, was somehow charming. Beyond that there was a small road, followed by open countryside and, just as the top of the uppermost field met the horizon, a collection of buildings nestling together to form another small village.

The road outside was quiet and she could hear sounds usually drowned out by the drone of human life – birds calling to one another, a rustle in the hedgerows. She pushed the window open a little and felt a swell of warm, fresh air enter through the gap. Breathing deeply, she tried to centre herself, banish her nerves. She was here, she was doing it. She was capable.

Then suddenly there was a flutter of wings and a pigeon, seemingly out of nowhere, shot through the open gap and flapped noisily past her head.

'Shit,' she said. 'Come on, little... um pigeon.'

But the pigeon was having some sort of avian panic attack. It flew up to the high ceiling, bumping against the fan, which thankfully wasn't on, then shot off into one of the rooms. The room marked *Privé*.

She took a step towards the slightly open doorway, then paused. What exactly was she going to do when she got there? The idea of a panicking bird flapping around her head was terrifying. There was no way she'd be able to catch it.

Besides, she told herself, the room was private. Strictly speaking, she shouldn't go in there. As she watched it, the open door moved gently as if in a breeze. Robert must have his window open. That decided it. The bird could find its way out from there.

Instead of entering into a game of catch-the-pigeon, she gently pulled the *Privé* door closed and made her way down the second flight of stairs to the ground floor where, by process of elimination she finally opened the door on a sizeable kitchen with a tiled floor, two mismatched dressers and a square pine table with a plant at its centre.

Robert was there, pushing the plunger on a coffee pot. He turned as she entered and gave a brief upward inflection of his lips which may have been intended to be a smile. There was something awkward, almost forced about it. 'Hope you like it strong,' he said, bringing the cafetière to the table. 'Take a seat.' His accent was strange, a soft northern undertone with what sounded like a French overlay – a hybrid of his past and present.

She obediently sat and he delivered a cup of coffee and a bowl of sugar lumps with tongs. Then he sat opposite her with a glass of water and looked at her silently.

'There's a...' she began, then felt embarrassed. Perhaps it would be better not to tell him about the pigeon just now. He might think she'd been looking into his room if she mentioned it, which wouldn't necessarily get them off to a good start. 'Um, I mean, lovely place,' she said instead, trying to smile.

'Yes, thank you,' he said. 'Look, I realise it's not in the best state. I've let things go a little bit over the past few years... Personal circumstances. That sort of thing.' He cleared his throat as if there was more to say.

She waited, but he didn't elaborate. Silence began to fill the empty space around them until it felt almost oppressive.

'Well,' she said, 'that's why I'm here! You know, to help you bring things up to speed.'

He nodded. Then, 'Oh, did you want some milk?' he said, noticing her grimace as she sipped her black coffee. Under the table, Buster, who'd been curled up, stood abruptly and began to sniff at her shoes.

'Yes please,' she said, reaching and patting the dog's head.

Robert jumped up and went to the fridge, bringing out a small carton. 'Sorry. I'm not great at hosting.' Behind him, she could see the contents of his fridge. Two small cartons of soup, another pint of milk and a butter dish. A tin of dog food with a fork in it. He caught her eye and she looked away, embarrassed.

'Not great at hosting?' she said. 'Aren't you running a B&B?' The words had escaped from her mouth before she'd had a chance to think them through and she felt herself begin to blush. 'I mean...'

He reddened. 'I suppose... I haven't really been at – um – capacity yet,' he admitted. 'I have a few guests in the summer, but off-season, well, I guess this place isn't people's first choice. Tripadvisor reviews have been a bit... brutal.'

'Sorry to hear that.' She'd had a quick look at TripAdvisor before coming over and seen his two-star average. But it seemed mean to admit she already knew.

He shrugged. 'Well, they mostly have a point. I'm a bit out of my depth with all this.'

'You do it all alone?'

'Well, yeah. For the most part. I have a cleaner in the summer, you know, when it gets busier. But otherwise... yes. I mean, I'd never cope in the UK, doing the full-English, that sort of thing. But it's croissants and cereal here, so...'

'Wow. Big job though.' She could see, now, why he needed some help. She wanted to ask what had possessed him to take on such an enormous task on his own, but it felt too personal, for now at least.

She sipped her coffee; it was well brewed and delicious. A silence fell over them which once again began to take on an awkward edge. She wracked her brain for something to say.

'So,' she said at last. 'Four guest rooms, the paperwork said?'

He straightened: 'Oh, yes. I understand. You're here to work, not socialise.'

This was socialising? 'No, it's fine, I was just...' she began. She wasn't quite sure how to say that she'd just been desperately filling the uncomfortable silence, not prompting him to get to work.

'Well, I'll give you the tour!' he said, nodding and getting to his feet.

'No rush...' she started to say, but he was already striding from the kitchen. She scurried in his wake, carefully carrying her coffee with her.

She caught up with him in the corridor where he stopped abruptly and pushed open a door to his left. Following him, she stepped into the room and gasped.

The dining room was enormous – a large rectangular space with exposed stone walls and a wooden beamed ceiling. The floor was laid with what must have been the original parquet – faded and slightly worn, but still beautiful. Four breakfast tables – each designed to seat four – were arranged in the centre, each in a different design, with mismatched chairs and, on one, a pot of wilting flowers.

The windows were adorned with enormous curtains which – even when flung open as they were now – blocked the edges of the glass, giving the room a feeling of being somehow underground despite the glimpse of field she could see when she focused on the gap at their centre.

It looked like a room that had been hastily thrown together – nothing matched, nothing was quite finished or in any way refined. A room that, with time and money, could be beautiful, but which was bowing to time and neglect.

'Oh,' she said.

'Yes.' He nodded.

'It's...'

'I know. It needs some work,' he said; he ran a hand through his hair and looked slightly pained. 'I just—'

'No.' She put a hand on his arm to stop him. 'I mean, it's beautiful. Or at least, it could be beautiful.' He looked at her hand on his arm, and she withdrew it. 'Sorry,' she said.

'Well, glad you think so.'

'Well, yes. But I mean, it needs...' she waved her hands around slightly as she looked for the right word, 'sprucing up?' *Sprucing up? Who was she? Her dad splashing on the Brut in readiness for a night out?*

'Yes. Yes. You know, we did have plans when we moved in,' he said, slightly defensively. 'But...' He trailed off, seemingly unable or unwilling to fill in the gaps.

'Sure,' she said. 'When was that by the way?'

'About twelve years ago.' He blushed.

Buster trotted through the open doorway and sniffed Robert's leg interestedly. He reached and patted the dog's head. 'That's right, Buster,' he said, in what seemed like a completely different voice – its sharpness and hard corners removed. 'We're doing a tour.'

'Twelve years?' She made a face, then regretted it. She wasn't here to judge him after all. Only it seemed like an awfully long time to let things crumble around you. Especially if you move with the intention of creating a decent business.

'Yes.' He sighed. 'But I suppose life had other plans. And now. Well, it's as you see. Not in the best condition.'

'You say, "we"?'

'Yes, Marie. My wife,' he said shortly. He walked over to one of the tables and began to adjust the tablecloth. 'We had all these plans – renovation, putting in a pool. We saved up for ages. Sold our old house in England. Bought this.'

'But she's not...?' Nicky pressed, although really it was none of her business she supposed. It was hard, though, to place him. His manner was confusing – one minute fairly friendly, the next brusque. Comments that could be jokes, but not accompanied by a smile. She wondered what on earth she'd got herself into.

'No, she's not part of the picture any more.' He made a face – a kind of downward inflection of distaste. 'I probably should have sold it. Not really my thing. Not my... skill set. But I don't know. I suppose I've become fond of the place in a way. And you know – it seems wrong to quit.' His gaze wandered to the window and he seemed to fix his eyes on something in the street. She turned her head but couldn't see anything.

'Oh.'

'I mean. It's OK. I do get guests. But I suppose some might say it's not successful,' he said, clearing his throat again. It seemed like a kind of awkward habit, rather than a result of a health problem and she wondered whether he was as unsure about what they were doing as she was. 'I do a bit of this and that to make ends meet. Handyman stuff.'

'Oh.' She looked at him anxiously, hoping any changes they made would make enough difference. She was a business advisor with a penchant for design, not a magician.

'Yeah, so I guess... well, then I saw the ad for the programme and a friend convinced me to apply. I'd been telling them how... well, if things don't improve, it might be curtains for this place. And they'd seen an ad for volunteers... Stupid really.'

She looked at the dining room, a sinking feeling in her stomach.

'I don't use the room myself,' he added, unnecessarily. 'Just eat in the kitchen. Hopefully you'll be OK to do that while you're here?'

'Of course,' she said.

'And you know, just help yourself to food, drink, whatever. It's going to be a month, so treat it like your own home.'

'Thanks,' she said, thinking of the open can of dog food and meagre fridge contents. For starters, it sounded like she'd need to do some shopping. Her dream of having meals cooked for her or being treated like a paying guest vanished, and a feeling of dread began to creep over her as she considered the month ahead. If all the rooms were in similar disrepair, if he didn't have any capital; if there were no staff and reviews were terrible, she'd have her work cut out. And he wasn't very saleable as a person either. He seemed to be one of these people who created an atmosphere around them, as if their emotions seeped out of their skin and infected everyone else in close proximity. For someone who'd been invited, she hadn't felt very welcome so far.

'I hope you're not regretting coming here?' he said, looking at her pointedly. 'Because they did say that they wanted properties that were a challenge.'

She looked around the room. It had so much potential. But when it came to Robert, as a host, she wasn't so sure. He'd mentioned terrible Tripadvisor reviews. He clearly wasn't a natural at small talk. He was friendly enough, but it was as if on some level he resented her presence, despite the fact she was here to help.

'Of course I'm not,' she said, not knowing how else to answer.

'Right,' he said, starting up the stairs. 'I'll show you the rest of the rooms.'

'Great.'

'This one's mine at the moment,' he said as they reached the top and curved into the corridor. 'But I'm thinking it might be better to convert it into a guest room – you know, move up to the attic to make more sense of the space?'

'Oh, I mean if you've got your things in there, I don't have to see it right now...' she said, noting that it was the door marked Privé – the pigeon room as it would henceforth be known.

'It's OK, I think it's important to see the whole of it,' he said. 'Today the rooms, tomorrow the books. To get a full measure of it.' He smiled, properly for the first time and she sensed he was starting to relax.

'But maybe we should start...' she began, desperate to prevent the disaster she knew was coming.

'We're here now,' he said. 'Don't worry, there aren't any nasty surprises,' he added, with a touch of self-deprecating humour.

Then he pushed open the door, only to be greeted by a rush of squawking, feathered terror as the pigeon, desperate for freedom, flew directly into his face.

4

She was running towards it again, the orange of the lamp post light, ice sparkling like frosting in the beams of headlights. Everything familiar down to the feeling of dread that tensed in her stomach; her own car door left open behind her, the car parked haphazardly on the hard shoulder. The blue lights reflecting on the damp tarmac, her breath misting in the air. The man being carried on a stretcher; one of his shoes achingly familiar.

Then to the emergency room, where the machines whirred and beeped and staff ran frantically; where people walked too slowly in front of her and curtains hid him from her view. Until she was next to him and could see for herself that he was OK. His face, unmarked. Eyes gently closed. Oxygen pumping from a machine. His body gowned into anonymity – like an actor in a hospital drama. The flood of relief as she pushed his hair back from his forehead – as she had a thousand times before.

Then the little room, the doctor's face as she sat down. That pathetic box of tissues nudged closer. And then she was screaming; screaming; screaming.

* * *

She sat up abruptly in bed in the cool, early-morning air, gasping for breath. The silence was stifling, and she sensed that at least one of her screams had been out loud.

When had she last dreamed of the crash? It must have been at least a year ago. She'd thought, perhaps, she was done. Yet here she was, five hundred miles from home, ten years away in time and the moment that had shaken her world was back with her.

She got up, her skin sticky in the cold air, and pulled her T-shirt over her head before reaching into her case and finding some fresh clothes. She already knew that staying in bed after one of the nightmares was pointless; she'd simply fall into a fitful unrefreshing sleep, or lie there letting the renewed grief crowd her.

She'd learned over the decade since Steve's death, that action was best. That getting her mind focused on something else was the way forward. That she'd never delete the terrible events of that day, but she could overwrite them. She pulled back the curtains and opened the window. Wooden shutters covered the glass, but splits and gaps in the wood let enough grey light in to reassure her that it was nearly morning.

She thought about Steve. How, after a decade, could her body still miss the reassurance of his arms around her? The familiar loneliness she always felt after a dream began to take hold. For a moment, everything she'd built had been removed; her grief newly exposed. She breathed. It was a lifetime ago. It was yesterday. He was still here. He was gone.

She picked up the fat notebook she'd left on the dresser last night and opened it up, trying to still her mind and focus on the day ahead. She'd be taking another tour of the house then going through Robert's books today, seeing exactly how bad things were. She'd already written a list of improvements that could be made, but they weren't meant to start anything in earnest until the initial filming session had taken place.

Last week, Robert had had a couple of visitors, arranged by the show to pass judgement on the place and his hosting skills on camera. They'd be given an edited version of the footage to react to when the first session took place. She'd add to her notes then. When she'd asked him how it had gone, he'd shrugged, which hadn't exactly filled her with hope.

She tried to forget about the cameras and Jenny, to just approach it as she would if a friend had asked for help. To tap into her long-dormant design skills. She thought again of the plans she'd abandoned – the dreams she'd had about being a professional interior designer. The folder stuffed with vision boards. This had been everything she'd wanted once. And perhaps it wasn't too late.

She wrote a list of people she'd need to contact:

1. Cleaners – deep clean?
2. Glaziers for broken window
3. Decorator – strip wallpaper/paint
4. Ask patisserie for deal on croissants
5. See if local restaurants want to collaborate
6. Local soft-furnishing stores?
7. Buy chalk paint

As she wrote down scribbled notes next to numbers, she felt this morning's nightmare fade away, and the memory was soon back in her subconscious as she focused on the day ahead.

An hour later, she made her way down to the kitchen to see if there was something to eat. The day was only just coming into itself and a gentle mist was rising from the distant forest at the edge of the horizon. The sun was shining, but its benefit could not fully be felt. Looking out of the window as she filled the kettle, she was surprised to see Robert, sitting on the wooden bench outside, reading a well-worn paperback, Buster curled at his feet. His expression was unguarded and as his eyes ran over a page he gave a small smile and shake of the head. The smile transformed his face; made him look younger, less careworn. Then he turned the page and his expression returned to neutral.

She tapped lightly on the window and, as he turned, waved at him, grimacing slightly as she saw the scratch marks on his face from yesterday's encounter. Once they'd applied some antiseptic to his scratches and cleared his room and the hallway of feathers and bird poo, she'd been unable to admit it was her who'd shut the pigeon in his room. Meaning he'd spent a great deal of time after they'd managed to guide it out of the window with a flapping blanket, trying to work out how it had got in through a window that he'd remembered closing and into a room whose door had been shut.

'You don't think,' he'd said at one point, 'it came down the chimney?'

She gestured at him now with the kettle and he shook his head, indicating his cup was still full.

Once her coffee was made, she stepped out onto the terrace and took a seat at the table, placing the notebook in front of her.

'Hard at work already?' Robert said, nodding towards it.

'Something like that.' She smiled. 'I mean, nothing much. Just a few notes. Ideas.'

He shook his head. 'I've never been that business minded, really,' he said, apologetically. 'I mean, I was on board for the move to France, running a B&B. But perhaps I didn't think it through properly.' He set his book on the table, face down, his long, neat fingers resting on the spine for a moment.

She nodded; she could appreciate that.

'Good book?' she asked.

He looked at it, as if becoming aware of the novel for the first time. She saw to her surprise that he was reading *Pride and Prejudice*.

'It's... yes,' he said, shortly.

'Austen fan?'

He shrugged. 'Sometimes.'

She nodded. It was breakfast time and she was already running out of things to say. This did not bode well.

He cleared his throat again. 'I suppose you just think that it's going to be easy. But when you're doing it on your own... Well, front of house. The washing and cleaning. The stress. I'm not what you'd call a natural,' he said, making brief eye contact then turning his face away.

'Yes, I can see that,' she said, blowing steam from her coffee and breathing in its rich, earthy smell. Then: 'Sorry, that was rude. I just meant...'

'It's fine,' he said. 'I mean, I used to... it used to come more naturally. But...'

There was a silence for a moment and the air settled around them again. In the distance, Nicky could hear a clock chiming seven. Traffic rumbled on a distant road. Somewhere a dog barked.

'Do you mind me asking,' she said at last, 'why you keep at it?'

He looked at her. 'That's a rather personal question,' he said, an eyebrow raised.

'I mean, you don't have to...'

But he sighed, his shoulders softening and held out his hands in a gesture of surrender. 'I'm not honestly sure. I suppose I must like it, underneath it all. Or aspects of it.' He shrugged a shoulder.

She nodded.

'I was a teacher in the UK,' he said. 'Maths. Rather stressful. Not sure if I'd want to go back to that.'

'I can imagine,' she said. 'I mean, all those teenagers with compasses. Could be dangerous.'

He looked at her for a moment, his brow furrowed. Then relaxed. 'Ha. Yeah.'

She wanted to ask why it was that Marie – whose dream he'd said it had been – had evidently been the one to walk away when their marriage had fallen apart. She wondered why he hadn't been the one to leave the business in her hands. But she opened her mouth and found she couldn't quite bring herself to ask. If he'd thought her question about why he ran the business was too personal, then this would surely be another step too far.

'So,' she said, instead. 'How are the scratches?'

'Scratches?'

'Yes – from the pigeon. Still sore?'

'I'll live,' he said, shortly.

'Yes. well let's hope,' she said.

'Besides, it's the business we're trying to renovate, not my wizened old face.'

She laughed, then looked at his expression, which remained serious. Had he been joking? Or fishing for compliments? Or did he really think that his tanned, smooth skin was wizened? 'You've got a great face!' she said. Then blushed at her own words.

'Um... thanks,' he replied awkwardly.

'I mean, it's not wizened...' she added.

'Right.'

'I don't mean to say,' she said, 'that you have no wrinkles at all. I mean time waits for no man and all that! But I wouldn't say wizened. You're... I mean, around the eyes there's... but we've all...' She trailed off feeling his eyes on her.

'So lightly wrinkled then?' he said, which sounded like a joke. But his face remained impassive and she wasn't sure.

Her skin felt as if it was on fire.

'Ha,' she said. 'Anyway, I must just...' And she got up hurriedly, indicating her half-empty coffee mug, and disappeared into the house before she could embarrass herself further.

Walking up the stairs afterwards, she had a sudden flash of a memory pierce her mind. That glove she'd seen by the rubber tyre marks. One of the girls' gloves – pink and sparkly, with a stitched-on koala. And she'd thought, looking at it, *thank God it wasn't them.* Thank God the girls were back at home, tucked up in bed, with Pam from next door sitting in the living room, a coat pulled over her pyjamas. *Thank God it had only been Steve.* She'd felt guilty about that later.

'Are you OK?' came a voice from below. Robert was looking up at her, his face full of concern. 'You seem to have... well, paused.'

'I'm fine,' she said. 'Just... thinking for a moment.' She let out a breath, steadied herself and focused on getting up the stairs to her bedroom. The feeling would pass. It always did.

When she reached her room she could hear a strange buzzing sound which got louder as she opened the door. It was her phone, set to vibrate, wobbling on the top of the chest of drawers, its screen lit with Jenny's name. She quickly raced to it and picked it up.

'Hey, Jenny,' she said, feeling the last of her anxiety seep away at the familiarity of her friend's voice.

'Hey yourself. Good sleep?'

'Yes, pretty good.' Nicky smiled.

'How's that Robert bloke?'

'I'm not sure,' she said, frowning. 'He seems OK. A bit... well, offish, if that's even a word.'

'Not the gregarious host then?'

'No. If anything, I feel as if I'm a bit of a nuisance.'

'Good looking?'

'Jenny!' she said, surprised to feel herself blush. 'I mean, I hadn't thought...'

'So, yes, then,' her friend said, a smile in her voice.

'Well, I suppose. I mean, he's obviously... he spends a bit of time in the sun. So quite tanned. Nice eyes... I guess.'

'You guess?'

'Anyway, I'm not here to give him a makeover. It's the B&B I'm interested in.'

'OK, if you're sure...'

'Anyway, even if he *is* fit. He's either socially awkward or... well, a bit rude, to be honest.'

'Oh. Well, he's probably just nervous. I expect he'll warm up once he gets to know you. It can be weird, you know, having a TV star in the house.'

'I am not,' Nicky said, 'a TV star.'

'Ah, but he doesn't know that, does he!' Jenny replied. 'He's probably in awe.'

'Not sure if that's what it is. But I'll take it.' Nicky felt her face relax into a smile. Things never seemed so bad when she spoke to Jenny.

'Plus, it's not all bad, I'm sure. Lounging around on a four-poster in Provence. How the other half live, eh!'

'Well, you know. I do like my luxuries,' she joked. 'Anyway, what's up?'

'What do you mean? Can't I just ring my bestie to see how it's all going?' Jenny's voice took on a mock-hurt tone.

'At eight o'clock in the morning your time,' she said, checking the time. 'No offence but, it's not your usual style.'

There was a silence. Then, 'Yep, you got me,' Jenny said, her voice slightly more serious.

'So? What's up?' Nicky sat on the bed and lifted her legs up, shuffling her body until she leaned against the headboard. From here, she could see the view through the window, a clear blue sky underlined with green fields.

'Now, I don't want you to panic...'

'Jen!'

'What?'

'If you don't want someone to panic, the LAST thing you should do is tell them not to panic,' she said, half exasperated, half-amused.

'Sorry. Bad choice of words. Look, it's nothing. It's just schedule stuff. Boring really.'

'Schedule?'

'Yes. And. Well, and budget. Nothing much. Just boring admin, if anything.'

A beat.

'Jenny?'

Nicky felt a sense of rising panic at her friend's silence. She stood up abruptly, unable to relax.

'Yes?'

'What exactly are you calling to tell me?' She walked to the window and looked out at the pattern of greens and the streak of clear blue at their peak.

'Well,' Jenny said. 'There's been a bit of a hiccup. I mean, it's quite normal for TV stuff. You know. I'm always complaining to you about how things change around and...'

'Jenny?'

'OK, OK. Short answer. Filming actually starts tomorrow.'

'You... what?' Nicky felt the kind of lurch that only usually happens when you're in an ascending plane. 'Tomorrow? Filming?'

'Yes.'

'Here? *Me*?'

'Well, yes. You, the bloke, the house, watching the footage, that kind of thing. Don't worry, it's all the 'before' stuff – nobody expects you to have done anything!'

'Jenny! I mean, I've got nothing to say. Nothing planned. I don't even have... I was going to get something to wear. I thought I had more time... I—'

'Now,' interrupted Jenny, in the kind of forthright tone that reminded Nicky a little of the headteacher from the girls' secondary school. No-nonsense and pretty intimidating too when she wanted to be. 'Calm down. They aren't expecting *anything*. They're going to ask you for your initial thoughts – not what you're going to do. Not yet. And you'll watch the footage with Robert and they'll film your reaction.'

'Right.' Nicky tried to steady her breathing. 'Still, is there no way we can...'

'Sorry, chick. It's all planned out.'

'Oh God.'

'I really don't get much say in the day-to-day stuff,' Jenny said apologetically. 'I did try to get your place bumped to the end, but flights worked out that way – it was easier to do yours first.'

'Right.'

A silence.

'So... you'll be OK?'

'Looks like I'll have to be.' It was a shock, Nicky reasoned. But she had, after all, signed up to a TV reality show. She knew both from watching and hearing the behind-the-scenes chat from Jenny that these things happened. 'I'll have to go shopping... and well, yes. I'd better get on, I guess.'

'Oh, and there was the other thing too?'

'The other thing?'

'Yes, just... well, admin really.' Jenny laughed. The laugh did not fill Nicky's chest with confidence.

'Why are you doing your nervous laugh?'

'What do you mean?'

'Jenny, the last time I heard you laugh like that, was when you told me you'd pranged my car a bit when doing a reverse manoeuvre. It's your guilty laugh. The one you used when you knocked over my dad's drink at my wedding, or do you remember that time you realised you'd accidentally picked up someone else's handbag?'

'Yes.'

'And vomited in it in the taxi.'

'Well, yes.'

'And that the woman whose handbag it was was…'

'Yes. Stacy Baxter, TV exec extraordinaire. That haunts me to this day.'

Handbag gate, as they'd since styled it, had happened at the start of Jenny's career, when earning the good grace of those higher up was everything. But as usual, she'd somehow managed to talk her way out of it.

'So forgive me if I don't find your laugh reassuring…' Nicky continued.

'I mean, a laugh's a laugh, so really…'

'Jenny?!'

'Yes.'

'Tell me.'

'OK. Well, look. You know budgets being what they are? Flexible things really. There's been a meeting and I'm afraid everyone's has gone down a little.'

'How much by?' Nicky asked, a feeling of dread creeping over her.

'By half.'

'What?'

'Well, 52 per cent if you're going to be…'

'Jenny! The original budget was bad enough!'

'Look, it's not just a cost-cutting thing. It's sort of one of those curveballs the show likes to throw. To be honest, I'm not really meant to tell you in advance, so do act surprised when they give you your budget amount on camera tomorrow, won't you?'

'Jenny, it's not possible… I can't.' Nicky felt her breath quicken. 'I can't… I mean, seriously?'

'Darling. You'll make it work! I have every confidence in you!'

'No. You don't get it,' Nicky said. 'I'm not doing it for that. I can't. This place is… it needs… I just can't.'

'Ah, where's my girl with her can-do attitude?' Jenny said. Nicky heard a click in the background and sensed that Jenny was already checking her emails, confident that Nicky wouldn't kick up a fuss. She felt annoyed.

'Not here.'

'Nicky? Come on. This'll be great. All of the others are taking the same hit. You'll only be competing like for like.' A beat. 'Nicky?'

'Uh huh.'

'Nicky?'

'All right,' she said, not knowing quite how she'd got herself into this but sure she was going to fail spectacularly. 'I'll do some sums. I'll…'

'Atta girl.'

The line went dead.

Nicky sat down on the bed with a creak and a sigh. She should have known, really, that this would happen. That Jenny would throw her curveballs, move the goalposts. She knew how production worked – Jenny was often regaling her with tales of disaster from her TV shoots. It was just… perhaps she'd thought it would be different. Because they were friends.

Only – other than this tiny heads-up – it seemed that it wasn't.

She was just beginning what promised to be a month of twists and turns and stress. Provence or no Provence, she wasn't sure if she was up to it.

Resting her head in her hands, she groaned.

5

'Down the hill, second right,' Robert said half an hour later, standing behind her in the street and pointing in the direction of the town centre. Apparently, there was only one acceptable women's clothing shop in Roussillon and she'd have no time to go anywhere else. 'A friend runs it. It's quite reasonable. Hopefully,' he added.

'Thanks,' Nicky said. It was hardly a ringing endorsement. She wondered whether Robert's shop-owning friend had similar taste in clothing to Robert himself. In which case, she'd be better off sticking to her faded jeans and crumpled T-shirt. 'A girl friend?' she asked, hopefully.

'No, she's just a friend,' he said, frowning.

Nicky blushed, realising how her question had sounded. 'No, I mean. I was just wondering if she was female, not...'

'If you need me to take you there... show you. Well, I can. If you like,' he said, stepping forward again. She could smell a hint of shower gel on him, and another scent. Maybe suntan lotion?

It was not the most enthusiastic of offers and she shook her head. She found shopping for clothes traumatising enough on her own. She couldn't imagine how tricky it would be with a practical stranger trailing in her wake.

'No, don't worry. Anyway, I guess you've got to tidy up?' she said. 'Make everything camera friendly?'

He shook his head. 'They've actually asked me to leave it as messy as possible. Something to do with the optics.'

'Really?'

'Yeah. I mean, I'm still going to clean up the rest of the pigeon shit,' he said, frowning.

It was almost a joke. At least she thought it might be. She gave a kind of half smile to cover all bases.

Last night, he'd stuffed newspaper into the small unused fireplace chimney in his room 'just to make sure' after he was convinced he'd heard the sound of another pigeon flapping away.

In retrospect, she should have told him about the bird straightaway, she thought. But it was far too late now. And he was hard to read – he might have been annoyed with her and that was the last thing she needed. Instead, she'd helped him by screwing up the paper and passing it to him as he'd blocked the potential pigeon entrance.

It was still only 9.30 a.m., but there was definite warmth in the air. Soon, she removed her thin cardigan and tied it around her waist as she walked along the narrow roadway, bordered on one side by rust-coloured houses with shutters opened wide to welcome the new day and on the other by a traditional stone wall over which a patchwork of green trees, houses, fields and small roads was visible. She felt suddenly amazed that, without Jenny's intervention, she would currently be studying spreadsheets in her office in St Albans. Yet here she was, worlds away, in a little town in Provence, hoping to change the fortunes of a ramshackle B&B, and her own, in one fell swoop.

Her heart flipped slightly as she remembered that this was more than a little trip to the shops; that tomorrow she would be on TV, filmed for the world to judge not only her design expertise, but everything about her. How she looked, spoke, acted, reacted. Just as she'd sat with a cup of tea or glass of wine and laughed, or eye-rolled or cringed or gasped over the actions, looks, voices, reactions of other poor souls thrust into the limelight in the past from the safety of her sofa. But they hadn't seemed like real people to her. 'They chose to be on TV,' she'd say, 'they must expect to be judged.'

It felt slightly different now she was – or at least would be – on the other side of things.

Back in the day, she'd enjoyed getting into a reality series – from celebrities eating bits of animals that definitely should never be served up, to business wannabes sitting in boardrooms being pointed at by a grumpy, bearded man. She and Steve had used to like dipping in and out of a series, laughing at various contestants. She wondered, for a moment, what he'd think of what she was doing now. She shook her head. She couldn't let herself go there today; she had work to do.

As she approached the centre of Roussillon, she began to pass more and more people. Some would nod in acknowledgement as they passed, and she even prompted one or two bonjours. She'd smile or mutter a shy bonjour in response. She wondered whether all the people she passed knew each other and could tell there was a stranger in their midst, or whether the population of what was after all a holiday destination, was full of others like her – not quite knowing their way to the shops, not quite sure what they'd find when they got there.

She found the boutique after walking past a row of shops and taking a turning to the right, onto a cobbled pathway. The buildings on one side looked rather residential, their stone walls covered in thick green foliage and peppered with tiny flowers. On the other, a small row of buildings sported tiny signs – a boulangerie, some sort of insurance place and a little *brocante*. Then finally, just as Robert had described, she found herself at the end of the little row, where an arched door opened onto a metal fenced balcony, on which a couple of mannequins covered in silk guarded the entrance like extremely well-dressed, but headless, security guards.

She climbed the tiny set of stone steps to the right of the entrance and made her way onto the tiny outdoor space. Inside, through the arch of the stone doorway, she could see clothing in a myriad colours neatly hung on rails around the little room. She felt suddenly shy: the clothing was colourful, bold in a way she'd never been fashion-wise: a riot of oranges, magentas, bright greens that would look brilliant on someone confident enough to carry them off, but not quite the colour palette she usually stuck to. She'd lived in an off-work outfit of jeans and T-shirts for as long as she could remember, and her work stuff had looked so dated when she'd laid some of it on the bed to pack, she'd decided to bring barely any of it with her.

She'd thought she'd have a few days in which to find some nice clothing shop in a bigger town, where she could get herself looking more business savvy and creative, as opposed to the two looks she favoured currently. Look one: 'mum on a day off' consisted of jeans or jogging bottoms and a T-shirt or jumper, paired with trainers or boots. Look two: 'small town business advisor' saw her dressed in navy or black trousers with a white or cream cotton blouse and two-inch heels. Neither look was particularly inspiring – and certainly neither said 'up and coming TV star' or even 'temporary TV fill-in'.

Now, she was left with a choice: with cameras coming tomorrow, should she face them in faded denim or a riot of orange silk?

A movement in the shop's interior caught her eye and she realised she'd been staring into space, lost in thought, for a moment or two, and now she'd been spied by the owner, a woman who looked to be in her thirties, sporting and somehow getting away with a long, pleated floral skirt teamed with a white lace top. The woman looked typically French with neat, brown hair hanging glossily in a shoulder-length bob and the kind of year-round tan that could never be achieved with the bottled orange fake stuff everyone back home seemed to favour. She was chic in a way only a French woman could really be, and as she approached, Nicky became even more aware that her trainers could do with a clean, her hair with a trim, her make-up with... well, a little application and her look with a complete revamp. She ran her tongue over her teeth relieved to feel that, at least, she had remembered to clean them this morning, then summoned up the tiny amount of French she'd retained from school.

'Bonjour,' she said to the woman. '*Er, je regarde... um...*'

'Are you English, love?' said the woman, her eyes sparkling with amusement.

'Oh. Yes,' said Nicky, taken aback. Not because the woman spoke English but because the woman spoke English in an unmistakably northern accent. 'And you are...?'

She looked again at the woman, the effortless chic of her outfit, her glossy hair, the poise that she'd assumed had meant she had to be French. Perhaps there was hope for a revamp after all.

'Guilty as charged,' the woman said, sticking out a hand. 'I'm Michelle.'

'Nicky.'

'Right. You looking for anything in particular?'

'Kind of.' Nicky had prepared herself for an awkward conversation where she'd fend off the saleswoman and be left to finger garments, try things on and have a mini crisis in the changing rooms, as was her usual clothes shopping method. But now, looking at the well styled Michelle and realising that there were no language barriers, she did something that would ordinarily be completely alien to her. 'Actually,' she said, 'I could do with some help.'

* * *

She was already feeling a bit doubtful as Michelle rang the total up on the till. 'Are you sure these suited me?' she asked, as she handed over her card.

In the changing room she'd felt amazing in the long-sleeved green dress Michelle had picked out for her, and when slipping on a silk blouse to pair with linen trousers, matching them with some wedge sandals that would give her height without sending her toppling down the two flights of stairs in the B&B. But now, back in her friendly, comfortable jeans, she wondered whether she was making a mistake.

'You looked amazing,' Michelle said. 'Honestly. You'll knock 'em dead.'

'Thank you,' Nicky said, uncertainly, taking the receipt.

'Look, I get it,' said Michelle. 'You're – what – about forty?'

'Forty-nine,' Nicky admitted.

'Well, similar to me then,' Michelle said. 'And when I moved over here about ten years ago, I was like you.'

'Like me?'

'Yeah, you know. I mean, in my twenties and thirties I was really into my clothes. Then, forties came and I think I got sort of stuck in a style rut. Like you said, you wear jeans, T-shirts, maybe a jacket to work, but they're all sort of the same, right?'

'Well, yeah.'

'Then I came here and I kind of... There was a day when I caught sight of myself in a shop window of all places. And I thought 'who is *that*?' I realised that I'd let go of so many parts of myself.

That I'd kind of stopped enjoying my clothes. I used to really love picking out things to wear, but I'd sort of lost my way.'

'I know the feeling,' Nicky said.

'Yeah, and I just thought "right that's it". I mean Pierre – my husband – was all "oh but you're beautiful the way you are" but I just knew I didn't want to stay like that. I kind of re-educated myself: what I like, what looks nice, what's in fashion. That kind of thing. And I feel brilliant now. Better than ever, really.'

'Well, you definitely look great.'

'Thanks. And three years ago I started this shop. It's a real passion project for me.'

Nicky nodded, glancing again at the bright flash of material inside her paper carrier. 'I just... I always felt these sorts of colours. Well, they're not really me.'

'Course they are.'

'Well, not for people who... feel like me. I just... I don't know if I've got the confidence.'

Michelle nodded. 'You're not the first one to say that. But I think confidence comes, after a while. So many women are made to feel like fashion should stop once you reach forty, and you ought to wrap yourself in a tracksuit and be done with it.'

'That sounds very familiar!' Nicky said, smiling.

'But I guess I've kind of learned to value myself. Like, all of that was in my head, you know? Like I can be the sort of woman who wears this stuff. That's kind of where the shop came from. You know? Because I felt a bit self-conscious at first, I guess. But now I love getting dressed. Kind of treating myself. Instead of feeling past it all the time.'

Nicky nodded. 'That's exactly how I feel,' she admitted. 'Sort of like dressing up was something I could do when I was younger, but now—' She gestured at her faded jeans.

'Yeah, but you know. Here – in France, I mean – older women

are seen kind of differently. Like, we're valued for our experience. Not seen as past it, but you know, properly worth something,' Michelle said.

'Really?'

'Yeah. And you know, we should be, right? I mean, it's not all about youth, is it? I like myself more inside than I did twenty years ago. So the package is a bit rougher, but I reckon I'm a better person. People seem to see that here. Men, even.'

'God, that's hard to imagine,' Nicky said. 'I mean, I feel pretty much written off – like, I don't know, I don't have the same value as I used to.'

'Right? And then you think, why?' Michelle responded enthusiastically. 'I mean, who made these stupid rules about what we should and shouldn't wear or that a couple of wrinkles make you less than you used to be? And I realised, for me, it was just my own stupid thoughts that were stopping me. Or, like, society's thoughts. What society wants me to think.'

Nicky nodded, feeling a little like she'd attended some sort of TED talk on women's fashion. 'Well,' she said. 'You look great. I mean, you completely suit that outfit.'

'Thank you.' Michelle smiled. 'That's another thing Pierre taught me,' she said. 'To stop being so British and batting away compliments like they're bluebottles. To accept compliments instead of saying "this old thing" or whatever.' She laughed. 'We Brits need to learn to stop apologising.'

Nicky nodded. Steve had always loved how she looked. She'd drawn a lot of confidence from that. That confidence in herself had disappeared the night when he was stolen from her.

She quickly moved her thoughts away. 'Well, thank you,' she said. 'It's been a boost.'

'You're welcome,' said Michelle. 'When did you say you're filming again? Robert didn't say exactly when things kicked off.'

'How long have you known Robert?' Nicky asked, curious.

'Oh, years.' Michelle grinned. 'I was so thrilled when I heard he'd got a place on the programme. It was me who found the advert online and I insisted he had a go – at least apply. Of course, I didn't expect him to actually get in – you never do, do you? But I was so pleased for him! He really deserves it. Poor guy.'

'Poor guy?'

'Ah, you know. Such a nice person. Just never seems to catch a break.'

'Oh. Um. Right,' Nicky replied, politely. Robert seemed OK, but his gruff manner hadn't exactly endeared him to her so far. She wondered what Michelle meant about his deserving a break, but it didn't seem right to ask.

'I mean, it's obvious why they've selected him for the show though,' Michelle continued.

'It is?'

'I mean, his back story... and well, his looks...' Michelle gave a wink.

'I suppose,' she said. Objectively, she had noticed that Robert was good looking, with his even features and wide smile. But his scruffy clothes and slight brusqueness hadn't exactly made her warm to him.

Michelle laughed. 'You should see your face! Honestly, trust me. He's a great guy once you break through that protective shell he puts up. He's just an awkward bugger, not a nasty one.'

'Good to know...' Nicky wasn't sure exactly what she should say. 'Anyway, filming's kicking off tomorrow morning.'

'Well, good luck. Tell him I'll pop over soon for a glass of wine.'

'Will do.'

'And listen, come back – I don't mean to buy more stuff. Although do that too, obviously.' Michelle grinned. 'But you know, if you want to chat or anything. It can be hard here at first.'

'Thanks.' Nicky smiled.

'And sorry. I know I go on a bit. It's just, well, my French is OK, but it's nice to talk with one of my own sometimes.'

Exiting onto the now-sun-drenched cobbled pathway, Nicky realised she was smiling. She tried to commit what Michelle had told her to memory. That she could embrace something new, and find new confidence.

She might not be in her youth, but maybe Michelle was right. She had more to offer than she'd had back then; more value than what was etched on her skin.

It was hard, sometimes, remembering that she existed at all as an individual. A decade of being a single, working parent had meant she'd been squeezed out of her own picture. But maybe like Jenny'd said, this would be her chance to take on the world.

And if Michelle was to be believed, the best outfit for battle would be made of green taffeta.

6

The following morning, they were sitting at one of the tables in the dining room when a loud rap on the door made them both jump. Nicky and Robert looked at each other, eyes widening, before Robert jumped up. 'I'll get it,' he offered.

'OK,' Nicky replied, trying to sound confident despite her racing heart. She'd slipped herself into the green dress and felt alternately glamorous and ridiculous, her self-consciousness fighting with the smaller, inner voice that quietly reassured her she looked fine. Either way, it was too late now, she told herself, getting to her feet and trying to embody her new role 'Nicky Green, Design Guru and TV Sensation'.

Shyness kept her rooted to the spot as the rumble of noise in the hallway got louder. She could hear voices, Robert's, another man's, a woman's and then a louder, more confident voice that she recognised as being Ryan Camberwell's. 'Well, morning to you too!' he cried. 'Fabulous place you have here. Just Fab-u-luuus!'

She forced her rather stiff legs to walk forwards rather than having the crowd of people burst in on her in the empty dining room and made her way to the door. In the hallway was a brown-haired man with a camera, a tall woman with a clipboard and – larger than life – Ryan, whom she'd watched a zillion times on reality programmes and who seemed simultaneously like a stranger and an old friend.

'You must be Nicky,' he said, eyeing her as she appeared through the crack in the doorway. He grinned, showing a perfect set of teeth which flashed brightly against his fake tan. He'd removed his habitual goatee and was instead sporting a black moustache which he'd styled with little twists at the end.

'Like the tash?' he asked her, with a wink. 'I've tried to French it up a bit. Got a beret for later.'

'Oh... well, yeah, it's great.'

'Fab-u-luuus dress by the way,' he added, looking her up and down approvingly.

'Thank you,' she said, and blushed.

Robert, who'd not yet commented on her outfit despite it being worlds away from the way she'd been dressed in his presence so far, looked at her as if for the first time. 'Oh yeah,' he said. 'Very smart.'

'Thanks,' she said. Then, 'You too,' she added on autopilot, despite the fact that Robert was wearing a fairly tatty pair of jeans and a checked shirt – pretty much the uniform he'd been in ever since she'd arrived.

She'd wondered why he hadn't got changed, but then had felt too shy to ask. Times were tough in the B&B business, but she hadn't realised they were *this* tough. Perhaps these were his smart clothes? Or perhaps he wanted to appear authentic? It was none of her business.

'And spot on!' Ryan said, turning to Robert. 'I was going to ask you to wear something awful, you know, the hard-up struggling business owner, unable to buy decent clothes.' He patted Robert on the back. 'Well done, mate! You look a total state!'

Robert blushed. 'Thanks,' he said, looking at his shirt as if for the first time.

'Ooh,' said Ryan, looking more closely at Robert's face. 'But we'll have to do something about those scratches. You look like you've been in a cat fight. Don't worry, Mo will fix it.' He glanced over at another woman who'd walked in, carrying a bag heaving with what Nicky presumed was make-up and accessories. She looked at Robert's face and nodded grimly, accepting the challenge ahead.

'It was a pigeon,' Robert said, after a moment's silence.

'What?' Ryan seemed to have forgotten what they'd been discussing.

'The face,' Robert said. 'I was attacked. By a pigeon.'

'Riiiight,' Ryan said, obviously used to dealing with 'characters' and assuming Robert was one of them. 'Well, hard luck, mate. Happens to the best of us.'

Then he strode into the hallway beyond them all. 'So where shall we set up?' he asked.

* * *

Six hours later, when the crew were packing up to leave, Nicky finally had time to take a breath. She sank into one of the kitchen chairs, feeling the material of her dress sticking slightly to her sweaty back. She was absolutely exhausted. But despite this, she was buzzing with a kind of heady euphoria. She'd done it. She'd actually done it.

Talking to camera had felt surreal. 'Hi, I'm Nicky Green and I'm here to turn this business around!' they'd made her say. Then they'd accompanied her on a tour of the house where she'd been encouraged to run her finger over (admittedly, dusty) shelves and shake her head, and sit on the beds to test the mattresses.

'The more disgusted you are, the better,' Fern, the on-site producer, told her. 'It makes for more of an impact later.'

She tried her best, hamming it up a little for the camera. But it felt awkward having to be so brutal with Robert literally standing there. 'Sorry,' she mouthed to him on occasion and he nodded.

Once they'd spent two hours shooting and reshooting footage and she'd got to the point where she no longer knew exactly what she'd said or actually cared any more, they took them to the kitchen, where an iPad was propped on the table.

'Now,' Fern said once Nicky and Robert were seated, a little more close together than was comfortable, in front of the little screen. 'Nicky, you need to explain to Robert about the secret filming. Robert, if you could act surprised – as far as you knew they were just "ordinary" guests, right? And then we'll play the footage and if you could perhaps exaggerate your reactions by 50 per cent or so, just to make things clear to the viewers...?'

'But...' Robert began.

Too late, the camera started rolling.

'So, Robert,' Nicky said, turning to him and trying to sound professional, yet friendly. 'You don't know it yet, but a couple of your customers last week weren't exactly who they said they were!'

'What?' Robert said, looking so horrified Nicky wondered for a minute whether a murderer had entered the room. Or perhaps, a pigeon.

'Yes,' she continued. 'But don't worry. It's important to get guests' reactions to things so we can really understand what's working and what isn't.' She reached forward, as she'd been told to, and pressed play on the footage.

'At this point,' Fern interjected, 'the viewers will see the footage, but we'll pan back and forth to shots of you guys, so keep your facial expressions strong, please.'

Robert had just enough time to glance at Nicky with a raised eyebrow before the footage started to roll. She wondered whether it was raised in shock, or amusement. Was it a friendly eyebrow? Or a facial-hair distress signal?

She had her French-to-English dictionary with her, but what she really needed was an eyebrow-to-English dictionary.

She watched as the footage played out. Even if Robert had had a full quota of guests, the two 'mystery customers' would have stood out a mile. They were a rotund couple, each with an apparent penchant for floral prints and Bermuda shorts – a sort of cut-out of a drawing of 'tourists' from a children's book. The footage showed them greeting Robert at the door from a weird angle that suggested a camera filming from a pocket or bag. Then once they got into the room, they went to work.

'Well, he's hardly friendly,' the woman sniffed once Robert had left them. 'Made me feel quite awkward.'

'Yes. Not the most welcoming of hosts,' the man agreed.

'Shower needs a clean,' the woman said. 'And this bed is far from comfortable.'

'View's OK,' the man responded. 'Good selection of teabags. But no sugar!'

This went on for about twenty minutes in which everything from the décor to the location was appraised. A particular bone of contention was when the woman found a long black hair in the shower drain.

'Wilbur, look!' she said to the man, 'this is a definite failing of Health and Safety Legislation, Point 2 paragraph b(i).'

He shook his head in disappointment. 'And the tea's rather weak,' he added, seemingly unaware that he'd been managing tea strength himself with a bag on a string.

'But that's her hair!' Robert said in frustration. 'I've got, well, mine is much shorter. Hers is exactly that length and colour!'

'OK,' Fern said, in the kind of voice designed to sound tolerant but with an undertone of irritation threatening to break through. 'But it's better if you don't talk over it. And you know, the worse things are...'

'I know, I know, the better they'll seem,' Robert said. 'But it's a bit rough being accused of poor hygiene! Can't you cut that bit out?'

Fern glanced at the cameraman who shrugged. 'We've kind of scripted a whole health and safety bit at this point,' she said. 'Sorry.'

Robert said nothing as they reset the footage and began filming again, but Nicky saw his jaw clench. She understood. It was one thing admitting you could market your business better, or accepting you needed to update the wallpaper. But dropping a hair in the shower then blaming it on your poor hygiene seemed one accusation too far.

By the end of the segment Nicky felt bone-weary, but rather than ending things, the filming apparently was set to continue. 'Can't we do a bit more tomorrow?' she asked.

'No, sorry, love,' Ryan said. 'The hotel's too far away.'

'Your hotel?'

'Yes, we're booked in over Nîmes way.'

'But... this is a hotel?' Nicky said.

'Yeah, no offence or anything, but I prefer my shower trays hair-free,' Ryan said. 'Right, Robert?' He laughed uproariously at his own humour then slung an arm around Robert and pulled him in. 'Dirty bastard.' He laughed, affectionately.

'Eh, right,' Robert said, frowning. Nicky had never seen anyone look quite so uncomfortable in an embrace.

'Right, we're now going to do a piece with Nicky, where she takes a call about budget cuts,' Fern said. 'You'll have to improvise, my love,' she said, picking up Nicky's phone and shoving it at her. 'Just act natural, think about what you'd say.'

'Budget cuts!' Robert said, aghast, and Nicky realised she'd failed to mention them. At least his reaction was authentic, she supposed as she tidied up her hair and prepared to act the part.

'Brilliant!' Fern said as the camera cut. 'You really looked annoyed and... well, more than a bit terrified!'

Nicky, who'd just re-enacted one end of the call she'd had from Jenny smiled tightly. 'That's because I *am* terrified,' she wanted to say. But bit her tongue.

At least then, it was time for a break.

'Talking of budget cuts,' Fern informed them. 'We're cramming both days' filming into one then shooting across to Bordeaux to the next place. But you know, take a bit of time for a drink, freshen up. Maybe get changed. I mean, we'll have to say it's the next day and all that, so...'

'Right.' Nicky nodded, feeling about as drained as it was possible to be. They certainly didn't make it seem that way on the TV.

'So, five minutes, people!' Fern announced loudly to the six people in the room. 'Then the piece with Robert. Everyone for tea?'

There was a series of yeses and nods. 'Tea for everyone then, Robert, there's a darlin',' she said.

'Oh... right,' he responded. He was heading dutifully towards the door, presumably to freshen up. 'I was just going to...'

'Oh, no. Don't *you* change, Robert,' Ryan said. 'We're painting you as a sort of dirty, neglected, lonely B&B owner. You know, to make the transformation even more startling.'

'But... I mean, it's my *house* that's getting the makeover so...'

'Can you leave the bag in,' Fern called. 'I like mine black.'

'Two sugars,' Tom the cameraman said.

'Do you have any mint?'

Resigned, Robert retreated to the kitchen.

Nicky felt a little sorry for him as she watched the soon-to-be-branded stinky, health and safety incompetent B&B host disappear through the door, shoulders-slumped. But then she remembered that her reputation too was on the line and raced upstairs, glad that she'd managed to find two suitable outfits at Michelle's shop rather than just one.

Minutes later, she breezed downstairs, feeling quite glamorous in her new top and linen trousers. She caught a glimpse of herself in the mirror on the way, and liked the way the high waist accentuated the flattest part of her stomach, and how the rust-coloured top seemed to chime in with the slightly lighter shade of her auburn hair.

She appeared in the dining room where Robert had set out mugs of tea and people were standing around talking. Ryan was leaning against the wall, eyes closed, his face furrowed in concentration.

'Is he all right?' she said to Tom. 'He looks... is he in pain or something?'

'Meditating,' Tom said in a whisper with an eye roll that told her exactly what he felt about the practice. 'Helps his energy flow apparently.'

'Right.' She grinned, lifting a full mug from the table and taking a sip. The hot, sweet liquid was refreshing and began to revive her. She realised they hadn't eaten anything yet today. 'Do we get to break for lunch? It's three o'clock?'

'Usually,' he said. 'But I think we're trying to wrap things up and grab a snack on the road. More driving.'

'Oh,' she said, feeling her stomach rumble but concluding it was probably a good thing as far as the high-waisted trousers went.

'Sorry about all this,' Tom added, unexpectedly.

She turned to look at him. He'd pushed his earphones back on his head and they'd gathered his mid-length brown hair back like an Alice band.

'About what?' she asked him.

'Well, this. All the last-minute stuff. It never used to be like this at the channel. It's got a bit shit since... well, we're under new management.'

'Don't worry,' she said. 'I get it.'

'Feels rude though,' he said, with a shrug, lifting his mug to his mouth. 'Usually it's nice to... you know, take a moment to get to know people a bit.'

'I can imagine.'

'I mean, I haven't seen you before, for instance,' he said, leaning against the wall, then seeming to think better of it, straightened up. 'Have you been on anything else I'd have seen?'

'No, I'm... well, I guess it's my first time!'

'Ah, a TV virgin,' Tom replied, then went about as red as it was possible to go without someone feeling the need to call an ambulance. 'I mean, you know...'

She laughed. 'Ah, a fellow blusher,' she said. 'Nice to know I'm not the only one who colours up the moment they say something awkward.'

He grinned, still scarlet. 'It's a bloody nightmare,' he said. 'It's impossible to try to be cool when your face gives everything away. It happens every time I'm talking to someone, you know... Well, someone I find attractive.'

Now it was her turn to go red. 'Oh,' she said, feeling a shiver of surprise. 'You do know I'm a forty-nine-year-old grandma,' she wanted to say. But then she remembered Michelle's words. Why shouldn't she simply accept a compliment without batting it away?

Before she could say anything further, Fern clapped her hands together. 'Come on, people!' she said. 'Final push and we can get away from this... from this...' she looked at Robert, 'er, lovely place and on to the, um, hotel. Anyway. Maybe if we could do that piece we discussed, Robert?' Fern looked at him. 'Is there somewhere

quiet, maybe your private rooms, where we can talk about all the...
history?'

He nodded. 'Upstairs,' he said, a strange expression flickering
across his face.

Nicky had gone to follow as Robert, Fern and Tom had begun to
climb the stairs. But Fern had turned. 'This one's an interview with
just Robert,' she'd said. 'Don't take this the wrong way but it'll be
more "intimate" if you sit this one out.'

'Oh, OK,' Nicky had said, feeling a little like she'd been kicked
out of a playground game. She'd hoped they wouldn't be talking
about her. But suspected strongly that they would.

* * *

'Well, that was... something else,' Robert said now, walking into the
kitchen and pulling up a chair opposite. 'I never realised...'

She looked at him; he looked absolutely shattered, eyes almost
bloodshot. Almost as if he'd been crying. 'Was the interview OK?'
she asked.

'Yeah. Bit... you know,' he said, gesturing to his eyes.

'Oh.'

'But I guess that's part of it,' he said.

'Yes.' She wanted to ask what it was that had tipped him over
the edge into tears, but couldn't find a way to say the words that
didn't sound nosy or intrusive.

'Didn't realise it would be so... full on,' he said.

'Me neither.'

'And it was really...'

'Yep.'

Robert shook his head. 'Careful what you wish for,' he said
sadly. 'I mean, I was desperate to find a way to... well, revive the

place. Get more attention, you know? Put the B&B on the map. But I just hope...'

'What?' Nicky asked gently.

'Well.' He fixed his deep brown eyes on hers and she saw that they were still glistening slightly. 'I wanted to give this place one last shot, you know? Because... well, if this doesn't work...' he drifted off. 'I just hope that it doesn't make things worse.'

'If it doesn't work...?' she prompted.

'Well, I mean, the handyman stuff I do doesn't pay much. And this place – well, old properties, they need maintenance all the time. If I'm honest, if this thing doesn't help, well, change my fortunes, then... well, I'll have to close up. Move back...'

'Oh!' Nicky felt her heart somersault. Nothing like raising the stakes, Robert, she thought. 'And would that... I mean, you said you're not a natural host. Maybe moving on wouldn't be so bad?' she ventured.

He looked at her, his expression hard to read. 'I know. It seems daft, right? I just... it'd be saying goodbye to a dream and I don't think I'm ready to. Plus, you know, I'd feel as if I hadn't given it a proper go. I'd always... well, I'd always wonder.'

She nodded. She knew a lot about roads untravelled and how the 'what-ifs' could haunt a person.

'Anyway,' Robert said, slapping his legs and standing up as if decisively moving the conversation on. 'I don't know about you but I'm starving!'

Half an hour later they were tucking into a pizza that Robert had heated up, teamed with some bagged salad. It was such a welcome meal that Nicky could have sworn it had been knocked up by a top chef rather than the local convenience store.

'This is great,' she said.

'Thanks,' Robert said. 'Quite a day.'

'God, you can say that again,' Nicky said, picking up a drooping slice of cheese laden dough and stuffing it into her mouth. A bit of it dropped onto her blouse and she wiped it off with the back of her hand.

'You've spilled a bit,' Robert said, looking almost horrified.

'Don't worry,' she said. 'It's OK. Tomato won't show up anyway on this orange.'

'Good point!' Robert nodded, then reached down and fed a bit of pizza to Buster, who trotted happily into the garden with the triangle hanging from his mouth.

'Does he like pizza then?' Nicky asked, surprised.

'That thing?' Robert said, affectionately. 'He'll eat anything. Although he has a habit of burying pizza in the garden for some unknown reason.'

'Yum.'

He laughed and shook his head. 'God, you're different from what I'd expected.'

'What do you mean?'

'Well, you know, the hotel inspector type. I expected some stern, judgemental, perfectly presented, terrifying business dynamo. And you're... well...'

'Not?' she asked.

'Well, you're some of it,' he said.

'The dynamo bit?'

'What I mean is you're... well, normal.'

'Thank you,' she said. 'I think.'

He nodded and bit into another piece of pizza. The silence descended again.

'Suppose I wasn't quite what you were expecting either,' he said.

'What do you mean?'

'Well, I guess I'm not very business-like,' he said, looking down at his clothes. 'What was it that Ryan said? "A total state" I think he termed it.' He smiled, but there was a sadness behind it, as if deep down he was quite upset.

'Ah, ignore him,' Nicky said. 'We can't all spend four hours gelling our hair into place every morning! And honestly, not many people can carry off a twizzled moustache.'

Robert laughed. 'Still,' he said. 'I guess I hope people aren't put off by my... well, my look.'

She studied him. 'I'm sure they wouldn't be,' she said softly. It was true, she realised. Yes, perhaps he could do with a bit of a spruce-up. But Robert was the sort of good looking where a bit of neglect didn't detract from the overall package. She wondered how to put this into words without looking like she was either patronising him or trying to get him into bed. 'Look' she said, instead. 'If you want I can... well, help you a bit? Maybe pick out a few bits?' She blushed.

He looked at her. 'You'd do that?' he said, sounding incredibly grateful.

'Yes. Of course,' she replied. 'After all, I'm helping to give the whole business a makeover; and you're an integral part of that!' She grinned. 'Can't have you letting the side down by *being a total state.*'

He smiled. 'Well, it's appreciated,' he said. 'Living here, not having that many guests... I suppose it's easy just to pull on the same old gear day after day. I mean, Michelle's offered to help once or twice. But it was hard... it's been a while since I've felt good enough to want to try.'

'Believe me, I completely understand,' she said, thinking of the drawer at home bursting with jeans, all a similar colour and fit.

Later, when she was showering off Nicky 'Business and Design Dynamo' and completing the transformation back into Nicky 'Middle-Aged Mum' she thought again about the cameraman, Tom, and what he'd said. That he found her attractive.

That had been shock enough. But what had surprised her more

was the way she'd felt when he said it. Pleased. Flattered. But also... Also, for just a minute, she'd felt something too. Some sort of reciprocal pull.

And she wasn't sure how to feel about that at all.

7

They kicked off their shoes and flung themselves onto the hotel bed, giggling at all the extravagance.

'Certainly beats Newhaven Premier Inn,' Steve said.

'Still, this is pretty posh,' she joked. 'I might get used to luxury at this rate.'

'Well, you'd better,' he said, rolling towards her and reaching up a hand to brush her hair from her face. 'Because you, Mrs Green, are going to have only the best from now on.'

She smiled. 'Careful,' she said.

'What do you mean?'

'Well, you know. Careful what you wish for,' she said. 'That's what they say, isn't it? Don't want to jinx it.'

He laughed. 'Don't be daft. We are going to have the best life together. And nothing is going to stop that.'

* * *

She came to slowly in the four-poster bed, feeling aches in her body as she stretched her legs and arms and tried to wake herself up properly. Last night had been difficult – the nightmares had returned, not once but twice, and she'd spent an hour downstairs, making notes at the kitchen table to distract herself before returning to try to sleep one more time.

Picking up her phone from the nightstand, she discovered it was eight o'clock – and forced herself to sit up and swing her legs out from under the covers. While the little kettle boiled, she showered in her tiny ensuite and slipped into a pair of jeans. She eyed the green dress hanging over the back of the chair like the cast-off skin from a reptile. She'd shed her identity as interior designer and was back being plain old Nicky.

She thought about what Robert said. How she'd offered to help him up his look a little. Perhaps it was time to do the same for herself. See whether she could find a state in between mum and designer. A hybrid in which she could embody some aspects of her more confident persona without having to go full patterned silk. She'd have a little browse in Michelle's shop again soon and see what she thought. In any case, she'd need to get a few more outfits sooner rather than later with the crew back to film again in under a fortnight.

Kettle boiled; she poured the hot water onto one of the stringed teabags. Then, as she waited for the reluctant French branded teabag to yield enough colour to meet her thoroughly British tastes, she scrolled through emails on her phone.

There was the usual mix of nonsense – offers from stores she rarely visited, emails from websites she couldn't remember ever using. And another, from Jenny, which just said 'how did it go?' in the title. She opened it, but her friend hadn't bothered to write anything inside but a series of question marks.

Call you in a bit.

She responded and pressed 'send'.

Back in her inbox, there was another new mail, sent late last night from an account she wasn't familiar with. F. Wiseman. Fern from yesterday. The title was 'Footage'. She clicked on it and found a link and the words 'few pics for social media' and a little smile emoticon. The link led to a series of cloud-stored files, featuring stills from the filming the day before. Her eye was drawn instantly to the woman in the green dress, with her red, shiny hair and confident expression. Was that really her?

She flicked through more – her speaking to Robert, her pointing at a damp stain in the bathroom. In a couple she cringed at her facial expression – not used to seeing herself mid conversation – but objectively she had to admit she looked pretty good. Not just smart and maybe even a little bit pretty, but like a confident woman. Someone who actually knew what they were talking about and had been in the business advice game for years.

'Blimey' she said to herself, shaking her head.

Before she'd even removed the teabag from her much-needed brew, the phone began to buzz, the name 'Jenny' displayed on the screen. Of course her friend hadn't waited, she thought. When did Jenny ever wait?

'Hi, you,' she said, answering the call.

'Hi yourself!' came the familiar voice – annoyingly chirpy for what was only 7.20 a.m. back in the UK. 'Hear you were quite the hit yesterday!'

'I *was*?' An image of Tom flashed into her mind and she pushed it away.

'Yes. Wrapping up all those different scenes in a day. Word on the street is that you must be a seasoned professional. I've been asked where I found you!'

'Well, that's good,' she said, feeling quite uplifted. 'And some pics have come through from Fern too.'

'Yes, I saw those. Love the dress. Very fancy!'

'Thank you.'

'And the orange blouse was... well, brave.'

'Brave good?'

'Brave,' said Jenny, all seriousness, 'is always good.'

'Well, thanks. It was that or the threadbare jeans.'

'Ha. Quite.'

'Everything OK your end?'

'Oh, yes. Yes. Always,' Jenny brushed her question aside. 'Apart from things going tits up in Bordeaux with some of the secret guests. But I'll regale you with that story another time.'

'Oh dear.' Nicky smiled. Jenny had a way of making even a disaster sound entertaining. No wonder she'd done so well in TV land.

'And, look. Good luck with the next bit,' said Jenny. 'Sorry about the budget.'

'Yes, I'm a bit unsure...'

'You'll be grand,' Jenny shut her doubts down instantly.

'But there's so much to do. So much...'

'Anyway, how is Provence? I hope you're going to make time for sunning yourself and making the most of the plentiful wine.'

'Ha. If I get a chance... But can we talk about the budget first. I'm just...'

'Sorry about it,' Jenny said briefly. 'But that's a done deal, chick. I can't change it.'

'OK.'

'You know how it goes.'

'I'm beginning to realise...'

'Sorry. But hey ho! You're brilliant. You'll nail it, I'm sure.'

Another thought caused Nicky's smile to fade a little. 'Look, Jenny, if I tell you something will you promise to keep it to yourself?'

'Oh yes?'

'Seriously. It's just between us, right?'

'OK.' Jenny's tone was more serious. 'You know you can trust me, Nic.'

'It's just, the cameraman yesterday. We got talking and... well, he seemed to be flirting with me.'

There was a click of fingers on a keyboard. 'What? Tom?' Jenny asked, clearly bringing up details on her PC. 'Do you want me to have a word. He didn't... try anything, did he?'

'No! No. Please don't. Not in a creepy way. In a... well, sort of subtle way. He might not even have been flirting. It's probably me. I'm not great at recognising the signs...'

'OK. So...?'

'It didn't bother me. I'm not complaining. It was... well, nice if anything to be noticed. It's just...'

'Yes?'

'Jenny. I kind of felt something too.'

'You felt something?'

'Yeah, I mean, I liked him.' Nicky felt the familiar heat in her cheeks and raised her hand to her face. She felt her eyes begin to tingle and blinked quickly in an attempt to stave off tears.

Jenny was silent for a moment. 'Honey, that's good. It's not as if you need to do anything about it.'

'I know... it's just... You know how I get.'

'I know.' Her friend was quiet for a moment. 'God, Nicky, I'm sorry. I know how this stuff makes you feel. I really do. And I understand. Sort of. It's just... you know deep down, don't you, that it's OK to feel something? Even if Steve... even if he was still here and you were still married, you're allowed to have a little flirt, or meet someone good looking. Blimey, if I had a pound for every time I'd batted my eyelashes at someone at work, well, I wouldn't need to *be* at work.'

'I know,' Nicky said, trying to smile as she sat on the edge of the bed. Her tea, now forgotten, was taking on a rusty brown colour on the cabinet. 'And I know what you think. What I'd think in your shoes, too. That most people would have moved on a long time ago.'

'Well, not necessarily.'

'It's just... Look, I know Steve's not coming back. And I'm OK with that – well, at peace with that.'

'OK...'

'It's just...' she tried to explain. 'This was different. Different from before.'

'Different how?' Jenny prompted.

'Look, it's hard to explain, but you know I never properly dated anyone after Steve. Despite your... help. And I know you thought it was because I was being loyal, or still grieving,' said Nicky.

'Well, yes.'

'But it was never that. Not really. It was more... I just never felt like it. I never found anyone attractive. I just wasn't interested. Even if... even when I tried.'

'The Tinder experiment?'

'The Tinder experiment,' she said, grinning momentarily in spite of herself, thinking back to last year when Jenny had convinced her to join the site. She'd gone on two disastrous dates and received more than a lifetime's supply of dick pics for her trouble before she decided it simply wasn't for her. 'I just never felt... anything. For anyone. I wasn't drawn to them, I wasn't interested. And I tried – you know I did. But I guess after a while I just figured, well, that was OK. That maybe that part of my life was over. That I didn't need anyone.'

'Oh, Nic.'

'I guess I thought that... that part of me had died.'

'What? You thought your vagina had died?' Jenny interjected.

'Jenny! No!' But she was grinning a little more now. 'Not my *vagina*! My heart! Or my head! Or whatever it is in people's bodies that makes them drawn to other people.'

'Still sounding a *lot* like a vagina to me,' said Jenny, clearly talking with a smile. Then, 'Look,' she said, more seriously. 'I guess it must feel weird to feel something like that again – but surely it's good weird, right?'

'Maybe.' Nicky stood up and walked over to the tea, saw the state of it, and put the kettle on to boil again. 'It's just... it's kind of a surprise I suppose. I just assumed. I guess I thought that part of my life was over. And you know what? I was fine with that. I was fine in myself, fine looking after the girls. I wasn't *looking* for anyone, anything. Then suddenly this guy... And I'm not intending to do anything about it, but it shocked me, that this part of me is still well, functioning. Or maybe it's coming back from the dead.'

'Are you saying,' Jenny said, 'that your vagina is now Undead?'

'Jenny!' she said. 'Get serious for a minute. This is really bothering me!'

'Sorry, sorry. I know I'm an idiot. Look, perhaps that part of you—'

'My heart.'

'OK, your *heart* wasn't dead. Maybe... maybe it was on hold or something?'

'What do you mean?'

'Well, after Steve. You had to really keep your shit together, right? You had to keep functioning for those girls. You told me – remember – that you barely cried for the first year. You just... well, you'd had to bury everything.'

'True.'

'And I don't know... Now the girls are more or less independent. You're in a different situation. And maybe...'

'Maybe?'

'Maybe there's finally space for someone else again? Maybe, somehow, subconsciously you're ready to feel things again. And you know, it's good. I know you don't think you need *anyone*. But we all do, sweetheart. Even yours truly.'

'Lots of people are happy without relationships...'

'Well, I suppose there are different kinds. Of love, I mean. You have plenty of that. The kids, your mother... me.'

'Thank you.'

'But it's nice – more love, more connection. It's a good thing.'

'It just makes me sad, that's all.'

'Honey, that's natural. It's OK. But Steve would have wanted you to be happy. You know that.'

'I know.' She thought of her husband. The way he'd always put her first. The times they'd laughed together. 'I just... the thought of replacing him—'

'Not replacing him,' Jenny said firmly. 'You'll always have him. But love is... well, it's bigger than that. You won't be taking any love, or passion or whatever you felt for Steve and giving it to some new person.'

'No?'

'No. You'll still have all of that love for Steve; you'll just find more. You can have more. Darling, it's infinite.'

They were silent for a minute, Nicky holding back the tears that threatened her, trying to steady her breathing.

'So,' said Jenny, clearly smiling again. 'Want me to put in a good word for you?'

'No! Jenny, don't be ridiculous. It's not so much about him as about me. I suppose it shocked me that part of me was still open for business.'

'Your vagina?'

'My *heart*.'

* * *

Robert had disappeared out to the market, leaving her a note on the table, when she finally made it downstairs twenty minutes later. The day was already in full swing and she started to regret the jeans and wonder whether she ought to find a pair of shorts, or take a pair of scissors and create her own.

Instead, she sat down with a tall glass of water and opened her notebook. She tried to think of how she could work with the budget cuts. Perhaps things weren't as expensive around here as they were back home, she thought. She began to arrange the steps in priority order – the deep clean, the new sheets, the signage, menus, advertising. She'd get them priced up and then see where they were.

By the time Robert returned, carrying paper carrier bags full of fresh fruit and vegetables, she'd filled a page with her scribbles. He heaved the bags into the kitchen; all overfilled, the paper straining and threatening to rip. The muscles and veins of his arms stood out with the effort of carrying them.

'Morning,' he said, putting the bags down on the kitchen floor and shaking his hands to release the stiffness from them. 'You're hard at work.' He was wearing a blue T-shirt, a departure from his usual dark colours. It lifted him, making his brown curls and chocolate eyes stand out. He smiled, and she found herself smiling back, unexpectedly.

'Well, thought I'd better get things underway,' she said.

He walked behind her and leaned in, his eyes scanning the page. She resisted the urge to cover her notes. Close up, he smelled clean and fresh – laundry detergent and a splash of aftershave. 'Oh!' he said, looking at her scribbles. 'That is a LOT.'

'I know,' she said. 'But this is our... well, a wish list. Not sure we'll be able to do all of this.'

'You really think the place is that bad?' He grimaced.

'Well, no,' she said carefully. 'But it could do with a little... well, TLC.'

He sat down at the table, eyes still on the notebook. 'But all that? It'll be way over budget. Especially now.'

'Really?' He seemed more upset than she'd imagined.

'Do you know things are expensive around here?'

'They are?' Her heart sank.

He nodded. 'Materials especially. I mean you'll be lucky to get, well, the first two things on that list – the painting and the new dining tables – for less than a thousand euros.'

'Oh.' She felt a little sick. 'That expensive?'

'That expensive.'

All the positivity she'd built up seemed to drain away suddenly and all she felt was tired. Tired and stupid. She drew a thick line through her work.

'What are you doing?' he said.

'We can't afford this. You said so yourself.'

'Yes,' he said, sounding genuinely concerned. 'But I didn't think you'd...'

'I'd what?'

'Well, quit. I thought you'd tell me some great plan you had. Some way of making the money or cutting costs, or making it work. You know, the kind of thing they do on TV.' He shrugged, disappointed.

'Oh.' She felt suddenly guilty. 'I mean I guess I just need to start again. Rethink things. They told you this was my first programme?'

He leaned his head on upturned palms and fixed his brown eyes on her. She felt herself flush. 'Yes. Yes, they did,' he said. 'But you're a designer and business advisor, right?'

'Well, yes. A business advisor, at least. With a penchant for design.'

'So, this should be right in your comfort zone?' he asked, hopefully.

'But even I can't make money appear from thin air,' she said.

He was silent for a moment. Then, 'How about if I added something to the pot?'

She looked at him. 'What, money?'

'Yes. I could raise some extra somehow. Or... or call in some favours. See if anyone wants to slap some paint on in exchange for some handyman work?'

The positivity in his voice lifted her. 'I mean, if you're able to...' she said.

'I just want...' he said. 'I just feel that I need to do everything I can.' He shrugged. 'So I know, even if it doesn't work... if I lose the place. Well, I'll know I gave it my best shot.'

She nodded. 'Makes sense,' she said. 'Although... can I ask. Well, why?'

'Why what?' He frowned and she wondered whether she'd overstepped the mark.

'Well, why this place? I know it's hard to... admit defeat. I get it. But running the B&B, it was your wife's dream, right?'

'Right.'

'And it's not in your comfort zone, but you want to make it work? Is it... don't take this the wrong way, but it seems a bit like you're trying to prove something to her.'

'Well, yeah. I guess that's true on some level. Although I mean, I love living here, and...'

'But surely if she left you, isn't it quite a complicated way to... what? Get revenge? Show her what she's missing?'

Robert turned to her, shaking his head. 'No,' he said. 'It's not like that.'

'But it's not really your thing...?'

He shook his head. 'Not right now. I mean, I'm not exactly a great host. But I used to be. And I think, if I try, I can be again. I've kind of... well, stepped back too much, I think.'

'But you have other skills. I mean, if it doesn't work out why not sell it? Start again? Do something completely new? Maybe Marie should be the one to take it on!'

'You don't know, do you?' he asked, softly.

'Know what?'

'Sorry. I assumed someone would have said something...'

'About what?' she asked, confused.

'It's my fault,' he said. 'I haven't explained it properly.'

'Go on...?'

'Yes, it was Marie's dream. Yes, she's not here to help me. But she didn't leave.'

Nicky felt disorientated as the truth slowly dawned.

'Nicky, Marie died.'

8

Steve laughed delightedly, went to pick her up, thought better of it and instead wrapped his arms gently around her. 'Oh my God,' he said. 'Already?'

'I know.'

'I must have... do you think it's possible to have super sperm?'

She snorted. 'Trust you.'

'What?'

'I think my eggs may have had something to do with it.'

'Touché. Well, we obviously make a great team.'

'Other people have babies, you know!' she joked. 'It's a miracle... but it's an everyday one.'

'Yes, but in one month of trying!' He stepped back and gave a little fist shake of triumph. 'Way to go, guys!'

'Are you seriously talking to your sperm?'

They laughed again, neither quite able to take in the news.

'We are so, so lucky,' she said.

'No.' He shook his head.

'No?'

'Well... Luck is... well, not sure if I believe in it. Too random. But fortu-

nate. Nicky, this is all us. The universe hasn't got anything to do with it. We're fortunate.'

'To have the good sperm.'

'And the good eggs.'

And she laughed as he wrapped his arms around her again.

* * *

'Are you sure she'll be able to handle it?' Nicky asked doubtfully as they watched the elderly woman make her way slowly up the driveway carrying a bucket full of bottles and colourful cloths. 'It's a lot of work for one person... let alone...' She wasn't quite sure how to finish the sentence.

It was another beautiful morning, but the sun streaming through the windows only served to highlight the fingerprints, streaks and dust particles that scattered the glass. Tiny flecks of silver and white floated in the air, highlighted by the unflinching light. The brightness revealed new layers of neglect – the badly wiped tables, the sticky stain in the corner, the uneven patchiness of the parquet. Nicky had hoped to be able to book a cleaning team, but as the budget had reduced, so had her expectations. It was day nine of her visit and she still felt as if they were at square one. They'd spent a few days clearing things out of various rooms, making a pile for Robert to take to the tip. Then they'd booked a deep clean, with the aim of putting everything back together before they moved onto the next stage. Saving money on the cleaner had made sense on paper, but now, watching the woman's painful progress across the scattered stones in front of the house she wondered whether they'd made a mistake.

Robert's jaw clenched slightly. 'I haven't met her before. But Michelle reckons she's a good worker.'

'I've no doubt,' Nicky said. 'But we're on a bit of a tight schedule.

I mean, it's been a week since we filmed and I know we've worked hard but...' She looked around. If the film crew were to come back now, they'd be less than impressed. 'There's not much... well, evidence of that yet.'

'I suppose there's only one way to find out,' Robert said, raising his eyebrows as he walked to the door and opened it, still in ample time before the woman made it to the front doorstep.

She watched him leave, wondering at his optimism. After his revelation about Marie a few days ago, which had somehow made everything she was trying to do seem more important and precarious, she'd wondered whether the whole project was going to cause him stress – the stakes were suddenly so high. But he'd thrown himself into the clearing out with gusto and hadn't seemed at all fazed by the fact that everything seemed to take an inordinate amount of time.

She was still kicking herself for not mentioning Steve when she'd had the chance. To say she was sorry; that she understood more than he realised. But as time had passed, so had the moment. It wasn't the sort of thing you could bring up casually with a: 'Me too!' as you might if you discovered something else you had in common. She couldn't ask him for a high-five of solidarity – as if she was part of some sort of secret widows' society.

'Ah, it doesn't matter,' Jenny had told her on the phone. 'I mean, the programme isn't about you, your history, after all.'

But that wasn't the reason she wanted to open up. It was the chance to connect with someone else, someone relatively young, who was in the same boat. It could have brought them closer somehow. That mutual understanding. As it was, it felt simply like a secret she was holding from him.

Alongside the clearing out they'd spent some time looking at Nicky's list to see where they could cut corners, and Robert had called around a few sets of friends for ideas and favour requests.

The result had been several promises of help with the painting and a recommendation for a low-cost cleaner who could spruce the place up on a shoestring. If they were lucky, they might be able to make it work.

Nicky stayed at the window as Robert opened the door to the woman with a creak. After exchanging bonjours, the pair had a conversation in rapid French then the two of them appeared in the dining room doorway, Robert's grin rather too wide to be genuine.

'This is Monique,' said Robert. 'Apparently her daughter is usually the one who does the cleaning, but she isn't well, so she sent her mum.'

'Right,' Nicky said, trying to smile at the rather frail looking woman.

'Bonjour,' Monique said, placing the bucket on the floor and holding out a gnarled hand for a shake. She was wearing a long, cloak like coat that went down to her ankles, despite the warm weather. She indicated the buttons.

'Oh yes, let me take your coat!' Nicky said, smiling. 'Um... *manteau*?'

Monique nodded and deftly unbuttoned the black coat. Then – surprise. Like a superhero in a phone box she flung off the cloak to reveal that underneath its voluminous folds, she was dressed in a pair of tracksuit bottoms and a loose T-shirt that read 'Bonjour Mes Copains!' in rainbow stitching. She straightened up and looked at Nicky with bright, brown eyes. 'I to start now?' she asked in imperfect English.

'Um, yes please. Maybe with the bathrooms?' Nicky asked. '*Les salles de bains*?'

Monique nodded and Robert followed her out of the door to show her where everything was. He returned shortly afterwards. 'Well, she's made a start in one bathroom,' he said. 'She seemed very keen to get going.'

'Great,' Nicky said. Having someone to give the house a clean was ticked off the list at least, assuming Monique could handle it.

'She reckons her daughter, Sophie, will be back tomorrow,' he said. 'So, fingers crossed, she'll have some help.'

'Yes.' Nicky felt a little guilty having Monique clean for her at all despite her surprisingly vibrant ensemble – she seemed somehow too old and frail. 'Are you sure she's up to it though?'

'I think she might surprise us,' said Robert. 'She whizzed up the stairs faster than me.'

He sat down next to her at the table they'd repurposed for their planning and scanned the list. 'I've ordered some paint,' he said. 'And there's a few local lads should be able to help with that. And I've got an idea... well, I know we spoke about how we might raise some extra cash... Well, I thought of something last night.'

'Oh yes?' She raised an eyebrow, questioningly.

'Just leave it with me,' he said, with a nod. A look crossed his face, like a small cloud blocking the sun for a moment; then it was gone and he met her eye and smiled thinly. 'I have a plan up my sleeve.'

They sat in silence for a minute.

'How are you feeling,' she said, 'about it all?'

He glanced around. 'Well, we're getting there, I guess. I mean, it's not... I think we've got a chance – don't you? Of making a bit of a difference.'

She nodded. 'I hope so,' she said.

'I reckon Marie would be proud, at least,' he said. 'You know, that I'm trying. That I've got help. It means a lot, you know.'

It was the first time he'd mentioned Marie's name since she'd found out. This was her chance.

'You know the other day – when you told me about Marie. How she... that she died?' she ventured.

'Yes?' Robert's eyes were back on the list, avoiding hers.

'I'm sorry I didn't say... much. I just... it was a surprise. I'd had this whole scenario in my head and it was totally, totally wrong. You know, when you said she wasn't around any more. I mean, lots of couples move abroad and, well, don't make it. So I thought...'

'It's OK, you weren't to know,' he said with a dismissive shrug. 'I should have been clearer about it in the first instance.'

'Maybe. But you know, I should have asked. Or, at least, not assumed.'

'It's fine, honestly.'

'And I'm surprised that Jenny – you know, my producer friend – didn't tell me. Because I wanted to say that... well, I get it. More than you know.' She looked at him.

He looked at her, his brow furrowed. 'You do?'

'Yes,' she said quietly. She felt her heart thump against her chest. How was it that after a decade it was still hard to get the words out? 'I... my husband, Steve. I... well, you know. He. I lost him.'

'I'm so sorry,' he said, looking at her so tenderly that she felt herself crumble.

'Thanks, I mean, yeah,' she said, wiping unexpected tears roughly from her cheeks. 'This is so stupid.'

'Of course it isn't,' he said, reaching into his pocket and handing her a crumpled, but hopefully clean, tissue.

'Thanks. But it is. I mean, it's been ten years. It's not... it shouldn't be so raw. But sometimes it feels...'

They were silent for a minute. Robert reached out and put an arm gently around her shoulder, pulling her in for a hug. The gesture was a surprise; despite the fact he'd thawed a bit since she'd arrived, he didn't strike her as someone who was ordinarily touchy-feely. She leaned in for a moment, feeling something deep inside relax slightly. Her defences crumbling a little. Then sat up.

'Maybe you never... I mean, maybe it's good that it's raw sometimes,' he said.

'You think?' She looked at him.

'Look, I'm no expert,' he said. 'But I've talked to a few – experts, that is. And you know, grief is kind of proportionate to love, isn't it? Like, feeling that way still must mean you two had something special.'

She nodded, blinking rapidly, trying to push any new tears back into her ducts through the force of her will.

'But a decade,' she said. 'I mean; I'm fine. I'm over it, as much as I'll ever be, I guess. It's just something sometimes... well, brings it all back.'

'I know exactly what you mean,' he said. 'This stuff, with the B&B. I mean...'

'Yeah, I can imagine.' Now it was her turn to look at him sympathetically.

'Was it... was it cancer, like Marie?' he asked. 'If it's OK to ask?'

She shook her head. 'Car crash.'

'Shit.'

It was the first time she'd heard Robert swear. 'Yep.'

They were silent for a moment.

'How long ago was Marie?' she said, not sure how to phrase the question.

'Three years.'

'Oh.'

'I mean she'd been sick for a long time – maybe eighteen months. And we knew, the last six, well, that it wasn't good. That she was... terminal. So I suppose it wasn't so... unexpected. But it's weird, you prepare yourself for it... but it's still a shock, you know?'

'I know,' she said, putting her hand on his arm for a moment. They looked at each other. 'I don't think anything really can prepare you for... all of it.'

'That's why this place – I tried to keep it going. I wanted to do her proud. But sometimes the energy just feels like it's been drained from me. Like I'd get up, get dressed, keep breathing. But you know, that is *it*. I can't always be thinking about bedding or guests or croissants.'

'I can imagine.'

'I've got some... good friends around here. Lots of people came through for me. I've been really lucky. But I suppose when I did... come out of it, the worst of the grief, I looked around and things had sort of fallen apart around me.'

'I get it. I really do.'

'Then... when this opportunity came, I thought: maybe this is my chance? My chance to make it actually happen. You know, like she wanted. Well, like we *both* wanted.'

Nicky nodded. She felt suddenly even more guilty about the show and the budget and the 'curveballs'. This was someone's life, not a TV show gimmick. How on earth was she going to make a real difference to this B&B with such a small budget and in such a limited timeframe?

'And I know I sort of joked about being a bad host. About... well, not being in my element. But I do want to stay. My life is here... my friends. And this place. It's a lot, I know. But it's my home. It's who I am now. And I just can't...'

The silence between them became awkward and she shifted her chair slightly. 'We'll make it work,' she said, hoping she was right. 'I'm sure we can make it work.'

Her eyes scanned the list she'd made, desperately searching for something to comment on. 'Bedding,' she said at last, trying to move the conversation on for both their sakes. 'I don't think we can afford to change everything but maybe some bedspreads? You know, freshen everything up a bit? Maybe get enough to redo the master suite so they've got something to gush about in the filming?'

'Actually, I've got some bedspreads,' he said. 'Marie bought some from the *brocante*. They're in the attic. We never got around to airing them out but they're beautiful. Antique, I think.'

'Sounds perfect,' she said, scribbling in her notebook.

He was about to say more when the door opened and Monique walked into the room clutching something in her hand. She seemed to glare briefly at Nicky before leaning in and saying something in furtive French to Robert.

'Sorry,' he said. 'I don't understand. *Je ne comprends pas?*'

'I need to ask for where to you keep the toys for sex?' she said, stiltedly.

'Sorry? The what?'

'Your sexy toys,' she said. 'Where do you keep?' She waved the thing in her hand. It was pink, shiny and domed at one end. 'Le vibrator!' she said. 'I put it by your bed, monsieur?'

'Oh.' Robert blushed to his roots. 'No, it's, it's not mine. It... I haven't seen it before.'

'Madame? It is yours perhaps?' Monique waved the offending article under her nose.

Nicky, who'd been studiously averting her eyes ever since the mention of 'toys for sex' looked up once the question was directed at her. 'Oh, no,' she said. 'It's not...' Then, looking more closely, she realised that what Monique was holding was very much hers. The pink, silicone travel case she'd bought for her toothbrush looked, in the cold light of day, every inch something very, very different.

The other object Monique was clutching was her hair smoothing lotion, with its pink shiny case, its domed cap. Nicky had bought a bottle after seeing it on a TV makeover programme, and when it had arrived one Saturday in an enormous box she and Jenny had laughed their heads off at its suggestive shape.

'Oh my God, why is it so *penile*!' her friend had said. 'I'd seriously read the ingredients before putting any of that white stuff on your hair.'

'This is dildo,' Monique said, matter-of-factly, placing the tooth-brush holder in front of Nicky. 'And this is vibrator, non?' putting down the hair smoother. 'I think it better they are not in the guest bathroom. Not everyone like this.' She shook her head disap-provingly.

'I... No,' said Nicky.

'They are yours, madame?'

'Well, yes. They are. But they're not...'

Robert seemed to reach a whole new shade of scarlet. He began studying something on his phone, aiming for nonchalant and failing completely.

'I find them in upstairs bathroom,' Monique said, narrowing her eyes as if judging Nicky's lack of discretion. 'Shall I put them in your private room, madame?'

Nicky had used the bigger, shared bathroom this morning when putting on her make-up – the light had been better. And she had left her toiletries in a neat pile by the sink, meaning to pick them up later.

Robert was looking away, his ears flaming red.

'I'll take them,' Nicky said, at last. 'I'll put them in my bag.'

Monique's mouth twisted slightly, but she shrugged. 'OK, and when I find more, I bring them, yes?'

'You won't find any more... you didn't... And look,' she said desperately. 'It's a toothbrush holder.'

'Oui, it's dildo.' Monique nodded. 'I understand. I do not judge. I have at my home. But not in the family bathroom.'

'No. It's for my teeth.' Nicky bared her teeth at Monique who stepped back.

'Yes. I know this. It's dildo.'

'And my hair stuff.'

'This? *C'est un vibrator.* Oui?' Monique gave her a curt nod. 'But it is not good for bathroom.'

'Oui,' Nicky said in the end, giving up rather than drawing out the painful conversation for any longer.

'OK,' Monique said decisively, turning on her heel as if she'd simply returned a cup or pen or something completely non-sexual to its owner, rather than handed back what she thought was something far more personal.

'Oh my God,' Nicky said, once Monique had hobbled out of the room. 'You know those weren't... sex toys, don't you?'

'Yes they were!' said Robert.

'No, look. It's... just some hair stuff and...'

'"No, it's dildo",' he said doing a very good impression of Monique.

'Oh God.' Nicky felt her shoulders begin to shake with either laughter or residual embarrassment.

Robert caught her eye and then they were both laughing. 'The look on her face!' he said.

'I know!' Nicky laughed. 'Poor woman. She was so determined.'

'To be fair, they do look a bit... well, suspect.'

'Well, yes. Now that it's been pointed out.'

'Guessing you won't be applying that hair smoother in public any more...'

'That is the least of my worries. I'll never be able to brush my teeth again!'

And then, just for a moment they were lost in the delicious, all-encompassing laughter. The kind of laughter we experience every day in childhood, but that disappears as we age. That gets lost in a mess of self-consciousness, or preoccupation, or is brought down to size by sadness or grief. The laughter that somehow frees you from everything that is holding your spirit down. And just for a second there was no crash, and no Steve, and no girls to care for, and no TV show and no worries about turning a business around on a shoe-string. There was nothing except an inescapable tide of happiness.

9

'You look great,' Michelle said decisively as Nicky came out of the changing room for the eighth time. Her outfit of choice was a pair of navy jeans with a blue silk blouse adorned with a red, floral motif. The blue, she had to admit, made her hair stand out with new vibrancy.

The painting would start in a couple of days, just in time to make a difference before the crew came, and she'd be dressing bedrooms later on. Monique had done well with the initial cleaning yesterday and now her daughter, Sophie, had joined her, things were beginning to come together. Nicky planned to spend the afternoon looking at Robert's books and seeing where he could make savings but Robert, ever mysterious, had gone on some sort of secret errand this morning.

Left to her own devices and not wanting to be presented with any more apparent sex toys, she'd decided to go clothes shopping.

She was beginning to get a feel for this 'new her'. Or, at least, the her she was projecting when working the cameras. Where this person would go once the show stopped filming, she wasn't yet sure. But playing the part of a TV expert had released something in her – an alternative version she couldn't quite believe was her.

'Thank you.' Nicky smiled, now turning slightly in front of the mirror. 'I think this is the one.'

'So when's the next filming session?' Michelle asked a few minutes later when Nicky was back in her casual clothes, popping her pin number into the card reader.

'A few days,' she said. 'I'm just hoping we'll be ready.'

'Wow, you'll be finished that quickly?'

'No, it's just a kind of interim thing. How we're getting on. That sort of thing,' she said.

Michelle nodded. 'Must be a great job,' she added. 'Going here and there, transforming lives.'

'Oh, well, it's not my usual job. I just... a friend gave me the opportunity. I'm usually more... well, local rather than national. I've never even been on TV before,' she admitted, feeling her cheeks get hot.

Michelle nodded. 'First timer. Wow, that's brave. I mean, brilliant and brave.'

Nicky grinned self-consciously. 'Well, if it helps, I feel completely out of my depth most of the time.'

Michelle smiled. 'Ah, don't we all,' she said. Then, 'Must be nice though.'

'What... drowning?'

'No,' Michelle said, expertly folding Nicky's purchases into a paper carrier bag. 'Having a friend like that. Someone who can, well, give you an opportunity. Take a real chance on you. She must have so much faith in you to put you in the limelight like that.'

'Oh, Jenny? She's brilliant.' Nicky nodded. 'We've been friends for... well, donkeys' years.' It struck her then that it really was a great opportunity and, Michelle was right, it must have taken faith for Jenny to give it to her. She'd been so wrapped up in the impact everything was having on her life that she'd never really thought about the risk Jenny was taking in engaging her in the first place. She resolved to call her friend later; thank her properly.

'That's one thing I miss over here,' Michelle said. 'You know, I've got friends. But... they're all quite new. And the ones I had in the UK. They do come over sometimes but it's not the same. It's lovely when they're here, of course it is. But I miss those small, regular meetings with people who know me to my bones.'

Nicky nodded, thinking of the coffees she'd had almost weekly with Jenny, come rain or shine. 'Yeah,' she said. 'I know exactly what you mean. I mean, Jenny's been almost my other half, since...' She paused, feeling something stick in her throat. 'After...' she said. 'Um... after...'

Nicky had been talking about Steve's death for a decade. The first few months after the accident she'd been unable to say his name without bursting into tears. But in the years that followed, that part of her had become more resilient.

As time had passed, she'd become used to recounting brief information about her circumstances and what had led to them without feeling very much at all. And even when she did reminisce about life with Steve or talk about her years alone with the girls she'd been able to look back more fondly. Always with a pang, but with happiness too. That they'd had each other, even if their time had been cut short.

Yesterday was the first time she'd cried when talking about him for a long time. And she'd assumed it was because Robert really understood. That something in him had spoken to her.

Yet here, in this little stone building at the end of a row of quaint shops, in a place five hundred miles from home, talking to a virtual stranger, she suddenly found the grief – almost as sharp as it had been ten years ago – once again pushed through all the years of sadness, repression, acceptance and fond reminiscing and made its way to the surface. She felt a flush of heat, and raised her hand to cover her mouth. But nothing could stop the shoulder-shaking sob that rose inside her like hot lava breaking through stone.

'I'm sorry,' she said, half an hour later sitting in a café around the corner. 'I'm not sure what came over me. I... I'm not usually like that when I talk about Steve. About the accident.' She said the words carefully, scared that she'd be consumed again. But it seemed as if the moment for emotional explosion had passed.

She took a sip of her coffee and shakily placed the cup back in its saucer.

'Don't be silly,' Michelle said, concerned. 'You have every right to feel this way. God knows, sounds like you've been through a lot.'

'Yes, but years ago. I mean, to break down like that? You closed the shop for me!' Nicky said, feeling guilt well up in her. 'I'm so sorry, I have no idea where it came from.'

'Ah, what's the point of having your own business if you can't close it in a crisis?' said Michelle, simply. 'Plus I rarely get more than a couple of customers in the morning when it's not market day. And most of them are local – they'll be back. This was more important.' Her eyes, concerned, studied Nicky's face.

'Well, thank you,' said Nicky still feeling a little awkward. 'Do you want to get back? I'm OK, now.'

'Yeah, in a bit.' Michelle was seemingly not at all worried about her business. 'Thought I might sneak another coffee first. Maybe a pastry?' She looked at Nicky expectantly.

'Go on then.' Nicky smiled. 'But this one is my treat.'

Now that she'd recovered some sort of equilibrium it was nice taking a step out of the stress of the B&B and her imminent exposure as a fraud on national TV to talk about ordinary things.

'So you seem pretty happy here,' she said to Michelle, eager to turn the subject away from herself and her near-emotional breakdown at the till.

'Oh, I am. Although I do get homesick.'

'Really?'

'Don't get me wrong. I have lots of great friends here, lots of people to lean on,' said her new friend. 'But I think when you move somewhere new – somewhere far from your original location – you sort of split yourself in two. Part of me will always be in Otley.' She shrugged and took a bite of her apple tart.

'Do you ever think about moving back?' Nicky asked.

'Ah, sometimes. But not in any real sense,' Michelle said. 'If I moved back to Otley, a part of me would still stay in Roussillon. I'm forever split in two.'

'I see,' Nicky said, with a sympathetic smile.

'Ah, it's not so bad. Choosing between two brilliant places to live. Could be worse.'

'Good point.'

'That's the problem with broadening your horizons, I suppose,' Michelle said, with a shrug. 'You never quite know where you *fit* any more.'

'I can see that.'

'Only I guess here there's better weather and a handsome Frenchman waiting for me at the end of the day.' She smiled.

'Seems like quite an easy choice when you put it like that!' Nicky grinned. She took a bite of the almond biscuit she'd bought and felt it melt deliciously in her mouth, filling it with a delicious mixture of sweet marzipan, butter and nuts.

'Yeah. So what about you? Ever think of moving away? Trying something new?'

Nicky shook her head. 'Never,' she said. 'Running away... sometimes. Especially when the girls went through the worst of their teens.'

'Ha. Yeah, nightmare.'

'But since Steve...' She paused, but the floodgates remained closed. 'I suppose it's been my job to provide some sort of stability for the girls. Well, stability for me too. After everything. I've built a kind of structure back home. I have a steady job, that kind of thing. So I never really looked for anything else.'

Michelle nodded. 'Sounds sensible'.

'Yes,' said Nicky. 'It does, doesn't it!' She set her cup back in her saucer and shook her head.

'Oh, I didn't mean to offend.'

'No, you haven't. It's just hearing you say "sensible" – made me realise how... well, how boring I've become.'

'Oh, hardly!'

'No, I mean it. Before, when I looked at my career I thought... well, I thought I'd be doing interesting things, having fun. I was dreaming of becoming a designer. I got the degree, a bit of experience. But now... well, I'm more on the financial advice side of things.'

'But start-ups are pretty exciting. You must have helped so many people on their way.'

'True,' she said. 'It's not that I don't value what I do. I suppose it's just part of me always felt that it should have been me taking the risk. Me with the fledgling business, helping it to fly.'

'But look at you now – if this isn't having an adventure, I don't know what is.'

'Kind of an accidental one, though,' said Nicky. 'I mean, Jenny sort of thrust it on me.'

Michelle nodded thoughtfully.

'I mean, don't get me wrong,' Nicky added. 'I'm happy in my day job. Well, content. It's just... sometimes I wonder whether I kind of lost some of myself in it all. When Steve... died, something had to give. And I suppose it was me... my dreams, ambitions, whatever. They went on the back burner.'

Michelle sighed. 'But what you did was amazing; selfless, really.'

Nicky nodded. 'Thanks. Only the more I think about it. Well... it wasn't really my need to look after the kids that drove me. At least, not just that.'

'No?'

'I think I was scared.'

'Scared?'

'Scared to ask too much of life maybe. I mean I'd had this brutal, sudden thing happen to my family. And I felt – well, maybe I'd just been too lucky before and sort of paid the price.'

The words, spoken aloud for the first time, shocked her. She thought back to the early years with Steve. Their marriage, their jobs. The way they'd fallen pregnant so easily. The fact that everything with him had seemed so simple, so natural. 'We,' he'd used to say, 'are unbeatable.'

Then the accident. And suddenly she was no longer lucky, but deeply unlucky.

On some level, had she thought that she'd paid the price for all that luck? Had she been scared to ask for too much in case the same thing happened again? She felt a shiver deep inside as if something had been unlocked inside her. *I've been on pause*, she thought. *I've been... frozen.*

'Are you OK?' Michelle said, reaching a hand across the table. 'You look a bit pale.'

'I'm fine,' she said, snapping back to the moment. 'Really.'

Michelle held her gaze for a moment, then nodded. 'Well, look.

You know where I am, don't you? If things get too much. I'm here. I know we don't know each other that well yet. But I mean it. Honestly.'

'Thank you.'

Ten minutes later, they exited the small café into the shock of the late morning heat. The pavement outside was full of people milling about, rushing along on errands or to work meetings; others strolling, looking, taking pictures. A mixture of different people, their lives blended together, coinciding in the same place for a moment, by chance. Faces she might pass again; faces she would probably never see twice.

In her conscious mind, she didn't really believe in luck. Things were too random. You made your 'luck' by taking chances, by being unafraid. But somewhere on a subconscious level she'd held onto a more primitive, childlike belief, that the universe was even-handed and if you expected too much, you'd end up disappointed.

She looked at Michelle at her side and caught her eye. 'Thanks again,' she said, as they approached the shop and Michelle began rummaging in her bag for her keys. 'Truly.'

'Any time,' her new friend said. 'I mean it.'

'And look, let's meet up for another chat soon.'

'I'd like that,' Michelle said. 'I really would.'

She smiled as she watched Michelle climb the stone steps back to her shop then, waving goodbye, began the walk back to the B&B.

And as she walked, handbag bouncing against her hip, Nicky looked anew at her surroundings. The rust-red of the stone houses, the shock of green trees behind a stone wall. The blue sky with its reliable golden sun. The colours, noises, sounds and smells of life seemed somehow brand new.

She'd found a little part of herself she'd locked away. A part that was a little braver, who wasn't afraid to want more from life. And she'd made a friend in the process.

She was, she concluded, incredibly lucky.

Well, not lucky.

Fortunate. Capable.

Somehow she'd arrived at a place of clarity. Maybe, just maybe, this was going to be her time.

10

'Nicky, I'm back!' The shout made her jump and she was glad that her coffee was firmly on the wood of the kitchen table rather than in her hand. Usually Robert entered the house quietly, and called a soft hello in the hallway. Once he'd even knocked on the kitchen door when she'd been in there, not wanting to shock her. Clearly, something was up. Buster, excited by his owner's tone, barked loudly to herald their return.

'Hi,' she called, slightly nervously.

She'd spent the morning applying rather thin emulsion to the hallway walls – trying to cover up the ancient, highly decorated wallpaper they'd thought would be easy to paint into oblivion. She'd found it strangely relaxing to do – watching the white cover the colourful, faded past – bringing it up to date and into the future. It had felt cleansing and lightened the passage to the dining room and kitchen beautifully.

Now that job was done – although three or four further coats might well be needed – she was sitting in the kitchen, paperwork spread across the table, drinking her second cup of coffee while trying to make sense of some of the plans she'd sketched out last night. Cost-cutting, sprucing up, improving service to guests – last night everything had made sense. This afternoon, she wished she'd written it out more neatly.

Robert came into the kitchen with an enormous and almost disconcerting grin on his face.

'Hi?' she said, a little uncertainly as the man who'd entered the kitchen with such gusto seemed to have very little in common with the Robert who'd left quietly this morning after breakfast.

'You are going to LOVE me,' he said, fishing around in his coat pocket and withdrawing a stash of notes. 'Show me the money!' he said in an outdated reference to one of her favourite nineties films. He fanned himself elaborately and accidentally touched his eye. 'Ow, sorry,' he said, sinking into a chair. 'I just feel kind of... wired.'

She looked again at the suspicious bundle of cash. Had he held up the post office? Been dealing crack behind the *bibliothèque*? But she couldn't believe he'd obtained it in any illegal way. It was just the sight of it once it was on the kitchen table, with no comment as to its origin, which unsettled her. All he needed was a black brief-case to stack it in and he'd have gone full *Wolf of Wall Street* on her.

Robert looked at the money, his expression suddenly unreadable. Smile gone.

'So this is for the... improvements?' Nicky said, uncertainly.

He nodded. 'Yes.'

'How much is—?'

'About three grand.'

The sum was hardly life changing, but it would triple the budget set by the show, which was now so squeezed it would hardly cover the cost of the deep clean and a few extra pillowcases. She was still a little nervous about cheating the system by injecting extra funds, but when she'd slightly hinted to Jenny that they might have some money from 'other sources' on the phone last night, her friend had simply said, 'keep it believable' and refused to be drawn. 'Don't tell me,' she'd said. 'Then I can deny everything.'

It made sense to inject a little extra capital if they could, Nicky had reasoned. It was Robert's business, his actual life and her career which would be at stake if things went badly. She ought to grab any opportunity to improve their chances. *His* chance to stay in France and keep his business.

'Well, that's great,' she said. 'But how...?'

He took a breath. 'Just... sold a couple of things,' he said. He didn't seem ready to divulge more, so she didn't push him.

'I see you've been working on your plans?' he said, looking at her notebook.

'Well, trying to,' she admitted. 'Might be easier now though.'

'Yes. And the wall looks good,' he added.

'You think?' She screwed up her nose.

'Well, the paint's a bit...'

'That pattern is going to take some covering up, that's for sure,' she said. 'And we've barely touched the upstairs.'

'We'll get there,' he said. 'Although you look as if you could use a break.'

'Yeah, that definitely sounds tempting,' she said. 'Do you want to... go for a walk or something? Talk about it all?'

'Yeah,' he said. He ran a hand through his hair, leaving it in disarray. 'Actually,' he said, glancing at her and snatching his gaze away. 'Do you mind if we don't? Not right now. I think... I might need a bit of a rest.'

She glanced at her watch. Two o'clock. 'Are you feeling OK?'

'Yes. It's... I suppose a headache?' he said, an upward inflexion making it pretty obvious he was lying. But she took him at his word. It was none of her business.

'Maybe a lie down then?' she said.

He nodded. 'If you don't mind?'

'Of course. I'll get calling around and we can chat about it later,' she said. 'Maybe do another coat if this one's dried too.'

He nodded, stood and then looked at her again. His mouth moved as if to speak, but then he shook his head and straightened up. 'Well, see you in an hour or so,' he said, avoiding eye contact.

'Sure.'

* * *

An hour later, she heard the sound of him moving around upstairs through the open window above.

She got up from the patio chair, almost knocking over the glass of iced water she'd made for herself. She'd been tempted to add a slosh of wine to the glass, especially after the stress of her latest round of phone calls. But knowing her luck, if she let her guard down the TV crew would turn up unannounced and bring her entire fledgling career crashing down.

Over the last couple of days she'd spent hours phoning and emailing, and had even roped in Michelle to make a couple of phone calls for her in French. But to no avail. Today, she'd finally made it to the end of her list of potential tradespeople. Every single artisan, painter, builder and even odd-job man seemed booked for months in advance. Even when she'd offered more money, the answer had been a firm 'non'.

Robert appeared, now looking dishevelled, at the back door. His T-shirt was even more crumpled than usual and he'd changed into a pair of tatty shorts. Somehow the ensemble together with his scruffy hair made him look cute and boyish rather than less attractive. 'Sorry about that,' he said. His eyes seemed slightly red and she wondered whether his headache 'excuse' had actually been genuine.

'Not at all,' she said.

'So, any luck?' he asked, nodding at her scribbled notes.

'No,' she said. 'No... luck at all. I just can't get anyone to do it,' she said, feeling her mouth wobble slightly. She pulled herself together. 'Nobody seems to want to take anything extra on for months. Nobody seemed to understand the... well, the urgency of it. I asked whether people could make an exception and well, people seemed to find it weird. Or... well, one guy laughed at me.'

'I was worried that might happen,' he admitted. 'Not the laughing bit, of course. But I did think you were a bit... ah, confident, when you talked about getting people in.'

'Oh,' she said. 'You didn't say.'

He shrugged. 'I suppose it's been so long since I hired anyone... you know, living on a shoestring... that I thought I might be wrong. I mean it was worth trying.'

'I suppose,' she said. It would have been nice, though, to have had a heads-up. Because if they had to take the bulk of the work on themselves it was going to take every spare hour they had left. 'I just don't get it,' she admitted. 'You'd think people would be crying out for some extra hours, a bit of spare cash.'

'Maybe in the UK,' Robert said. 'Here, you'll be hard pressed to find anyone working extra hours. And lots of them pack up altogether in August.'

'I know, what is it with that?' she asked. Already having shared the problem with him she felt a little better.

'I used to think that,' he said. 'But the longer I've lived here, well, I've started to think they've got it right when it comes to work. They work to live around here. You know, value time with family. Don't like to make it all about money the way we Brits do sometimes.'

'True.'

'But it's not ideal if you actually want to get a job done.'

'Well,' she said. 'Exactly.' They smiled at each other in mutual frustration.

She'd thought she'd at least be able to recruit someone to do a bit of labouring on a part-time basis, or some students for evening work, but so far she'd been unable to get anyone to agree to do anything. One plumber had told Michelle it would be three months before he could even give an estimate for changing the shower attachment on the bath.

They smiled at each other for a moment, before anxiety welled again in Nicky's chest. 'But seriously, what am I going to do? We need to be ready to film again in a few days – to show the "progress",' she said, gesturing around as if to highlight the fact that their net progress was completely and utterly zero.

'No,' he said. 'Not what are *you* going to do. What are *we* going to do.'

'Oh.' The simple correction startled her. She was so used to problem solving alone.

'We are going to put our heads together, we're going to get on the phone again, we're going to call in favours – hell, blackmail people if we have to – and we're going to make this thing happen,' he said, looking in her direction (possibly at her, it was hard to tell as his eyes were screwed up against the light).

He was right, she realised, when she looked at him. She wasn't sure exactly what they'd do, but at least they were on the same team. Over the years, she'd become used to sorting everything out for herself, and liked the independence and the feeling of self-sufficiency it had given her.

But that didn't mean she didn't sometimes miss having someone at her side telling her everything would be OK, or taking a difficult job from her when it became too much. The way Steve had sometimes done when she'd been tired and he'd sent her to the spare room for a proper sleep and taken on the baby duties for a night. Or when he'd taken the saucepan out of her hand and told her he'd order a takeaway. The way he'd stick up for her when she'd had a falling out with her mum, or knew he'd be completely on her side when she'd relayed a difficult encounter from a work day.

She smiled at Robert. 'Thanks,' she said.

'No problem.' He smiled, eyes still ridiculously scrunched up in the light. 'And would you help me, too, to find something better to wear?' he said. 'I'm just so... well...' He gestured at his ragged shorts and she nodded.

'Do you want to carry on this conversation inside...' she said, before she realised how that sounded. 'I mean,' she added quickly, 'out of the direct sunlight.'

'Now that,' he said, 'really *does* sound like a plan.'

11

'Are you sure you're OK with this?' Robert asked for the third time.

She took a sip from her coffee. 'Of course!' she said brightly. Although in reality she wasn't 100 per cent sure she was going to be able to find Robert a new wardrobe they'd both approve of. Or whether they really had time for a shopping trip at this point in proceedings. Still, a promise is a promise, she thought, taking in his jogging bottoms and slightly greyed-out Aertex top. And it would be good optics for the TV show.

Optics? a little voice inside her said. Was she actually turning into Jenny?

In reality, she had almost called the whole thing off – they could focus on painting the skirting board and door-frames, or dressing the tables or doing one of the many 'snagging' jobs on her hit list. But when he'd come downstairs all enthusiasm and gratitude this morning, she hadn't the heart to cancel.

Robert had chosen to drive them to the centre of Avignon rather than visit the rather ropey 'men's clothing store' in Roussillon. It was raining lightly as they drove along, enough to need the window wipers on, but not so much that it prevented them from squeaking every time they cleared the screen. Robert would turn them on and off periodically and every time Nicky felt a sense of relief when the annoying noise stopped.

She looked out of the window across the open fields, the colours washed out under the grey sky; a few brown, dishevelled cows huddled under an enormous tree, and in another field, sodden sheep grazed on, despite the weather.

They passed stone houses with immaculate gardens, others set back from the road and surrounded by clumps of trees. As they drove, the sun began to break through the clouds determinedly and although the rain persisted, it became lighter and began to ease off. By the time they reached the outskirts of Avignon, the rain had ceased entirely and the day had settled into itself – warm, but not sunny. Perfect for wandering and shopping. It took a while to find a parking space, and as they drove down streets flanked with enormous sand-coloured buildings housing everything from insurance companies to municipal services and turned into smaller, one-way roads peppered with small boutiques and glass-fronted medical centres, Nicky began to imagine she was in a film. On the arm of a burly Jason Bourne type, making their way through an unfamiliar city together, looking for somewhere to blend in. Cutting and dyeing their hair to protect their identities, and emerging dressed like chic locals, her with a jet-black bob, him clean-shaven and handsome. Running over rooftops being pursued... Making out in a hotel room, high on adrenaline...

'...About three hours?' Robert was saying when she came to.

'Eh?'

'Do you reckon, for the parking?' he said, as he finally pulled into a space.

'Um, yeah. That'll be fine,' she said, snapping back to reality.

'You were miles away,' he remarked, unclipping his seatbelt and grinning at her.

'Yes,' she said. 'Lost myself for a minute.'

'Planning your shopping route?' he queried.

'Not quite,' she said, then felt a need to fill the silence. 'I was just thinking,' she added quickly, 'how French everything looks.' She heard her own words spoken aloud and blushed. 'I know,' she said. 'That sounds ridiculous. I just mean that even though there are the normal shops and restaurants and insurance firms or whatever, everything – all the buildings, the people – are unmistakably *French*.'

Robert looked at her. 'Who'd have thought things would look so French in France?' he joked. 'But I know what you mean. It's kind of beautiful, isn't it?'

She nodded. 'It is,' she said.

He even looked a bit like Matt Damon in that moment, she mused. She'd never seen it before – the shape of his face, the eyes – albeit brown not blue. His hair was a little longer, more unkempt, but there was definitely a resemblance there. She watched him get out of the car and make his way to the meter to pay and felt suddenly just how much difference she could make to his appearance with well-cut clothes, a haircut, a closer shave. He was a bit like the B&B, she thought. Beautiful, but neglected. Shabby chic.

What was she, a poet? She shook her head and got out of the car, trying to keep her mind on the job. Sitting in the passenger seat for almost an hour had made her feel slightly fuzzy headed, made everything dreamlike. She needed to get her focus back. She was not an actor in *The Bourne Identity*. Nor was she a personal stylist. She was Nicky, middle-aged design enthusiast. And he was not Matt Damon, he was a B&B owner in crisis. The only similarity between the film and her situation really was that both Robert and Matt needed to find out their true identity – but in very different ways. In Robert's case, on the racks of a French boutique rather than in some secret government file. Which was eminently preferable and almost certainly safer.

She wondered what fancy boutiques he'd take her to in the historical town. Having lived nearby for so many years, he'd know all the backstreets, the little markets, the cute independent stores and the hidden secrets. It would be like having her own guided tour.

'So I thought we'd start with H&M?' he said, as he popped the ticket on the front dash and locked the car.

'H&M?' She was incredulous.

'Yes, they do have ordinary shops in France too, you know,' he said. 'It's not all boutiques and haute couture.'

'I know, but *H&M*,' she said. 'I shop there all the time. I might as well be back in St Albans.'

'All right, where would you like to take me,' he said, grinning.

'I mean, H&M's OK,' she said. 'But I guess I'm here and it would be nice to at least go to a shop I'm not familiar with.'

'Something French?'

'Oui, yes. Something French, monsieur,' she said in her best French accent. Which admittedly wasn't that impressive.

'Superdry?' he suggested. 'Although I guess, it's another chain store, so maybe not quite what you were thinking of?'

'It sounds a bit like a deodorant stick!' She wrinkled her nose.

'OK, how about some sort of independent boutique, like Michelle's but for men?' he said.

'Yes!' she said. 'I mean, if you know one. If it's OK with you,' she added hurriedly.

'Coming right up, m'lady,' he said in a mockney accent. Which made the whole thing rather confusing but did result in her letting out a little laugh.

'Idiot,' she said.

Then she wondered whether she'd overstepped the mark. She was here in a professional capacity, almost, to spruce up the owner of a B&B not out shopping with a friend. Not really. 'Sorry,' she added.

He led her along a small back road to a pedestrian area teeming with people. She walked past a chocolatier, a small home furnishing shop whose window featured a chair draped in fabric samples, a shop selling make-up and another that boasted the title 'fromagerie' – although in all honesty the sign was hardly needed; she'd smelled the heady scent of mixed cheeses in the air about ten metres before finding the source.

Finally, he led her into a men's clothing store, with black signage that read 'La Mode'. This was more like it.

The shop was almost empty; a salesman was standing in the corner, moving jackets on a rack and checking sizes. Another man was browsing a small selection of shoes at the back of the store.

Unsure where to start, Nicky tried to take on the air of one who knew what she was doing, perusing racks of trousers and jeans, pulling the odd pair out for inspection. She looked up to see Robert studying her, looking amused.

'What?' she said, half offended.

'Nothing,' he said. 'Just hoping you're not going to get me to try those on?'

She looked and saw that she was holding a pair of faux leather trousers in a tiny size. 'Oh, I don't know,' she said. 'It is apparently *La Mode*.' She grinned.

'I thought you were serious for a moment,' he said, looking relieved. 'Are you sure we shouldn't be in H&M?'

At the mention of the store, the man in the back snapped to attention, looked at them and seemed to glare, his nostrils widening as if insulted.

'Whoops,' Robert mouthed.

The man began to walk over to them, flicking a scarf over his shoulder and taking on a haughty air. 'You are looking for something, perhaps?' he said to them, his eyes running up and down Robert's ensemble and clearly finding it wanting. 'I cannot imagine that you would find anything better in H&M than you can 'ere.'

'We're just... I mean, looking at clothes,' Robert said, shrugging awkwardly.

'It's just...' Nicky said quickly. 'I'm doing... well, a makeover,' she said, not quite knowing how to describe it.

The man's nostrils flared in approval. Before meeting this particular guy, Nicky had had no idea that nostrils could be so expressive. He nodded. 'Ah! Le Glow-up!' he said approvingly. 'Yes. Yes, I can see that he does need some help,' he said. 'Perhaps I can guide you. I am considered quite, how you say, le guru in Avignon, I can assure you.'

Nicky was about to say no, when she thought – why not? After all, she'd relied a lot on Michelle's help for her own outfit choices; as a result she had a couple of items in her wardrobe she'd never have considered otherwise.

'Yes please,' she said, nodding reassuringly at Robert whose face had grown pale with alarm.

Minutes later, she was standing outside the dressing room with the man – whose name, she'd now discovered, was Théo – waiting for Robert to exit in one of his new outfits.

The curtain was drawn back reluctantly and Robert emerged, looking uncomfortable in a pair of black jeans and a vibrant blue shirt. He pulled at the collar slightly as if it was strangling him. The jeans were rucked up at the knees and so low at the back she could almost see a cheeky glimpse of bottom cleavage as he moved.

'Not sure it's quite me,' he muttered self-consciously.

'Maybe not,' she admitted. 'Next!'

'*Ce n'est pas vrai!*' Théo exclaimed loudly, making them both jump and rushing forwards. 'How is it that the English men do not know how to dress himself?' he said, pulling the shirt where Robert had tucked it in, opening a few buttons – revealing a surprisingly smooth chest – and redoing them deftly. He pulled the shirt slightly at the back, tugged at the trousers, disappeared suddenly and came back with a scarf which he flung around Robert's neck with a flourish. 'Voilà,' he said, confidently.

'Wow,' said Nicky.

'I'm not sure about the...' Robert said, turning towards the mirror, then stopped. Clearly he had seen what Nicky had. That he looked absolutely amazing. The blue of the shirt, which now fitted flatteringly around his taught midriff, complemented the deep brown of his eyes. The jeans were well cut and narrow without being clingy. The scarf, well, it was a flourish that set off the outfit brilliantly. She doubted he'd go for that accessory for day-to-day, but he could buy it to wear on the show perhaps. 'Oh,' he said. 'It looks OK, actually.'

'Pah! OK.' Théo was affronted. 'It is better than OK! It is a triumph! Monsieur, you no longer look like the English man, huh? I have in fact worked a miracle!' He looked at Nicky and winked, and Nicky suddenly saw that he wasn't haughty at all, that not only did he know his stuff, that he had a sense of humour about it that she hadn't seen until now. Even his nostrils looked more friendly than they had previously.

She smiled. 'Théo, you are indeed a miracle worker. Come on, Robert, let's see the next one.'

As Robert turned back into the changing room, Théo said, 'These British men, they do not know how to flatter their bodies. And your boyfriend, he is very good looking. A handsome man, but he hide it, non?'

'He's not my...' she began, then wondered why she felt the need to clarify that to Théo. It didn't really matter what he thought. 'We're just friends,' she said.

Théo winked at her as if in on a secret. 'But of course,' he said. 'But of course.'

* * *

An hour later, they were sitting in a café, their table surrounded with paper 'La Mode' bags. Robert was studying the receipt, his face slightly contorted. 'Wow, remind me not to go shopping with you again,' he said. 'I'd need to take out another mortgage!'

'Ah, but it's worth it,' she said. 'You look…' It felt awkward to say it, so she let it trail off and took a sip of her coffee. 'It'll be great for the programme,' she said more decisively after the caffeine hit.

'And at least it's done,' Robert said, nodding. 'Want to get some lunch before we head off?'

She shook her head with a grin. 'Oh, it's not over,' she said, looking at his hair and pulling out the little card from a local salon Théo had given her. 'Yes, to a bite of lunch. Then we're getting the hair done.'

'We are?'

'We are.'

He nodded. 'Anything for the ratings, I suppose.'

'Exactly,' she said. 'I mean, now I know what you looked like under those clothes I'm keen to see what else you have going on.' Then she blushed, hearing herself. 'I mean,' she said. 'You know. In the new clothes you look like… the best version of yourself… not… I mean, I didn't… I only saw your chest so…' She felt her cheek with her hand and almost burned herself.

He laughed. 'Don't worry I know what you mean. It's been a while since I had a glow-up.'

'Have you ever even used the word glow-up before?'

'Well. No.'

'Probably for the best.'

They smiled at each other and finished up their coffee. 'Right,' said Robert, standing up and reaching for her hand as if to pull her to her feet, then clearly thinking better of it. 'Where next, boss?'

12

———

'So, how's it going?' Amy asked the following morning.

In the background Nicky could hear the chatter of the radio in her daughter's house, and the clink of plates or bowls being stacked.

'Really good, thanks,' she answered. Although in truth, well, that simply wasn't true. They'd managed to slap another coat of paint on the hallway, but the wallpaper was still, stubbornly, showing through in places.

Yesterday, Nicky had started to clear moss from the front step, using a scraper to remove the stubborn green growth – it had been a satisfying job, but had taken her over two hours.

They still needed to get someone to sand the floor in the dining room; someone to print and laminate the new menu cards they'd created with tick-boxes for vegetarian and vegan options, as well as a space for those on special diets to request their chosen breakfast.

They needed to find someone adept with a paintbrush to revamp the walls in the dining room and upstairs corridor. They needed to shop for accessories and perhaps replace some of the ricketier chairs. She'd hoped to get others to do a lot of the actual

DIY and concentrate on soft furnishings and finishing touches. As it was, she and Robert had worked until midnight last night after returning from their shopping trip. She'd also had a chat – half in English, half in mime – with the local baker and thought at least she'd sorted something out regarding croissants for the guests, only to have a box of twenty-five of the things delivered at 8 o'clock and realise he'd clearly not understood what she wanted at all. She was stuck. But there was no point in worrying her daughter – she had enough on her plate with little Rose.

'You managed to get everything sorted OK?'

Nicky could hear water pouring as Amy made herself a cup of tea. She felt a pang of guilt that she wasn't there to pop in after work as she usually did. 'Yes, yes. It's great,' Nicky replied. 'But how are *you*? How's my favourite little granddaughter?'

'Your only granddaughter.'

'Well, yes.'

'She,' said Amy firmly, 'is in the doghouse. You should have seen the state of her cot this morning.'

'Oh?'

'Let's just say there was a nappy incident.'

'Oh dear.'

'Yep. Code brown. In fact, many, many things were brown.'

'Oh love. Look, are you coping OK? I can always...'

'Don't be silly. Mum, it was a dirty nappy, not a crisis,' Amy scolded. 'Besides, I'm enjoying telling all my friends my mum is now a famous TV guru.'

'You're not!' Nicky felt her face flush. 'Seriously?'

'No. Well, maybe a bit. I'm really proud of you, Mum.'

'You are?'

'Yes!' Amy took an audible sip of tea. 'You're out there, doing something fantastic.'

Nicky felt a spike of anxiety. 'It's not fantastic... it's...' She wanted to tell her daughter things weren't going to plan, that she was worried that she was going to mess everything up and on national television. But she swallowed her words. 'Anyway, glad you're managing to cope OK with Will back at work.'

'Are you kidding? It's much easier now it's just us girls.' Amy laughed. 'Will's only contribution to things was to be forever standing in front of the drawer or cupboard I was trying to open, asking if I needed any help.'

Nicky laughed. Amy was always able to cheer her up, somehow. 'Sounds just like your dad.' There was a silence as both of them acknowledged their loss. 'Still, it's hard work with a little one. So let me know. I can easily come back if you need...' Nicky continued.

'Not a chance,' Amy said firmly. 'You go conquer the world, Mum.'

'Um. OK.'

'That's the spirit!'

As she ended the phone call, Nicky felt a flush of pride at how easily Amy seemed to be coping with motherhood. The pregnancy had been unplanned; Will had just started his first job, and Amy had only just finished her teaching qualification. But somehow they were making it work and Rose had brought so much happiness to the family already.

It was still a bit disconcerting to think she was a grandmother at forty-nine – Jenny never let her forget it. But being a young gran would at least mean she'd have years to help with Rose and watch her grow up.

She sat on the bed and looked at herself in the mirror. Her red hair was falling softly around her face, and her skin looked almost luminous in the light that shone gently through the voile curtains. She didn't look like anyone's grandmother. At least, she didn't think so.

In a second, she'd go down to have breakfast and start her day properly. She and Robert had managed to rope in a few of his friends to help get the work done. Hopefully they'd be able to make a little difference to the place before Ryan and the crew turned up next week.

She'd decided to focus mainly on the dining room for the initial revamp. It was a blank palette, just waiting to be brought back to life. Elsewhere, they were freshening paintwork where they could, but the bedrooms could stay almost as they were for now – new bedding would bring them back to life, perhaps new curtains or voiles for the windows. After the deep clean, if they added a few cute accessories, a selection of teas and coffees for the welcome tray and fresh vases of lavender on arrival they'd do just fine. 'We just need something to give a 'wow' factor,' she'd said to Robert, sounding more like Jenny than she was comfortable with. 'Something for them to do a decent 'before and after' on. And I think we could really make the dining room look spectacular.'

She picked up her phone and flicked briefly on social media – nothing new. And emails – something from the bank, a couple of spam, a message from Chloe – usually the more communicative of her two daughters – apologising for missing her call and saying she'd call later. And a message from Jenny, the title of which read DON'T PANIC.

'Shit,' she said to herself, clicking on the message title.

Quick heads-up. I've just heard that the schedule's been rejigged again. Film crew to arrive tomorrow – just for a quick update. Don't panic – they are not expecting to see the finished job. Just a few shots of the work underway. Best, Jenny.

'No, no, no, no, no!' Nicky said to herself. She knew she and Robert were behind, but they'd thought they had a few more days in which to catch up before the interim 'how are you getting on' episode. She knew that nobody expected a finished job. But they'd want at least a few shots of work underway.

The only thing she'd achieved was probably hundreds of pounds in roaming charges on her mobile, a semi-painted hallway, a new outfit and a few scribbles in a notebook. Nothing TV-worthy at all.

She'd originally planned, by the time the interim shoot took place, to have the dining room spruced up – or at least be mid-spruce, to have worked out a better price point for the B&B. To have looked at social media strategies, had a go at the website. Even to have spoken to other, more successful, local B&Bs to see how they did it. As the date had drawn nearer her aims had become more modest – simply to get the dining room sorted. As it was, all she had to show at this point was a slightly cleaner premises, a box of rapidly drying-up croissants and the beginnings of a migraine.

She could probably cobble something together or at least make up something about the business accounts, make a few suggestions for an improved breakfast, re-watch the footage of the 'mystery guests' and make sure she addressed the points they made (however petty) in the next twenty-four hours. But that was IT.

There would be nothing to film.

Nothing at all.

She knew better than to write back to Jenny. Partly because she was sure her friend would not be able to do anything about the situation and partly because she was a bit embarrassed to be in the situation in the first place.

Instead, she rushed downstairs to find Robert, who was in the kitchen, whisking eggs in a Pyrex bowl. He'd tied an apron around his waist and was wearing shorts, his midriff and chest left bare. She felt almost embarrassed at his partial nakedness, and found her eyes drawn to the muscles on his back which gently moved as he whisked. His new, shorter haircut, tousled from the night, made him look cute and boyish.

'Morning!' he said. 'Coffee's in the pot!' Then he turned and noticed her face. 'Is everything all right?'

'Um, yes,' she said, feeling a little hot. Then she remembered that actually it really wasn't all right. 'Actually,' she said. 'Actually, not really.' She showed him the email on her phone.

He took the mobile from her and squinted at the screen. 'Oh.'

'Yes.'

'Shit.'

'Quite.'

He was silent for a minute before handing back the phone. 'Well, look, it's not the end of the world. I mean, they're not expecting anything to be finished... and we have done some of the paperwork stuff.'

'I know,' she said, trying to calm herself, 'but it's not very *visual*, is it? I think they're expecting to see real changes. And... well,' she said, gesturing around the rather messy kitchen.

'We've had the deep clean,' he said.

She snorted. 'Yes, there is that.' The place was looking shinier after Monique and Sophie's efforts. But in some ways, the deep clean had only served to highlight the shabbiness of the walls underneath the finger marks, the wear on the wood underneath the dust.

They were both silent for a moment, Robert whisking the eggs thoughtfully in the bowl. Then, 'I've got it,' he said emphatically, putting the whisk and a big string of egg batter onto the wooden surface.

'You have?'

'Yes.'

* * *

'This doesn't feel right,' she said, pushing the cart laden with bottles of vodka and wine and other spirits along the supermarket aisle two hours later. 'I feel as if we should be back there, you know, making a start.'

'I know,' Robert said. 'But if we're hosting a party, we at least need to pretend it might be fun.' He grabbed some tortilla chips and dip from a shelf.

The idea, once he'd fleshed it out, had seemed like it just might work. 'All we need is to have things in progress,' he'd told her. 'So how about I invite as many friends and acquaintances as I can around on short notice, and call it a painting party. You know, where people have a drink and socialise, but flick a bit of paint around too.'

She had been a bit uncertain about the wisdom of the vodka and paintbrush combination. But she'd gone along with it – after all, it seemed like their only feasible option.

They'd already bought off-white emulsion for the dining room and, as it was already practically unfurnished, it seemed the best place to host the party. They'd moved the tables together and thrown a sheet over them in the centre to protect them and to use as a place to put glasses and snacks.

They'd been to the DIY store and bought cheap paint trays and rollers and masking tape for taping off the skirting board. And now they were in the local supermarket, stocking up on supplies.

'That was €256,' Robert said, inspecting the receipt as they rolled the trolley to the car. 'Not bad for the labour of ten people.'

'Depending on the quality of their work?'

'Definitely depending on the quality of their work,' he said.

They agreed on the way back that they'd both stick mainly to soft drinks that night so they could spot any potential problems and nip them in the bud. Then they spent the rest of the afternoon writing up lists and plans and trying to work out what they'd say to the cameras.

Finally, it was 6 p.m., and she stepped into the small shower in her ensuite and stood under the warm water, letting it cascade over her skin and relax her a little. She was jangling with nerves. It was about fourteen hours until the crew would be on the doorstep and they still had nothing tangible to show for their time together. Just war stories about unavailable artisans and cut budgets.

Robert, for his part, seemed more confident. An hour ago, he'd changed into a pair of slightly ripped jeans and a faded T-shirt for the painting then emerged, looking relaxed, from his private quarters and had begun making punch in an enormous bowl that looked like glass but was (thankfully) made of plastic.

She'd been so tempted to go and wrench the bottle of vodka from his hand and have a slurp that she'd decided, instead, to get herself ready. According to him, there'd be 'quite a crowd' including Michelle and her husband, and several other couples and singles she didn't know. In normal circumstances, she'd have been quite happy to meet some new people, have a couple of drinks and relax. But as she was expecting an enormous favour from strangers, and was going to be supervising slightly tipsy people with paint rollers, she couldn't look at the evening ahead with anything other than dread.

She walked from the shower room to her bed, glancing at the green dress hanging on the wardrobe door. She debated whether to put it on – after all, she wasn't intending to get covered in paint. But decided instead on her old jeans and the baggy T-shirt she'd brought to wear at night.

With her limited wardrobe, this was as good as it was going to get.

She jumped slightly as the doorbell rang downstairs and she heard Robert's steps as he went to answer it. Then a murmur of voices, the sound of the door closing and several pairs of feet making their way to the dining room.

'I guess it's now or never,' she said to the woman in the mirror.

The woman looked back at her as if to say, 'Well, looks like you've really done it now.'

13

Someone was making an awful racket. 'Shut up,' she murmured and turned over in bed. Only to find herself landing face down on the parquet floor with a bang. It took her a moment to right herself; pain exploded in her head as she sat up, her eyes bleary.

Then, gradually, she began to get her bearings. She was lying on the parquet floor of the dining room, having rolled off a pile of cushions, still wearing her now paint-splattered T-shirt and jeans, her head throbbing from a combination of last night's excesses and this morning's floor encounter.

She sat up carefully, feeling the room shift around her. For a second she thought she might vomit, but managed to calm herself and the feeling passed.

The bang came again.

She looked around the room and felt her jaw drop. It looked like the aftermath of a horror movie – bodies were strewn everywhere, in various states. Only these bodies were alive... just.

A bang.

'OK, OK!' she said, realising it was someone banging on the door. Then she froze.

It was Tuesday. It was – she checked her watch – 8.30 a.m. And the film crew were at the door. She looked around the room – paint was splashed haphazardly on the walls. Someone had picked up a pot of the wrong colour and attempted some sort of paint flick design. Bare patches of off-white grubbiness showed through. There was paint on the floor, on the skirting board, doorframes. Nothing matched, nothing was finished, the job was uneven.

It looked, to all intents and purposes, as if the room had been decorated by a group of drunken partygoers.

Gradually her memories returned. The party had started off quite civilised. Michelle arrived in a pair of jeans and an enormous shirt, with a handsome man on her arm, who kissed Nicky's hand in greeting. Then a couple of blokes – one in his sixties, the other who looked to be about forty-five –turned up. 'That's Henry and Chris,' Robert whispered. 'They run an Irish themed pub over in Gordes.'

She felt shy and self-conscious, especially as everyone seemed to be so thrilled to meet her – as if she was a TV star rather than a jumped-up fake from a high-street business advisory service. And she'd said to herself she'd just have one small glass of punch to take the edge off her nerves. Robert had followed suit.

The rest, to be honest, had become a bit of a blur. She remembered laughing; remembered caring less and less about the quality of the painting, or the imminent arrival of the film crew as time went on. Some sort of paint flicking competition...

The knock again. This time more insistent.

She staggered to her feet then noticed Robert, slumped in a chair and somehow managing to lean against the wall and sleep in a position that many would describe as a torture pose. 'Robert,' she said, walking over to him and giving him a poke. 'Robert. We are in trouble!'

His eyes snapped open then crinkled up as they met the harsh light of day. He, too, had helped himself to too much punch last night. 'Wha...?' he murmured.

'Robert,' she hissed, leaning close to him, then moving slightly further away as she realised her breath was probably about 80 per cent proof. 'The film crew are At The Door! And look!' She gestured around him.

The sight of the slumped bodies and the sound of knocking seemed to act like an adrenaline shot to the heart for her host. He leaped to his feet, stumbled slightly then said, 'Right. You open the door. Keep them talking. I'll get this lot out the back way.'

'But what about the room?'

He looked around, registering the state of the painting for the first time. His eyes widened. 'I suppose, we'll just have to sort of... style it out.'

'What does that even mean?'

But the knocking came again. 'Cooeee,' she heard Ryan say. 'Anyone hooome? Iiiitttt'ss Ryannnn!'

She nodded in agreement with Robert's plan and, smoothing her hair down and scraping a paint stain from the front of her T-shirt as best she could with her thumbnail, took a breath and went to open the door.

Outside, Ryan, Tom, Fern and a couple of other people she didn't recognise were clustered together on the doorstep. It was raining lightly, and all of them had been gradually saturated as they'd waited for her to answer.

'Hi,' she said. 'Oh, I'm sorry. Just...' She couldn't think of how to finish the sentence to explain the delay so simply let her words fade out as she gestured them into the hall. 'Sorry about...' she added as

Tom wiped his camera with an enormous cloth and the others shook droplets from their clothing.

'No worries, no worries,' Ryan said, beaming and leaning in for a cheek kiss. 'You look well,' he said. She saw his expression change as he got a little closer and clearly picked up her scent. But like a consummate professional, he straightened without comment and looked around. 'Where should we set up?'

'Well,' she said, wondering how to answer that. But before she could, there was a bang as the back door closed in the kitchen behind them, and Robert appeared at her side. Somehow, he'd managed to pull on one of his new shirts and despite the fact it, and his trousers, were crumpled, he looked relatively smart.

'Ryan!' he said, sounding much heartier and more welcoming than he must have felt. He stuck out his hand for a shake. 'Sorry about the delay, do come through.' He waved his hand towards the dining room.

Wide-eyed, Nicky followed at the back of the group. Why was he showing them straight to the scene of carnage? Then she discovered that the room had been miraculously cleared of bodies; windows had been flung open to remove the smell of stale, sleeping, drunken people. But Robert had obviously been able to do nothing at all about the splattered paint in different shades which adorned the walls, nor the massive mural someone had tried to fashion over the fireplace with confident, dark-blue lines.

'Oh,' she heard Fern say.

'Wow,' Ryan said, looking around, hands-on-hips. 'Someone's been busy.'

'Yes,' Robert replied, looking at Nicky, his eyes pleading with her to say something.

She had no idea what she was meant to do. But something in Robert's desperate expression made her speak up. 'Yes,' she said.

'Well, we're just... trying something. You know to... revamp the eating area. Something a bit... experimental.'

Ryan was nodding. 'I can see that,' he said. It was hard to read his tone.

'I...' she said, desperately trying to keep the panic from her voice. 'So, one of the things, um, we are looking at is how to make Robert's offering, um, *stand out*, in the current market. Lots of competition, etc.'

'Uh huh.' Ryan walked over to the 'mural' and looked at it intently. 'Well, it's certainly a plan.'

'So, we thought we might try something a little... out-there,' she continued. 'Like make the dining room like a... like a...' She wracked her brain, trying to think of something interior designy to say. 'Living canvas,' she finished at last.

'A living canvas?' Ryan said, holding his chin in his hand thoughtfully.

'Yes,' she said, gaining confidence. 'A... a living canvas. Rather than sticking to the more subtle colour scheme of the rest of the property, we've tried to create something that guests can... well, wonder about. Something that has... more to it than simple white walls.'

Ryan turned to her, his brow furrowed. He opened his mouth then closed it. Then turned back to the mural. Then looked at the splashes of paint, then the daubed swirls around the window. He shook his head, then turned again to face her. 'Well,' he said. 'I LOVE it!'

'You do?' Robert said. Nicky gave him a little poke in the upper back with her finger. 'I mean, yes! I'm glad you got the... the... concept.'

'Are you kidding?' Ryan said, his mouth spread into a smile. 'This is fabulous. The contrast of the blues – representing the blue skies of Provence, with the subtle creams reflecting the stone buildings, the beaches. And the mural!' he said, turning again to the daubed mess on the chimney, 'it's a representation, I'd say, of the hustle and bustle. The vibrancy of the area.'

'Exactly.' Nicky nodded, with a sideways glance at Robert. 'I mean, obviously it's not finished yet. This is just... a prototype, an experiment.'

'Yes?' Ryan said as if he had been sure that this was the Finished Article. 'What plans do you have going forward?'

'Well,' said Nicky, desperately thinking. 'We're obviously going to tidy up, or... um, enhance the paintwork. And introduce more objects – ornaments, mirrors, that kind of thing. A kind of... um, filling the space with items of interest. Making guests feel...'

'Like they're in a home from home,' suggested Robert.

'Yes. Rather than the clean lines of a hotel, we're going for a more comfortable feel. With some of the... the clutter that might exist in a normal family home.'

Ryan was still nodding as if they were sharing deep truths and intelligent insight. Nicky glanced at Robert and felt giggles rise up in her, as if she was ten again and talking to a teacher. She looked away.

'But consciously,' she added. 'Not simply flinging things in, but adding touches. A kind of um... conscious recluttering.'

Ryan nodded. 'A conscious recluttering,' he said, thoughtfully, as if in the presence of a design genius.

'Yes,' said Robert. 'Exactly that.'

'Well,' Ryan said, turning back towards them, 'I knew you two would be making great progress, but I didn't think you'd have gone to quite this level. A sort of Marie Kondo eat-your-heart-out design movement.'

They glanced again. 'Um, yeah,' said Robert.

'Fabulous,' said Ryan. 'Right, let's set up and get some of this on camera.'

Later, when they'd done a couple of interviews and the crew had filmed their 'designer' renovations, Robert booked a table in a local bistro for them all to enjoy dinner together before they departed for their next assignment; Nicky was looking forward to being able to finally relax. After another day with them all, she felt more comfortable – even Ryan, whom Nicky had watched on several reality shows and who'd seemed at first like a caricature, had softened and become more human as she'd got to know him better.

It was six o'clock, and while Fern and Ryan went to check into the hotel they'd booked for the team (nobody opting to stay in the empty rooms at Robert's) leaving Tom and Mo to tidy up their equipment, Nicky went to sit in the garden with a cup of tea. She wandered onto the grassed area, which was uneven under its apparently smooth surface, and over to a wooden bench set underneath an old cherry tree, its trunk covered in a light green moss. Moments later, Robert walked out, saw her and came over.

'Not interrupting?' he asked.

It was the first time they'd been alone together since the knock on the door that morning. She smiled. 'Not at all.'

He sat next to her, still smelling vaguely of punch, and she realised she probably had a similar odour. They'd rushed off to change before the filming had taken place, but there'd been no time for a proper shower. She shifted slightly. 'So, quite a day,' she said, taking a sip from her tea.

'You can say that again.'

She grinned. 'God, when I woke up and realised... well, what had happened...'

'I know. So much for abstinence,' he said, shaking his head. 'It was the punch I think. I just poured stuff in... and it was...'

'Potent,' she said.

'Yes. Exactly.'

'Never trust the punch.'

'Quite.'

They fell into silence again, listening to the sounds that existed under the hum of daily life – the birds, the loud buzzing of insects in the grass and bushes. The sun had come out, driving away the unseasonal rain clouds by late morning and now everything was already dry and parched in the heat. The sky was a bright, light blue and any clouds that had existed earlier had melted away during the course of the afternoon.

'Conscious recluttering,' Robert said, out of nowhere.

She snorted. 'Yup. Looks like we're stuck with that one.'

'Still,' he said. 'I like the idea of it in a way.'

'What? Filling a house with clutter?'

'No, but the idea of... things. Having things around. Sometimes I think we're so intent on cleaning everything out. On being kind of... sterile as humans. When we're not, are we? We collect things, we add meaning to things, you know?'

She nodded. 'I know what you mean. It's kind of comforting to hold onto stuff.' She thought of the jumper of Steve's she still kept in her bottom drawer, the fact she would never part with the ridiculous collection of frog ornaments he'd had since childhood.

'Anyway,' Robert said, after they'd lapsed into silence again. 'Thank you.'

'What for?'

'Well, for taking this... ridiculous situation and kind of making something of it.'

'Well, thank you TOO in that case.'

They looked at each other.

'It's nice,' he said, 'not being in this on my own. For now, at least.'

'A problem shared,' she said.

'Yes. But it's more than that. It feels like... we're really in this together. Like a real team. And it's nice, isn't it, to feel that some-one's in your corner.'

'Yes,' she said. 'Yes, it is.' She'd always had friends around: Jenny and the girls a phone call away; her sister, Liz, in Scotland always asking her to visit or sending her silly text messages to make her snort. But she too missed the feeling of being part of a team.

Robert got up suddenly. 'Well,' he said. 'I'll leave you to your tea. Just wanted to say, you know...'

'Thanks,' she said. 'See you in a sec.'

She watched him return to the house, with a smile. He stopped at the doorway and someone else stepped past him.

Tom. The cameraman. He stood for a minute and looked over the garden, then his eyes clocked her, where she sat on her bench. He smiled and lifted his hand in a little wave. She waved back.

He really *was* handsome, she thought. And there was something else. Something friendly and approachable about him. He'd had his hair cut since their last meeting, and it was spiked up in a way that seemed a little too young for his forty years, but somehow cute at the same time.

As he started walking over to her, she felt herself get tense. She really should have prioritised the post-filming shower instead of opting for a cup of tea first. Hopefully the scent of the nearby bushes and flowers would overpower what was left of her drunken excesses the night before.

'All OK?' he said, standing in front of her, hands in pockets. 'Filming went well.'

'Do you think?'

'Yeah. You're... I reckon you're a natural.' He made eye contact, then focused on something close to his shoe. 'Camera loves you, you know?'

'Come on, now you're lying,' she wanted to say. Instead, she opted for 'Thanks.'

'Coming to the meal in a bit?' he asked, still looking at his shoe.

'Yes, looking forward to it.'

'Good,' he said. 'I mean, it'll be nice to chat a bit... more.'

He's nervous, she thought. This handsome, successful TV cameraman is *nervous*, talking to a middle-aged grandmother, who stinks of vodka. Wonders will never cease.

Then she thought of the way she'd seen herself in the mirror last night. Not a grandmother, or even a mother. But a woman. And a woman who was just on the cusp of something exciting. And she thought, maybe I have got something to offer. Maybe he *should* be nervous talking to me. And it felt good to talk to herself that way rather than listening to the doubting voice that usually drowned the other out.

'Yes,' she said. 'Yes, it will.'

And although she still felt a frisson of the guilt she'd experienced last time, she tried to remember what Jenny had said. That it was OK to feel things.

You can have more. Love is infinite.

Not that she expected this attraction with Tom to go anywhere.

It was just nice to think that perhaps she was open to the idea of something more.

14

She awoke and stretched her arms above her head, luxuriating in the comfortable bed. Relief flooded through her. Relief that yesterday they'd somehow made the filming work, got away with the painting party disaster and that now the crew had departed, they had at least a fortnight this time (Fern had assured her) to get their act together properly before the final reveal.

How they'd explain the changes she hoped to make to the dining room when the crew returned – covering up the mural for starters – she wasn't sure. But the problem wasn't pressing. They had time to work it all out.

The sun was already shining brightly outside heralding another hot, summer's day. She was in France, in a four-poster bed, in a room that – while a little shabby – was now dust free and gleaming. And last night, for the first time in over a decade, she'd found herself drawn to someone and been excited about it.

She and Tom had sat next to each other at dinner and she'd found herself talking about how nerve-wracking this assignment was, and how she'd spent most of her career advising small businesses on the high street. Tom had listened sympathetically then told her about his career as a cameraman that had taken him to the wilds of Africa and Antarctica when he was younger and now had him filming reality TV shows.

'It must be quite a comedown,' she'd said. 'After filming in such exotic places.'

'Maybe.' He'd shrugged. 'But I kind of enjoy connecting with people.'

She'd blushed, wondering if he meant her. 'True, can't imagine there was much banter between you and the lions,' she'd said, to deflect her embarrassment.

He'd laughed. 'It was the wildebeests that were the worst. Never had a pleasant word to say.'

But she wasn't interested in a relationship with Tom, she reminded herself. She was just enjoying his company, the feeling that he just might find her attractive. And his kind hazel eyes. And his soft looking tousled hair. And, if she was honest, his pert, infinitely grabbable bottom. Not that she would, but it didn't hurt a girl to dream once in a while.

She looked at her phone. It was 8 a.m. – she'd slept later than planned, but she'd needed it after the broken and drunken night she'd had post-party, followed by the next day's filming that had been both stressful and exhausting to get through. They'd left the restaurant at ten, and Tom had seemed to hesitate when saying goodbye – the way one might at the end of the date when not sure whether to kiss someone or not.

'Well, see you,' he'd said at last, with a little smile. 'Next time, I hope.'

'Yes,' she'd said. 'Look forward to it.'

She wondered whether he'd wanted to ask her for her number, or her social media handle. She wasn't sure how it was people connected these days. She imagined what she would have done if he'd leaned forward at that point and kissed her, in front of Fern and the crew, in front of Ryan, in front of Robert. She was glad he hadn't. But it was fun imagining what it might have felt like; the feeling of his soft lips on hers.

Then, abruptly, she halted her fantasy. She ought to be focusing on the day ahead, not daydreaming like a lovelorn teen. She threw back the covers and got up, feeling slightly unsteady at the speed, and began to think through the day.

She and Robert planned to visit a few other local B&Bs today, to look around the 'competition' and find out what they were offering. Robert had called a few people and they'd all seemed happy enough to chat.

'Aren't they worried we'll steal their business?' she had asked Robert.

He'd shrugged. 'I think here there's plenty of business for all of us,' he'd said.

'Unless you get slated on Tripadvisor?'

'Yes, unless that happens.'

The Tripadvisor page had been brutal. She'd pulled it up a few days ago to give it a proper read. There was a rant by one woman who had termed the B&B 'the worst night of my life'. Another had called Robert, 'witless' and a third had complained that the pain au chocolat they'd been given was stale.

Robert blushed when he saw her reading them. 'God,' he said. 'Don't look at that. So embarrassing.'

'Yes, but important,' she said, making notes. 'And you know, we ought to reply to each of them, saying how we've improved things. It will give people more confidence, you know, for the future.'

'Should we tell them about the refurbed dining room?' he asked with a grin.

'Maybe not right at this moment.' She smiled. 'But I'm sure we could work on the witless bit.'

She thought he'd laugh at her comment, but instead he looked downcast. 'You know, that was one of the first times I'd opened since Marie,' he said. 'I was kind of lost in my own head, rather than... anything else.'

'Oh God. I know,' she said. 'I was only kidding...'

'Still... witless,' he said, looking at her with such a hurt look that she felt herself grinning.

'Could be worse,' she said.

'How, exactly?'

'I don't know, gutless?'

He grinned, catching on. 'Gormless?'

'Legless?'

'Trouser-less?' he suggested, with a smile.

She laughed. 'I think we have a winner. See? Witless isn't so bad.'

He'd smiled and they'd locked eyes for a moment. And she'd felt good that she'd managed to make him laugh at something that had obviously upset him. It's what Steve had used to do for her, and what Jenny did for her now. Even the worst moments had a funny side if you knew where to look.

When she got downstairs half an hour later, Robert was already dressed and ready to leave. She grabbed a quick coffee and they set off in his small Nissan Micra, driving down the steep little roads with their red stone walls, past pretty houses and several boulangeries, past tourists and locals walking clutching their morning bread. After a few minutes in which they'd seemed to negotiate smaller and smaller roads, Robert pulled up outside a small *chambre d'hôte* which proudly displayed a three-star rating from 'Gites de France' by its shiny black front door.

The minute they knocked, the door was flung open and a little man in a neat shirt and chino ensemble welcomed them in.

* * *

Two hours later they were sitting at an outdoor table in a restaurant on the outskirts of Roussillon, sharing a basket of bread and sipping wine. Nicky had her notebook out on the table and they were reviewing their findings from the three visits they'd made.

The heat had intensified and Nicky was glad of the shade from the awning that covered the outside courtyard area. Their table was in the corner, against a peach-painted wall, over which she could see the tops of trees, their greens transforming from dark to almost yellow in the sunlight. Beyond, the ground became steeper and she could just make out the yellow of a house on the hill at the edge of the horizon. The place had begun to fill up with the midday rush but the quiet murmur of conversation made the venue seem homely and intimate.

Their tour of various successful businesses had been eye-opening. Both due to the ideas she'd been able to pick up and because she had realised that the gulf between Robert's B&B and the thriving businesses they'd viewed hadn't been as wide as she'd imagined.

Most of the places had a similar look – traditional stone, pointed or painted walls, clean white linen on wooden beds. Sure, they were fresher, more recently painted than Robert's, but the canvas underneath was very similar.

They were told that French guests now expected meat and cheese with their morning breakfast, that customers loved local products and the natural soap bars one place invested in. Nicky also learned that Robert's room rate – at €80 a night – was on the modest side. 'If we improve your offering,' she said, 'you could charge a lot more; really make this a viable business.'

All three of the places they visited offered guests the option of an evening meal with the host for an extra charge. 'I just can't,' Robert said when she looked at him hopefully. 'I haven't since...'

'What, since Marie?' she asked, softly.

'Well, yeah.' He blushed. 'I used to be OK at it, you know? I cooked for her the whole time, while she was sick. Healthy stuff. New recipes. Kind of trying to...' He continued to redden. 'Well, they say food can heal people, right? So it was all fresh, all organic. Took hours sometimes. But since she... and it's just been me, I've become more of a sandwiches or pizza man. Not sure if my skills would be up to it these days.'

She nodded. 'But do you think,' she said, 'you might be able to... well, explore that?'

He looked thoughtful. 'Maybe,' he said. 'I guess it's kind of... well, a block.'

'I definitely know how that feels,' she said. 'Well, we can decide about it a bit later. Give it some thought?'

He nodded. 'OK.'

'You know, I'm feeling so much better about everything,' he said, as they drove to the restaurant for a working lunch. 'And it's down to you.'

'Me?' She felt her cheeks turn pink. 'What, my painting prowess? The negotiations with the patisserie?'

He snorted. 'Well, maybe not. But the fact that you're doing something completely different with your life. You've embraced something new.'

'Oh.'

'It made me realise. I've been stuck in a rut. But I don't have to be, right? I can... well, things could be different. Just because I feel out of my depth sometimes doesn't mean I can't learn to...'

'Tread water? Stay afloat?' she suggested.

'No,' he said. 'Swim. Really move forward and swim.'

They arrived in the restaurant car park and he turned off the engine. 'I suppose maybe that's what I was doing. Trying to... somehow stay in the past. Stay still. And I've been so kind of wrapped up in it. But I suppose for the first time in... well, years, I'm looking at the future and thinking maybe... well, that maybe I *have* one.'

'Well, that's... good?' she said, carefully.

He nodded. 'Definitely. And you've kind of shown me that things can change even at...'

'My age?'

He smiled. 'Our age. You're forty, right? I'm forty-four, so not much older. But I was feeling about a hundred years old until I realised that was all in my head. That my life wasn't over... it was just changing.'

She nodded. 'Although I'm forty-nine,' she said. 'But thanks for the compliment.'

'Well, whatever age. You showed me I should just... well, go for what I want.'

She felt herself blush again. She wanted to tell him that it wasn't so much her own impetus but that of her friend. That she was here, but half the time she was making it up as she went along. But then maybe it was nice to let him believe that about her. If it helped him. And maybe, if she was truly honest, he wasn't entirely wrong. Maybe she was doing something brilliant.

'This place looks amazing!' she said instead. 'Have you been here before?'

And they had begun instead to talk about the restaurant and the menu, and then the plans they might have to improve the business, and what they'd learned that morning.

Now, as the food arrived, Nicky ticked the last item on her list. 'So we agree,' she said. 'Bedding, fresh flowers, possibly offer a laundry service of some kind. And we'll find somewhere to put the breakfast menu, perhaps in holders on the tables?' she asked, looking at Robert.

He reached over and took the pen from her hand. 'Definitely,' he said. 'But that's enough for now.'

'What do you mean?'

'Well, I may have made a mess of the business and be a bit... mixed up about the future. But one thing living here has taught me is to pause and... well, take in the moment.'

She looked at him, then finally acknowledged their little corner table, the blue of the sky just visible through the raffia of the sunshade, the greens and yellows and blacks and browns that tumbled away then rose up beyond the walled balcony. And acknowledged the fact she was here, living a brand-new type of existence, a different life. And that life, right at this moment, was pretty darn good.

'You're right.' She shut her notebook. 'I've always been rubbish at... switching off.'

'Well,' he said. 'How about you help with the business, and I'll teach you to stop and smell the roses.'

She raised her glass. 'Or the rosé,' she quipped as they clinked glasses together.

'Yes, or the rosé.' He grinned.

And as the waiter came over with their delicately arranged starters, she finally allowed herself to stop her head chattering about the past, to stop her worries for the programme and the work they had to do, and simply be in the moment in this beautiful place and take stock of how far she'd come.

15

The following day, as she drove into the car park of the out-of-town shopping centre she realised that, although France was romantic and full of cafés and boutiques and old stone houses, there was plenty of modernity here too. It felt odd to be at a retail park – almost as if she'd woken from a dream to find herself confronted with the cold, hard reality of ordinary life or stepped out of a dark cinema after an absorbing film only to find herself blinking in bright, afternoon sunlight.

Having discovered Robert had 'any driver' insurance on his car, she'd suggested she go alone to the shops this morning to buy dye for the bedding they'd decided to revamp instead of replace; told him to stay and mow the grass or do something to tidy the patio area up. She'd emphasised how important it was to keep the momentum up in case they were surprised again. But in reality she'd wanted to be alone to clear her head.

As far as the B&B went, things were progressing well: a couple of his friends had been roped in to come and help finish off the dining room and cover up the mural in a few of days' time; and she'd finally managed to get a local guy to have a look at Robert's website, tidy it up and make the place look like a going concern. It felt as if they were making progress and some of the worry in the pit of her stomach had dissipated, at least for now.

Later, she'd address the Tripadvisor reviews – replying politely (however hard that might be) to explain how they'd improved the business since the complaints had been made.

They were on the right track.

In all honesty, she probably could have used a bit of company on the trip. The short drive to Chanas had been easy enough – she'd driven past vibrant fields bursting with maize or tall green stems shielding cobs of corn; then livestock, brown cows with their wet noses to the fence as she went past and sheep grazing on endless green. Then the houses that had dotted her route had become more regular and she'd reached the outskirts of town and turned towards the retail park. But as the roads had become busier, she'd become hyper-aware that she was unused to driving on the right. Roundabouts had been a nightmare. And now she looked at the enormous, unfamiliar stores she wasn't sure exactly which she should be going to.

Shops such as But, Leroy Merlin, Boulanger and La Halle surrounded her, their glass windows revealing something of their content – electrical items, clothing, computers, homeware. But she wasn't sure where the best bargains were to be found, or in fact the exact wording for fabric dye. Hopefully it would be obvious.

She thought back to what he'd said to her yesterday and felt her anger flare again. She didn't want to argue with her host, or even let him know he'd upset her. He hadn't meant anything by it and she needed to calm herself and focus on the job in hand.

That was the problem, she thought, when you let the lines blur between work and friendship. She was staying in the guy's B&B, but in the absence of other guests, it had begun to feel like a home rather than a business premises.

Sitting having meals together, planning together and the fact they'd had to overcome some hurdles together had made him feel more of a friend. And that had been her mistake. Because she'd cared what he thought of her and that had been her downfall.

It had been lovely, sitting in the restaurant at lunch yesterday. Then Robert had driven back to the B&B and they'd spent the afternoon ringing around, making plans and budgeting for various aspects of the business improvement.

Afterwards, he opened a bottle of wine and they sat in the garden for a chat. It was hot and the bushes and shrubs were buzzing with insect life. She found a bit of shade and applied plenty of sun cream to avoid the burn, then sipped her wine, sighed and took in the scenery as the conversation moved from business practicalities to ordinary matters.

He offered her pizza for dinner, but she offered instead to cook a simple curry with him. It was nice, chopping onions and peppers together, crushing garlic and inhaling the delicious smell as the spices hit the melted butter in the pan. 'This is delicious,' he said when they were finally ready to eat it.

'Simple too,' she said, looking at him sideways. 'And you were a pro with those onions.'

He laughed. 'You're right,' he said. 'It's probably about time I got a little more adventurous in the kitchen again.'

'Man cannot live on pizza alone...' she joked and he shook his head and laughed.

As the sun began to sink in the sky, he talked about his time in France – the way he and Marie had enjoyed things before her diagnosis. The dreams they'd shared. Then Nicky spoke of her life in England, and how much Jenny had had to push her to take the chance on the TV programme. And the girls and how she still worried about them despite the fact they were in their twenties now.

Then, unwittingly, Robert pulled the rug from under her.

'Well, you certainly don't come across that way,' he said. 'You seem really capable from the outside.'

'Are you saying I'm not capable?' she joked, not quite understanding what he was getting at.

'Oh, not at all. You're very capable. It's just... I suppose you don't seem like someone who has doubts. Someone who had to be forced to take a risk.'

She snorted. 'Appearances can be deceptive.'

'It's sad really,' he said, almost wistfully.

'Sad?'

'Well, the accident obviously... changed your life. But realising you're ten years past it and haven't really moved on.' He shook his head. 'Wasting that much time...'

'But...'

'Sorry, I'm not meaning to offend you. Your journey is your journey,' he said, not realising that he'd ignited something in her.

'I didn't waste time,' she said, feeling something rise up in her at his words. 'Before Jenny gave me this chance... I may not have been doing my dream job. But I was completely happy. I had my life the way I wanted it. A good job, the girls, friends. No relationship, but not because I couldn't... I didn't want one. Didn't need one. I was happy. I am... I am happy,' she insisted.

'Glad to hear it,' he said, his voice so sympathetic she wanted to knock the glass of wine out of his hand.

'I'm sorry,' she said, after a moment, unable to let it go. 'Explain what you mean by "wasting time".'

He looked at her, his eyes earnest. 'Sorry,' he said. 'I didn't mean to offend. I mean, what you've said about raising your girls. How well they've turned out. It's amazing. Truly.'

'Right?'

'It's just... The girls moving out – well, a lot of people would have thought that was the moment, right? To get your life back. But you stayed the same. I guess it can be scary doing something different.'

'Oh.' She hadn't known what to say. This virtual stranger had been analysing her life over a glass of wine, and telling her she was – what? Some kind of loser? She'd made her excuses shortly after and had disappeared for an early night. Robert still hadn't a clue he'd offended her.

What did he know anyway? she thought cruelly, as she exited the car and walked to the trolleys, grabbed one and tried to insert a euro into the coin slot. He was trying to recreate his wife's dream to honour her memory. He was hardly an expert on moving on himself.

She'd held it together. She'd got the girls through school, their exams. She'd worked hard at a job she didn't mind, to pay the bills, keep the house, keep things going. She'd supported Amy through the pregnancy and in those first fractious weeks of Rose's life. She'd been the one cheerleading when Chloe had told her about her plans to start her own business – she had taken her to the bank to get her loan. Helped her with her tax forms. Helped 'Chloe's Chocs' into being.

She'd been there every step of the way. Been the best mum she possibly could. Been a rock.

She wrenched the trolley out of the rack, cursing as it struck her shin. 'Bloody hell,' she muttered.

Then something else had hit her, this time metaphorically. *Been a rock.*

She'd had to be both mum *and* dad to the girls, as much as was possible. She'd had to be strong when she'd wanted to crumble. And she'd had to throw herself wholly into supporting their existence – choosing a steady job, working overtime when it was available, been the one who helped the girls with their homework, their A-level choices, their exams. Been the one who listened to their dreams and tried to make them happen.

But maybe Robert was right. What was she now? Now that the girls had moved on. A rock in the middle of the ocean with no real purpose. Just sort of crumbling and getting covered in seaweed and barnacles.

As she pushed the trolley towards the entrance of a shop called Leroy Merlin that looked from the outside to be the kind of place she needed, she realised with a pang that Robert might have been right. Why had she kept things just as they were when she'd finally had the space – both financially and because the girls were grown – to take her life back? What had happened to the hopes and dreams she'd used to talk about with Steve long into the night? What had happened to the person she'd been the day before the crash that changed everything?

Yes, she was in her forties. And yes, nobody could be the same person they were a decade earlier. People's hopes and dreams fell by the wayside. Relationships ended. People ended up alone, or in a different life from the one they'd planned.

And that was OK. That was normal and fine and almost expected.

But that wasn't what had happened to her, not quite.

As she'd driven home shakily from the hospital to break the news to the girls, to start the endless work that comes with a bereavement, she'd taken part of herself and put it away. She'd set aside whatever she'd wanted, whatever she'd hoped. Because there hadn't been room. She'd focused on one task only – making sure her daughters were all right.

But now they were adults. They were self-sufficient. They had flown the nest. She didn't have to be that person any more.

Jenny had been right; it should have been *her turn* now.

Only she'd forgotten the person she'd used to be. And what that person had used to want.

How had it taken a virtual stranger to make her see that?

And what was she going to do about it?

16

'And Rose is well?' she said.

It was nine o'clock the following morning and she was making her daily call to her daughter, Amy. Back home, she'd usually check in at least once a day and try to pop in too. She felt a flash of guilt – should she be there rather than here?

'Mum, you've already asked that!' Amy laughed. 'Yes, she's well. Growing fast. Filling more nappies than I know what to do with.'

Nicky smiled, thinking of the little baby with her gummy smile and tiny sprinkle of blonde hair. She felt suddenly homesick, but pushed the feeling back down. She was only here until the end of the month – it was hardly a lifetime. And Amy seemed to be managing.

Nicky remembered too well the early days with both Amy and then Chloe – how emotions had washed over her in waves: happiness and despair sometimes only seconds away from each other. The exhaustion hadn't helped, but it had been the hormones that had proved the most difficult to cope with. She hoped that Amy wasn't simply putting on a brave face to make her feel better.

'Oh, she's a little monkey,' she said. 'But you're OK, yes?'

'Mum! Yes! I'm fine. Honestly. Anyway, enough about me and nappies and sleep deprivation,' Amy said. 'I want to hear about your exciting life in France!'

Nicky snorted. 'I wouldn't call it exciting.'

After the shopping trip two days ago, she'd arrived back at the B&B loaded up with more paint, a throw for one of the sofas and some fabric dye to stain the old, slightly greying, bed linen a gorgeous pale pink. Even with careful budgeting it had come to almost €200. But Robert had been pleased enough and they'd begun the process of soaking the cotton linen in the dye and crossing their fingers it would work.

Robert had been to a local second-hand furniture shop and found a dresser for the hallway where they'd put postcards and local guides and the welcome pack, as well as some new lamps to brighten the bedrooms. He'd shown his purchases to her shyly, as if pleased with himself and hoping for approval.

In a few days Robert's friends would have finished repainting the dining room, the floor would be sanded and they'd start dressing it and the bedrooms before moving on to the stage of her plan she thought of as 'final touches'.

'Then what would you call it? You're a soon-to-be TV star trans-forming a business in Provence!' said Amy now. 'Sounds pretty exciting to me!'

It did sound quite impressive when you put it like that, Nicky thought, picking at a thread on her cut-off jeans. She was silent for a minute.

'Mum?'

'Yes, still here. I'm sorry. I just... I suppose I was thinking how different things can feel from the inside to how they look on the outside,' she said. 'Do you think anyone ever feels confident or I don't know, successful?'

'Probably. Lots of men, I'd imagine,' Amy joked. 'Maybe not so many women. Aunty Jenny, probably.'

'Yes, maybe,' Nicky said. Although she knew that Jenny's relentless positivity was a veneer she showed to the world, she also knew that Jenny had moments of pride at what she'd achieved. Jenny had had a difficult couple of years in secondary school – she'd been teased for being a 'swot' and taken such pains to disprove it that she'd ended up with just a handful of mediocre GCSEs. While she'd then come into her own when A-levels and university had come around, she'd never really thrown off the feeling of having let herself down. 'It's what drives me,' she'd confided in Nicky once. 'You know, having to prove something to myself, to everyone.'

'If it's any consolation, you always seemed confident, you know when I was growing up,' Amy said now. 'Like you always had the answers.'

'I did?'

'Yeah. And the more I get used to this motherhood malarkey – you know, see things from the other side of the equation – the more I realise that you must have just felt like a child sometimes.'

'Just sometimes?!'

'Ha. Well, let's just say I'm glad I didn't know how hard you probably found it. Thinking you had all the answers – even if it wasn't true. Well, it made me feel safe, I guess.'

'Well, I suppose that was the point,' Nicky said.

Nicky could hear her granddaughter gurgling in the background.

'Yeah, I kind of took it for granted, that I'd feel capable as a mum,' said Amy. 'But it's a lot harder than it looks, isn't it?'

'I think everything probably is,' admitted Nicky.

'Maybe. You know, you've told me a lot about when me and Chloe were babies, but did you ever feel confident as a mum? You know. Did you grow into it?' The hope in Amy's voice was palpable.

'Yes. I mean, not all the time, but yes. I did. It gets easier,' she reassured. 'I suppose it's a case of fake-it-till-you-make-it when it comes to parenting.'

'I think you're right.'

'I hope you don't mind me telling you it was hard sometimes when you girls were tiny. I just feel like it helps to know that other people... well, have their doubts sometimes.'

'I think you're lucky, you know. Your generation is much more honest about that sort of thing. You don't have to pretend,' she added.

'Except on social media, where everyone's perfect.'

Nicky laughed. 'Yes, except for that.' She smiled. She'd loved bringing the girls up, but she was loving this phase of motherhood too. Where her daughter was more than someone she had to guide and feed and nurture, but was a proper friend too. Someone she could confide in.

After saying goodbye to Amy, she walked to the mirror. The afternoon sun streamed through the window onto its shiny surface and she had to tilt it away slightly to capture her reflection properly. She often shied away from looking too closely in the glass, especially in the unforgiving sunlight, but now she studied her face, taking in the signs of age – the sprinkled fine lines, the more angular cheeks, the auburn hair that she'd had highlighted to disguise the couple of greys she was in denial about.

Midlife, she thought. Neither old, nor young. Neither at the start or at the end of things. A time of self-doubt, but also self-discovery. She'd closed one chapter of her life recently, and had thought for a while that she was at the end of the book. That she would go on, but as a secondary character in the novel, not the heroine.

Now she'd begun to question that. She'd spent a decade underwater, swimming against the tide and just about managing to gasp enough breaths to keep going. And now she had washed up on a foreign shore. She had a choice. She could see this as the end of the book, or the beginning of a new chapter. The end of the road, or a fork in a much longer journey.

And she realised that it was up to her which way she went, what she did and how she decided to frame it to herself. That she wasn't drowning any more. Yes, someone had had to throw her a life-ring – an opportunity that might not have come her way otherwise. But now she was ready to kick against the water and swim to somewhere brand new. She thought of Amy's words 'TV Star'. She wasn't interested in stardom, but she was interested in new experiences, in helping people to achieve, in using her under-tapped potential to bring out the best in others.

And if that took place in front of a TV camera, so be it.

She drew a brush through her hair and tied it into a ponytail. Then changed her mind and let it fall softly around her face instead. She applied a little mascara, a slick of tinted lip balm; attempted to reduce the dark circles under her eyes with a little coverup.

Enough of holding her breath. Enough of low self-esteem. She was a fighter. She was strong. And maybe as with motherhood, it was about convincing the world that you had what it took, and gradually growing into the role.

She gave herself a small smile. 'You've got this,' she said.

* * *

Three days later, she stood in the corner of the room and snapped a photo with the oversized camera Robert had provided. Checking the picture, she nodded to herself. The room looked charming – clean, pale pink bedding offset the mahogany bed frame; she'd somehow managed to capture the right amount of light.

Originally she'd planned to use a professional photographer, but although they now had the funds, they no longer had the time. The website was almost finished and they needed to get the pictures sorted pronto.

'It looks great,' said a voice in her ear. Robert.

'Thanks,' she said. And, 'I think so too,' she added, remembering her new, positive mindset.

'The guys have finished in the dining room,' he said. 'It looks pretty good actually.'

'Oh great.'

'Less recluttering and more... well, tasteful redressing.'

'I like the sound of that.' She smiled.

'Sam said he'd bring his sander over tomorrow and have a go at the floor if we want. Just in the dining room. You know,' he said. 'What do you reckon?'

'Can we afford it?' she asked.

'Well, he's got family coming over at Christmas so I said I'd do a swap of a free room for a week if he did.'

'Brilliant!' she said, and watched his face break into a smile. Robert was one of those people who, when they smiled genuinely, radiated happiness. She felt herself smile in return. Things were finally coming together. They'd worked tirelessly for the last few days and now she was beginning to see how the transformation might come across to viewers. And you know what? It wasn't too bad. She'd even let herself believe that they were in with a shot at winning. But whether that happened or not, they hadn't disgraced themselves. And if it went well, who knew what other opportunities might come her way.

She'd silenced the doubting voices for now, and was bringing together each shred of energy and confidence she had to push the project to a good place.

Now she had to work on her presentation – tidying up her plans to present to camera; what she'd say about all the advice she'd given. She had a few more bedrooms to dress, but things felt possible.

The final filming would involve another round of 'secret guests' (or not so secret in this case) who were due to arrive in just over a week. The camera crew would arrive shortly afterwards, and this time she was excited.

She had a few jobs earmarked for the days between now and then: linen to iron, beds to dress, skirting boards to touch up... the list was long. She also hoped to find time for a tour of the small high street with Robert where they'd pop into local shops to find items to dress the rooms. It would be a chance for Robert to engage local suppliers for potential future collaborations. The market would be on and the road filled with artisans and local producers. She'd spent a morning there last week and had enjoyed the hustle and bustle, looked at stalls packed with fresh produce, a refrigerated unit selling so many cheeses she'd been unable to choose just one. A woman with silver jewellery and another with handmade pottery, thick and rudimentary but beautifully glazed and charming; a man selling carved wooden objects – games and ornaments and coasters and placemats.

She hoped Robert might be able to buy some items, and get others to offer them for display. 'That way,' she'd told Robert, 'we can bring some of them in for the final shoot – you know, let people see the wonderful culture you're living in.' Robert had told her that he was firm friends with Victor, an artist and gallery owner who might be persuaded to lend them some of his work.

She also had to finish her presentation, checking the work they'd done for any snags, as well as adding finishing touches to the new website. Another clean to remove any grime that had accumulated, some fresh flowers maybe. Then they'd be ready.

'Do you want to grab a coffee and debrief?' she said to Robert now. 'I think we're nearly there.'

And despite the fact that the little voice inside that she was trying to ignore these days warned her that she was tempting fate with her confidence, she pushed it down and smiled. 'I actually think we're going to nail this.'

17

Roussillon had more shops than Nicky had realised. As they walked towards the town centre, the roads narrowed, the red stone of buildings closing in from either side, but just as she was beginning to feel claustrophobic, they reached the end of a road to find it opening out into a large, cobbled courtyard, with several shops, a brasserie with maroon awning and a boulangerie with a hand-painted sign.

Nicky felt herself smile as the sunlight played on her face. After an afternoon spent crunching the numbers yesterday and several days prior to that helping with the painting, or dyeing linen, or – worst of all – ironing it before it went on the beds, it was lovely to get out and about and focus on finishing touches to the décor.

The market was on again and already she'd bought a set of smooth wooden coasters; a vase glazed in fiery orange; some mugs made with thick, local pottery and painted with flowers. She'd even used a little of her schoolgirl French and had felt gratified when stallholders had grinned, replied slowly and clearly appreciated her effort.

'Here's Victor's place,' Robert said as they neared a small building decorated with a sign that said 'Galerie'. They walked in to find a whitewashed interior, with beautifully painted watercolours depicting local scenes, scenic waterways and traditional still life subjects such as fruit and flowers in vases. Each picture was tastefully mounted with a white surround and wooden frame.

'Here he is!' Robert said, nodding to a man behind the counter. 'Bonjour, Victor.'

'Bonjour.' Victor walked over from behind the counter. 'It is a pleasure,' he said in broken English to Nicky. He leaned forward slightly and for a moment she thought he might reach for and kiss her hand and felt herself stiffen awkwardly, but thankfully he seemed to sense her British reticence and simply nodded at her with a smile.

'This is Nicky,' Robert said. 'She's a TV star from England.'

Victor's eyes widened. '*Mon dieu!*' he said, hand to his heart. 'Well, I am honoured, madame.'

'I'm not really...' she began, then saw the expression on Robert's face. 'Yes, nice to meet you.'

'I had not realised you had friends in such high places, Robert,' he said, seemingly astounded. 'You keep her quiet, yes?'

'Well, she's quite a new friend,' Robert admitted. 'She's staying with me to help me decorate the *chambre d'hôte*.'

'Ah, then you are lovers?' Victor said, with an arched eyebrow. How he'd jumped to that conclusion, Nicky had no idea.

'Oh, no, nothing like that.' Robert's ears reddened. 'She is just here for a TV show. You know, that competition I entered.'

This, too, was clearly astounding to Victor. 'Well, *enchanté*,' he said to Nicky. 'I am so glad you take time to see my little shop.'

'Actually, it's a bit more than that,' Robert said. He explained how they'd hoped they could hang some of Victor's artwork in the B&B for the filming. 'We'll buy some of course,' he said. 'But with the budget, I wondered whether you might loan some to us?'

'And they will be on the television?' Victor said, hand, once again, rushing to his heart. 'My little paintings, they will be famous, non?'

'Well, a little bit,' Robert said.

'Then you must take them!' Victor said, almost breathless by this point. 'You must take as many as you want!'

He laughed joyously and Robert joined in. Nicky found it hard not to laugh a little too. She wondered whether, like her, Robert's laugh had more anxiety than mirth at its core.

Victor, who was bald other than a little piece of painstakingly styled blond fluff on the top of his head and dressed in white chinos, sandals and a floral pink shirt, showed them through to an anteroom. 'I will pick out some of the works I think you might like,' he said. 'Perhaps some views of Roussillon, non?'

The pictures were beautiful and they soon earmarked a couple of recognisable buildings from the square, as well as a picture of a church and two countryside scenes. 'They're gorgeous, Victor,' Nicky said, smiling. 'Really.'

'Merci, madame,' he replied. 'To hear this from a famous celebrity like yourself, is a great moment in my life for me.'

She decided not to tell him that she was about as far from an art expert as it was possible to be.

'TV star?' she said to Robert as they stepped out into the fresh, warm air.

Robert shrugged. 'Nothing wrong with aiming high,' he said.

'Still...'

'Well,' he said. 'I can't say how the programme will go, obviously. But I reckon the viewers will come to love you just as much as I do.'

There was a silence as they both digested what he'd said.

'I mean,' he added awkwardly. 'I think you're very good at your job. And... well, it does feel like we're friends. Doesn't it?'

'Definitely,' she said, the warmth of his original words still fresh in her mind.

They were silent for a moment as they passed a café with tables set out on the cobbles and the steady rumble of conversation seeping from inside.

'You probably gathered when you first came. I sometimes... it takes me a while to warm to people. But with you it seemed... well, easier. Natural.'

She felt herself blush.

'Although I was a bit worried at first,' he admitted.

'Worried?'

'Well, yeah. The whole... underwear thing.'

Her stained, wet underwear handshake. She'd forgotten about that. 'Oh God. I nearly died.'

'*You* nearly died? I thought you were handing me some sort of dodgy housewarming present.'

'No, the housewarming present was the pigeon,' she said, looking at him sideways.

'Come again?'

'Yeah. I kind of... well, I let him in,' she admitted. 'I just... I was too embarrassed to say.'

'It was you!' he said, looking at her his eyes dancing with humour.

'Guilty as charged.' She reddened, hoping that he wouldn't be annoyed.

'All that newspaper up the chimney... the... I was checking that window for days.'

'Yeah.' She grimaced. 'Sorry about that.'

'You must have thought I was mad.'

'Maybe a little...'

They both grinned. 'Well,' he said. 'Knickers and pigeons aside, it's been lovely having you.'

'That's beautiful,' she teased. 'Maybe if this doesn't work out, you could get a job writing cards for Hallmark.'

They walked on, slipping into silence, past a café and a tourist-focused shop with racks of postcards outside the entrance, and the bistro from which gorgeous smells emanated. Nicky marvelled at the three-storey buildings, their smart, symmetrical fronts, at the reddish colour of the stone and the atmosphere of the square itself.

'I can see why you chose to live here,' she said. 'It's gorgeous.'

'It's strange, but after a while you stop seeing it. We – Marie and I – used to love walking around the little back streets and browsing all the tiny shops like Victor's and some of the other little places we've seen today. But it's weird how quickly you forget.'

They turned down another narrow roadway which shortly opened into a car-park area. They passed more market stalls selling fresh produce – its colours vibrant in the sunlight. As the morning went on, more and more people began milling around, that strange juxtaposition of those who lived in the town and were going to work or doing errands and the slower, marvelling tourists with their sunglasses and cameras and snail's pace walk.

'Do you ever get lost?' she asked. She picked up her pace to match Robert's as they found themselves once again in a courtyard of buildings in red and yellow stone.

'I used to.' He grinned. 'But I know it pretty well now. And you know, it's pretty small. So not any more.'

She nodded.

'Here's the candle place,' he said, minutes later, as they approached a small, stone building with a large window full of candles in various guises, vases with tall, silk flowers and glass ornaments.

Walking through the door, Nicky's senses were assaulted with a variety of smells; their combination sweet and heady. Behind the counter, a tall woman with short, bobbed hair was ringing something up on the till. She pressed a button and an enormous receipt began to snake its way across the counter.

'Clara,' Robert said as the door closed behind them. The woman looked up, a smile spreading across her face at the sight of him.

'Ah, Robert!' she said, giving a dramatic roll of the 'r'. 'And you have brought a friend!'

'Yes,' he said, 'this is Nicky.'

'It is nice to meet you,' Clara responded. 'So you are here to buy gift?'

'No, this is a business expedition,' said Robert. 'We'd like to buy a selection of candles please.'

In the end, their order of twenty candles seemed to have made Clara's day, as well it might, thought Nicky, looking at the prices. She'd never really been a candle person and while she could appreciate some of the gorgeous scents, she'd never justify spending €20 on something you ultimately burn away. Still, they'd be a good look in the B&B and would be another connection with the local area for the show.

'My husband can drive them to you later, if you want?' Clara said when they'd boxed up their various choices. 'They will be too heavy, I think.'

They thanked her and minutes later were stepping back onto the street. Nicky breathed deeply, inhaling the comparatively fresh, thin air of the cobbled walkway and Robert laughed. 'Bit overpowering isn't it!' he said. 'Not sure how she manages to stand in there all day.'

They were about to call it a day, when Robert put his hand on Nicky's arm.

'Let's just pop in here,' he said.

She looked. It was the patisserie where she'd tried to negotiate over croissants and ended up buying half the store in one fell swoop. 'Oh God. You do it,' she said. 'I embarrassed myself last time.'

'Don't be daft,' Robert said. 'They were delighted with the order, I think.'

'Well, yeah. I'm not surprised. So was Buster.'

She trailed behind him as he walked through the automatic glass door. Inside, the smell of pastries and bread made her stomach growl noisily.

Robert looked up in surprise. 'Was that you?' he said.

'Was what me?' she asked, all innocence.

The guy behind the counter was different from the man she'd dealt with before – older, with a reddish complexion and a kindly expression. He shook hands with Robert and smiled at her as they were introduced. 'Did you have a good party?' he asked her.

'Party?'

'Yes, all les croissants!' he said. 'For your friends, I think?'

'Oh,' she said. 'Yes.' it was easier than trying to correct him.

Robert and the man started to talk together in rapid French, which culminated with a strange half hug over the counter. 'Merci!' he said, as they left.

'Yes, merci!' she said, although she had no idea what she was saying thank you for.

'You're amazing, you know?' Robert said, as their feet once again met cobbles.

'I am? I didn't say a word in there,' she said, confused.

'Yes, but it's all your idea. I'd never thought,' he said. 'I mean obviously I bought croissants for guests. but I never thought to make a proper arrangement. You know, between businesses. He's given me 10 per cent discount and will deliver to the door each morning, when I want. I used to like the walk, or drive, to get them, but of course it makes everything else so hectic.'

'Ten per cent's pretty good.'

'Yes, and he's going to give us some cakes for the crew, provided we try to put one of his boxes prominently on camera at some point.'

She laughed. 'That's sneaky of him.'

'Yes, I thought so.'

The town seemed to be a real haven for artists – they passed several more galleries and a couple of murals, hand painted onto wooden doors. The sun had risen in the sky and the heat was intense whenever the roadways opened up. She began to get grateful for the shade afforded in the smaller back roads where buildings faced each other, barely a car's-width apart.

'Should we get a drink?' she suggested, eventually, pretending to refix her sandal strap so she could give her armpits a quick sniff. Luckily, despite the temperature, she'd managed to stay relatively fresh. But with the sun reflecting off the road, and the sun bearing down on them, she was now uncomfortably hot.

'Sure,' he said. 'I know a great place.'

By this time, her legs had started to ache, and her feet were sore from the uneven ground. They reached the edge of the shopping district; and her claustrophobia was relieved when the buildings opened out to reveal a stone wall, over which tumbled breathtaking views of open countryside.

His great place turned out to be the maroon-shaded brasserie they'd seen right at the beginning of their walk. They'd passed a couple of cafés and bars en route and she'd longed to say that their drinks would no doubt be as good as any. But he'd seemed determined to share a favourite destination with her and her politeness overrode her desire to sit and drink and recover.

'Here it is,' he said at last, lifting his hand to point out the very obvious awning of the 'Café des Couleurs' on the sunlit square. There were several tables outside, two of which were free, but he walked inside and she followed him wondering whether he, too, had had enough of the strong sunlight.

But instead of sitting at one of the comfortable looking indoor tables, Robert led her through to an enclosed courtyard terrace where several people sat, shaded by cotton sunshades at small glass-topped tables. 'Here we go,' he said, pulling out a chair for her.

She sank into it gratefully, although she supposed she ought to have objected. Were men meant to do that any more? She'd never really had a man be gallant to her and do all the chair pulling and puddle cloaking and all the other things men were meant to do for helpless maidens like herself. The closest she'd got was at school when Lawrence Morgan had pulled away her chair and she'd tumbled to the ground on sitting. It wasn't quite the same. And Steve, well he'd been gallant in his own way, but quite rightly realised she was capable of opening car doors herself. She'd always laughed at the idea of having a chair pulled, door opened, bag carried; but actually the gesture felt rather sweet.

'It's a lovely place,' she said as a waitress brought them tall glasses of ice-filled water. 'I can see why you wanted to live here.'

'Yes.' He nodded. 'It's the people too. I mean, even being alone here... I don't know. I don't feel properly alone, if that makes sense. Everyone knows each other, or at least recognises each other. You get bonjours from everyone. People take the time to chat, even though my French is pretty crap, you know? I suppose it's a small community thing.'

'Your French sounds pretty good to me,' she said.

'Thanks,' he said. 'My grammar's awful still, but I get by.'

Nicky nodded. 'Must be nice knowing everyone,' she said, thinking about how she rushed to work and barely made eye contact with anyone other than her customers. It was lack of time, probably. And a cultural thing. If you went around saying hello to people you didn't know in St Albans, you'd probably get sectioned.

'I guess I'm beginning to see why you stayed,' she said. 'I can imagine it'd be hard to walk away from this place.'

Robert sipped his water and looked around the courtyard, at the blue sky and trees visible beyond the peach-coloured walls as if seeing them for the first time. 'Yes,' he said. 'That's the problem with moving somewhere special. You get kind of caught. You know. It's so lovely here. You're right. And I bet if I moved back to the UK or to somewhere else, I'd miss it every day. The problem is I miss loads of things about England too. The people, family. Some of the culture.'

'What, fish and chips?'

'Ha, I was thinking more the sense of humour.'

'There is that.'

'So that's my advice,' he said, smiling. 'Don't expand your horizons unless you want to be torn in two.'

She laughed. 'Well, that's... um, inspirational. Another one for the Hallmark job?'

'Ha, yes.' He laughed. 'Reckon that would make the perfect greetings card.'

'I'll let you have one of mine,' she said, warming to the topic. 'Never drink the punch, unless you made it yourself.'

'Amen to that,' he said, smiling. 'Although I think I did make that punch.'

'OK, in that case "never let Robert make the punch".'

Just as she was about to move the conversation back to the project, she felt a hand on her shoulder. 'Hello stranger!' It was Michelle, dressed in a sleeveless polo neck and cream linen trousers. As always, her chic 'French' appearance was at odds with her soft northern accent.

'Oh, Michelle!' Nicky said. 'How are you?'

'Well, just about got over the hangover from the other night,' she said, pulling up a chair. 'Bloody hell. I hope we didn't ruin your filming or whatever. I was going to ask but...' She made a face to show she'd been too nervous about the answer.

'Actually,' Nicky smiled, 'the painting was a real hit.' She told Michelle about how Ryan had enthused over the messy work. 'It's even a movement now,' she joked. 'I've called it conscious recluttering.'

'Conscious recluttering?' Michelle's lips pursed in approval. 'I like it. Could catch on.' She grinned. 'Sorry about the penis by the way.'

'The... what?'

'The blue penis I drew on the fireplace. You know, for the dare. I was going to cover it up but...'

'You mean the mural?'

'Yes.'

'We couldn't make out what it was!' Robert said. 'That was you?'

'Yeah. I guess it's a good thing my artistic talents are wanting. It was meant to be a giant nob.'

'Remind me,' said Nicky, 'not to enlist you for any future painting projects.'

They laughed and Michelle waved at the waitress and ordered herself a Coke. 'Don't mind me joining?'

'Not at all.'

As they chatted about life in France and clothing stores and B&Bs and sunshine and what should or should not have been included in the punch, Nicky began to realise just how lucky she was that she'd been given this opportunity. Because whether or not she made it as a TV designer or got a break in her career, she would definitely come out of this with some fabulous new friends.

18

The following day, when she'd called Amy as usual at nine o'clock, she'd been worried when her daughter didn't answer. So, an hour later, she was relieved to hear the click on the line followed by a sleepy 'Hello?' when she tried again.

'Are you OK?' she said. 'You didn't pick up earlier.'

'Yeah, just up to my neck in washing. Then ended up dozing on the sofa with Rose,' Amy said. 'Just woke up when the phone rang.'

'Well, glad you're OK. You're not ill or anything?'

'No! Not at all. Feeling much more capable today. Been talking to some of the girls from the baby classes and have been thoroughly reassured that we all feel like we're drowning most of the time. So far, so normal. Anyway, today it's just usual mummy tiredness. I'm told it ends in about... eighteen years,' her daughter joked.

'Hopefully sooner,' Nicky said. 'But yes, I remember those days well!'

'Anyway, how are you, Mum?'

'I'm good! How's my granddaughter?'

'Yeah. Same as yesterday. Pretty good. If a little sticky.'

'Glad to hear it.' Nicky laughed, imagining Rose's little face as she'd looked last time she'd dropped in before her flight. The little girl's face had been covered with strawberry juice - her skin stained pink. Nicky longed now to hold her granddaughter's fat little body in her arms and hoped she wouldn't have changed too much by the time her French adventure finished. The odd moment when she'd managed to FaceTime Amy, her daughter had tried to hold Rose up to the camera, but she'd wriggled and squirmed. For now, she had to make do with pictures Amy sent her, and already she could see the little girl emerging from the sweet baby, time moving quickly on as it always did.

'So, did you get everything done yesterday?' Amy asked. 'You said you were going around the town to schmooze business owners?'

'Yes, it went really well, thank you. Oh, and Roussillon is beautiful.'

'Hang on, you've been there for – what – three weeks and you've only just noticed?' Amy laughed. 'What have you been doing?'

'I know. I mean I've been out and about a bit. But this was my first proper walk around it. It's all been a bit... hectic really.'

'I can imagine.'

The conversation took its usual course; they talked about their plans for the day. Nicky listened to her daughter and tried to read between the lines, make sure everything really was OK with her. She missed popping in after work, or coming to help out at the weekend and hoped her absence wasn't taking its toll on her daughter. But Amy seemed fine; chatting about mums' groups and the takeaway she'd been treated to the evening before.

'By the way, have you heard from Chloe?' Nicky asked as the conversation drew to a close. 'I've sent her a few emails and text messages, but she's barely responded.' Nicky's younger daughter, Chloe, wasn't the most reliable communicator, but it was unusual for so many missives to go unanswered. It was daft, really, asking

Amy. Obviously, if anything was wrong with Chloe, she would have told Nicky herself. But still, she worried.

She tucked the phone under her chin as she selected a T-shirt from the drawer to put on after her shower, and the green fitted trousers Michelle had persuaded her to buy yesterday afternoon. She doubted she'd look as chic as her new friend, but it was nice to be making more of an effort than she did at home where she'd been stuck in a wardrobe rut of safe favourites.

'Oh yeah. I think she's just busy. You know. She got that big order in just before you left?'

'From the spa?' Chloe had been thrilled when a local, boutique spa had got in touch with a chocolate order a few days before Jenny had flipped Nicky's world upside down and had her tearing to France. 'That's all going through?' she asked now, feeling a little guilty that she hadn't worked out the reason for Chloe's silence herself. The poor girl must be frantic.

'Yeah. They want her to do some sort of enormous order for an open day they're having. And she's rushed off her feet. But she said to say hi.'

'Well, I'm glad she's talking to you, at least. And you're sure she's OK?' Nicky asked again.

There was a silence.

'Amy?' Nicky prompted, feeling anxiety spike in her chest.

'Yeah. Look Mum, she's fine, honestly.' Was it Nicky's imagination or did Amy sound a little annoyed?

'Right.'

'She just... I mean, she's bombing around everywhere trying to get everything done perfectly. You know what she's like.'

'Yeah, that's true.' Nicky relaxed a little. Although it was still slightly odd not to have heard from Chloe at all.

'And she honestly did ask me to say hi. She told me the other night that she kept forgetting to call you, except when she was just on the way to bed at about one in the morning, and assumed it was too late.'

'Oh dear, poor girl.'

'Yeah, so I said. "Stop stressing. I'll take on the mum duties!",' Amy said with a laugh.

Then there was another silence.

'Mum duties?' Nicky asked quietly.

'Sorry, I didn't mean to put it like that,' Amy said. 'You know what I mean.'

'Actually,' Nicky said, feeling her voice crack a little. 'I don't… not quite. I mean, speaking to me on the phone. It's a *duty*?' She felt her heart begin to thump.

'No, Mum. It's just a little joke about it between me and Chloe. We don't mean anything by it,' said Amy. 'I mean. We worry about you – of course we do. Doing something so different in a new place. So it's only natural that we want to check up on you, make sure everything's OK.'

'Of course,' Nicky said, uncertainly. Unable to stop her voice sounding quiet and odd.

'It's only because we love you. We just – I don't know, *mum duties* is just our little joke. And kind of our way of making sure one of us is an attentive daughter at all times and we don't abandon you completely!'

'Oh.'

'And… it's not a duty really. I mean, it's a pleasure, obviously.'

'You worry… about *me*?'

'Yes. Of course we do. We love you, Mum.'

'But I don't understand. Why are you worried about me? This France thing?'

'Not the France thing, in particular. Just… well, everyday stuff. You know. You're alone. You seem… a bit lonely, I suppose.'

'Oh.' Nicky had never thought of herself as being lonely. Yet she felt a shiver of recognition. Perhaps in some ways, she had been – she was – lonely. 'That's... I mean, thank you. But... sorry.' Nicky tried to phrase her words carefully. 'It's just I always thought that. I mean, these calls we have... That I'm checking up on *you*. Making sure *you're* OK. Not... I don't need them for other reasons. I just know how tough it is, you know, looking after a baby and I just wanted to help...'

'Oh, Mum,' Amy said, her voice sympathetic and slightly patronising in a way that made Nicky both melt and bristle. 'It's always lovely to talk to you. But you know, I'm OK. I'm a grown up. I have friends, neighbours. A husband who's getting better at nappy changes by the day. I'm happy to chat. Of course I am. But I don't *need* you to check up on me. I really don't.'

'Oh.'

'I know you mean well...' her daughter added carefully. 'But if I'm honest, the idea that you think I can't cope with... well ordinary life. It feels as if you don't have much faith in me.'

'But it's not that at all! And, honestly, if the phone calls bother you...'

'Mum! Don't be silly. Of course I want to talk to you on the phone. But only because it's *nice*. Not because I *need* you to make sure I'm OK.'

'Yes. Yes of course.' Nicky had been offended by the idea the girls were worried about her. But perhaps she was guilty of the same thing. An excess of love, perhaps. But also a lack of faith.

'And you know. It's lovely when you pop in. It really is. We always love to see you – don't we, Rose? But you needn't put yourself out! It's important you... well, you know.'

'Important I what...?'

'Well. It's important that you have your own life.'

'Oh.'

'And I suppose it's important that you...' Amy sighed. 'Sorry

Mum. It's hard to say. But I suppose sometimes I wish you'd give me a little more space to live mine.'

'Oh.'

'I love you, Mum. And I know I'm so very lucky that you're always there. It's amazing. You're amazing. It's just... Well, since you've been in France and haven't been able to, uh, pop in, I've realised that I'm more capable than I thought.' Another silence. 'Mum? Are you OK?'

'I do have a life,' Nicky said, softly.

'I know. Look ignore me. Honestly, I've had hardly any sleep. And I've been watching breakfast TV for an hour on and off – my brain is mush. Forget I said anything.' Silence. 'Mum?'

Nicky took a shuddery breath. 'Yes. Of course! Well, lovely to speak to you. And glad all's well. Give Chloe my love, won't you!' she blurted out in a breathy run-on sentence before saying a brief goodbye and hanging up.

She threw the phone onto the bed where it bounced precariously close to the edge. Her body flexed as if readying itself to dive-bomb and rescue it. But luckily it finished its journey safely cocooned by the blanket she'd flung off when climbing out of bed this morning.

She tried to remind herself that Amy hadn't said anything wrong. Nobody had accused her of bothering them. Or being a nuisance.

But it had been there, hadn't it, in the sub-text? That slight irritation. The idea of 'duty'.

She was in no doubt that the girls loved her. But she'd also thought they needed her. Almost as much as they had a few years ago when they'd been teens and living under her roof.

But it seemed they didn't need her any more. At least, not in the same way. In fact, what she'd thought of as being helpful, they'd seen as being needy on her part.

Everything she'd thought had been turned on its head.

She was suddenly this figure of sympathy in their minds. Lonely old Mum, better check up on her.

At forty-nine. She looked in the mirror and glanced away. Yes, she was a grandmother. And yes, it was great to know that there were loving daughters ready to look after her if she faced a genuine crisis. But she was far from old. Far from needy.

What she was though, she realised with a horrifying surge of anxiety, was not *needed*. A huge part of her purpose had been ripped away by the call. And with it her confidence. Her sense of self.

You're alone. Amy's words came back to haunt her and she felt suddenly both indignant and embarrassed. Is that how her daughters saw her? Not as strong, independent and single. But alone? Lonely? Because she was alone through choice! She'd given up on that side of her for them. To support them!

People around her had often mentioned her 'self-sacrifice' but it hadn't felt that way. Or they'd say 'you give so much to those girls', and she'd feel embarrassed, but maybe a little proud too.

Only now she was becoming a burden. That was what Amy had meant, wasn't it? That she was the one who needed keeping an eye on. That she was a duty.

For a moment, her fingers twitched and she wondered whether she ought to call Amy back and have it out with her. But then she realised there had been no malice in what Amy had said. That if anything, she'd been kind and tolerant and had only actually let slip how she really felt by accident. And when you say something by accident, chances are you really mean it. She couldn't be angry at Amy for genuinely thinking something; for hurting her by mistake.

So she thought instead of what she was doing here in Provence. That perhaps, as everyone kept saying, this was a chance for her to embrace a new life.

The time had come not to be alone by choice, but to explore the options that life seemed to be giving her. Show the girls that she was quite capable of looking after herself.

She picked up her mobile and scrolled through to Jenny's number.

'Hi Jenny,' she said, as soon as her friend picked up. 'Quick question. Do you have mobile numbers for the guys in the film crew?'

Perhaps it was time to finally take her own life in her hands and give herself the attention she'd reserved for her daughters.

19

This time she was in the hospital. The corridors stretching endlessly in front of her as she ran through sets of double doors, past patients on gurneys and unresponsive nurses who looked away as she screamed, 'Where is he?'

She knew that if she didn't get to him soon he would be gone, she'd miss the chance to say goodbye. But the numbers on the doors kept changing and she kept finding herself back in reception or inside a different patient's room or finding a door with the right number but being unable to push it open.

Then she heard his voice calling her name. Faintly but louder as she ran and she was screaming his name in return. 'I'm coming!' she yelled. 'I'm trying to find you. Where are you? Steve?!'

* * *

It took her almost a minute to adjust to her surroundings when she woke up. Her heart was pounding and the room was dark. She wasn't sure whether she'd screamed out loud and hoped that Robert hadn't heard anything.

Gingerly, she pushed herself into a sitting position and clicked on the bedside light, flooding the room with an electric glow and pushing the shadows to the edge of the room. The dreams were always worse when she was stressed, she told herself. It was now just a couple of days until the secret guests arrived, she was just tense about making sure she finished everything on her 'to do' list.

Her body was tired and she didn't want to have to get up. Instead, she tried lying back down, light still on, and running her 'to do' list through her head. All she had left to do was to print the information she'd written down and practise presenting it so that she could make a good show when the cameras were running. She'd make sure that the paintwork that had been completed yesterday in the dining room was on-point – with no penis murals. She'd check the hallways in the light to make sure the wallpaper wasn't showing. Robert's friend had sanded the floor in the dining room, then returned two days ago to apply some varnish, and the patina in the ancient oak had broken through beautifully. She'd set out some of their new purchases and make sure everything was great in the guest rooms the 'secret' guests would be in. She and Robert were going to hang the paintings provided by Victor. There was quite a bit to get done, but these were mostly finishing touches and flourishes that would set the whole place off.

She'd finished costing up Robert's expenses, and had suggested he raised the room rate a little to give him a chance of turning a profit. The website was already live and looking fantastic. No bookings yet, but already several enquiries. And all before anything had been shown on TV.

'It's you,' she said to herself. 'You made that happen.'

Although thinking through the days ahead helped to move the nightmare further into the shadows, she found that instead of feeling ready to return to sleep, she was now wired with all the things she needed to do. Sighing, she got out of bed, checked her phone for the time – 2 a.m. – and decided to go downstairs to make a cup of tea. Hopefully half an hour or so of sitting in a different environment would reset her body ready for the additional sleep it definitely needed.

She made her way quietly along the now familiar corridor, tiptoeing down the stairs to minimise the creaks her movement inevitably made, and reached the downstairs hall without having made any noise. The low light outside from Robert's solar lamps and the three-quarter moon filtered through the glass in the door and window meaning visibility in the hallway was good enough – she'd avoid putting on the light which would flood the upstairs landing too and potentially disturb her host.

Quietly, she twisted the handle on the dining room door and walked in, hoping to grab one of the dip-in herbal teabags they'd set out in a basket next to the coffee maker, rather than rummage in the kitchen for the enormous box that Robert kept on a top shelf – reaching that would mean clambering on a chair and at this hour, she didn't fancy her chances.

The dining room was darker than the hallway, and smelled unfamiliar with its new mixture of drying paint, varnish and a strange, burning smell left by the floor sander. She fumbled around for the light switch and clicked it, then remembered that the electrician had just changed a fitting yesterday, and the click would do nothing until they'd been out to purchase the special bulbs they hadn't realised their new chandelier would need.

But it was OK, she thought. There was a little grey light still from the hallway giving a tiny bit of visibility and she knew roughly where everything was. She'd just use her other senses to navigate the room.

She stepped in, her bare feet enjoying the welcome sensation of the newly sanded and polished wood. The renewed surface felt almost soft under her feet, and so smooth she was tempted to push herself forward and glide like a skater on ice. She was almost across the room to the large oak dresser they'd set against the wall to provide a place for the toaster, the glass cereal jars, coffee machine, hot water urn and individual teabags when her foot struck something. Hard.

'Ow!' she hissed involuntarily, bending down to grab her injured big toe. Then there was a sound of a wobble and a heavy crash as something hit the floor and rolled across the wood. She leaned down to rub her toe, not too worried by what it had been. She'd pick up the box of tools or bin of DIY debris tomorrow. Anything sticky or dirty ought to come off easily enough. She'd have to check what she'd done in the morning – there was no way of seeing it tonight.

But when she returned her poor throbbing foot to the floor, she realised a great patch underneath her foot was covered in thick liquid. Stepping forward, her heel slid and she found her bottom coming into contact with the floor with a heavy, painful thud.

'Bloody hell,' she said, trying to stand up but failing and slipping again in the liquid.

She righted herself, clutching at one of the chairs, fell again, took a different route using a table to steady herself then cautiously made her way back to the dull grey light of the doorway, not caring now if she woke Robert up. Whatever had happened must be messy and she'd have to do something about it – for that she'd need light. With the light fitting out of order, she'd have to fling the door open wide and put the hall light on to give her a chance of seeing things properly. Perhaps one of the painters had left a flask of coffee? Or maybe it was a bucket of water from the mop Robert had used on the kitchen tiles earlier.

In the hallway, she snapped on the light, then turned to look at the slightly brighter dining room. And gasped.

It hadn't been a mop and bucket, or a flask, or anything else she'd speculated about. It had in fact been a large tin of paint. The paint they'd been using to finish off the woodwork and skirting board. The kind of paint you could only remove from paintbrushes with smelly chemicals.

And it was everywhere. The initial spill had created a large puddle in the centre of the room, but her subsequent struggles had spread the paint so that there were handprints, a bum print, a kind of mess where she'd scrabbled to her feet. One of the tables had white paint marks where she'd pulled herself up using a leg.

It was all that she could do not to scream.

Then she heard a slow creak on the stairs. Looking up, she saw Robert making his way blearily into the hall. 'Is everything OK?' he asked. 'I can... oh.' He took in her appearance – the fact that she was covered in splatters of white. 'Shit,' he said. 'Don't tell me another pigeon's got in?'

'No,' she said, shaking her head. She had a sudden urge to lie to him. To close the door on the dining room and leave all the mess until the morning when she could confront it with a clear head. But found herself simply stepping back and gesturing towards the dining room. 'I kind of... Well, I had a bit of an accident.'

When he saw what was inside, Robert's face fell.

'So, not pigeons then,' he said at last.

'No,' she said.

'Shit.'

'Yep. Look I'm so sorry I...'

'Oh God.' He whipped round. 'This isn't your fault. It's... I mean it was an accident obviously. A pretty... spectacular accident.'

She felt tears well in her eyes. 'But we're never going to get it off in time, are we? And people are coming. It's everywhere! What are we going to do?' She felt her breath coming in short, sharp gasps.

'It's OK,' he said, although his voice didn't match his words – it sounded uncertain, almost as worried as she was. 'We can fix this, no problem.'

'But we'd need...'

'Listen,' he said. 'I'll make you a drink. You get cleaned up. We'll close the door and figure it out in the morning.'

'But...'

'That's an order.'

She looked up at him, as he smiled at her. 'OK, sir,' she said, with a nod.

She was glad now that he'd woken up. Otherwise she'd have spent the rest of the night in a sleepless panic wondering what he was going to say or – probably worse – trying to clean the paint up in her pjs and failing miserably.

Obediently, she went upstairs and slipped out of her clothes. She washed her hands in the sink with lots of soap, although remnants of the stubborn paint clung on, pulled on a fresh set of pyjamas then made her way downstairs to the kitchen.

Robert – who'd been sensible enough to put the hall light on properly – had already made her tea and set it down on the table, nodding towards a chair. She sat down in it, and cupped her hands gratefully around the mug.

He pulled out a chair and sat opposite, his eyes resting on her still paint-splattered hands.

'I can get some paint remover for that.'

She shook her head. 'I'll do it in the morning,' she said. 'That stuff stinks and I'm still hoping for some sleep.'

'Good point.'

They were silent for a minute. Then, 'But you're OK, right? Not hurt or anything?'

'I'm fine. Just annoyed and, well, embarrassed,' she said.

'Bit of a fuck up,' he said.

She was surprised to hear him swear. 'Yes,' she said. 'I'm so, so sorry.'

'Don't be silly. Blame the person who left an open tin of paint in the middle of the floor with the lid just balanced on top. It was a recipe for disaster.'

'Even so.'

'Seriously, it's OK,' he said. 'It's done. We'll deal with it, somehow.'

'Maybe I can ask if we can delay the guests,' she offered. 'Just for an extra day or so.'

'Sure,' he said. 'But you know. If not. We'll find a way.'

She searched his face for signs that he was lying – just placating her. But he looked back steadily, confidently. She took a sip of her tea. 'OK,' she said. 'Thank you.'

'Don't be silly.'

A few minutes later they made their way back upstairs. 'Good luck,' he said as she moved to the next set of stairs and he stood at his *Privé* door.

'What with?'

'Just getting back to sleep,' he said. 'It can be hard when you're... stressed.'

'I think I'll be OK,' she said. And realised she meant it. She felt a lot calmer after their chat. 'And look, Jenny's a friend. I must be able to pull a favour from her at some point. Perhaps this is the time.'

'Maybe.' He smiled. 'Either way, don't sweat it.'

They said goodnight and she climbed the stairs to her third-floor bedroom. Inside, she flung herself on the bed, the scent of paint still in her nostrils.

Before trying to settle down she picked up her phone. Maybe striking while the iron was hot with Jenny would be a good idea. She'd send an email and Jenny would pick it up as soon as she woke tomorrow (this?) morning.

Hi Jenny,

Can I ask a favour? We've had a bit of a disaster here. Any chance of pushing the secret guests back a few days? And the filming too? Nearly there, but just had a setback.

Nicky

She thought of all the times over the years they'd been there to support each other. How much Jenny had done for her – from babysitting to midnight phone calls to even this opportunity in France. Despite that, she'd rarely asked for anything directly from her friend. Jenny had given her time and support freely, just as Nicky had done to her – just as friends should do. So if she actually asked? Cashed in a friend credit? Even though she was cautious about the filming schedule, surely Jenny would be willing to step up and support her.

As she finally lay back and drifted off to sleep, she felt relaxed. Suddenly confident in Jenny, in their friendship. And in Robert and his ability to tackle whatever mammoth task lay ahead in the cold light of day tomorrow morning.

It was all going to be fine.

20

The minute she awoke, she reached for her phone. Jenny, as suspected, had been up early and there was already a response to her email.

Hi Nicky,
Sorry about the setback. Can't change the schedule I'm afraid.
Sure you'll nail it though,
Jenny x

'Shit,' she said, shifting herself up into a seated position. She checked the time – 8 a.m., so only 7 a.m. in the UK. But then Jenny had written her response at six, so she must be up. She scrolled through her contacts and pressed the 'call' button.

The line rang a couple of times before Jenny picked up. 'Hi Nicky,' she said. There was a background rumble and murmur that suggested she was on the train. 'What can I do for you?'

'I just wanted...' Nicky took a deep breath. 'Look, I know you say you can't do anything about the schedule, and I know you hate to meddle with these things. But could you possibly make an exception. I've... well, I've messed up and it's my fault.' She explained about her midnight quest for a cup of tea and how it had gone horribly wrong. 'It's just... it's not really fair on Robert,' she explained. 'He's being really good about it, actually. But it seems awful if the room's messed up and it's not his fault. I mean, this is his business. His livelihood.'

Jenny was silent for a moment. Then, 'I'm really sorry, Nicky,' she said. 'I just don't think we can change things around at this late notice.'

Nicky felt tears prick her eyes – she wasn't sure if they were tears of anger or sadness. 'Seriously? You can't do anything?' she said. 'I mean... I did come out here for you. You know, at the last minute. It was... well, a favour, if anything.'

'An opportunity,' her friend said firmly.

'Yes, OK. And I'm grateful. But you know, it's not something I asked for. And what I'm asking of you is... can't you do *anything* at all? Even an extra day would help?'

'I really wish I could help... but—'

'And don't you think,' Nicky added desperately, 'that it'll make for a better programme. I mean, what we've done to the B&B on such a limited budget in a short space of time. It looks... it looked. It would be amazing TV. I reckon people will love it,' she said, trying to sell the favour from a different angle.

Jenny was silent and for a moment Nicky wondered whether she'd actually hit home with her latest angle. *Please* she thought silently. *I really need this.*

Then Jenny spoke. 'Thing is, chick, that the programme is going to be great.'

'I know, but...'

'No, hear me out. What you've done... what you *did* sounds brilliant. But as far as the programme itself, the audience, goes it's actually quite cool if you... well, mess everything up.'

'It's… what?'

'Yeah, you know. People like to see some radical business trans-formations, but it's also great if they see a couple of disasters. For contrast but also entertainment. Think of all the reality TV you've watched. Do you remember the vanilla people who just played by the rules? No. You remember the emotional disasters, the moments when everything goes to shit… That's what makes a good reality programme – even one like this…'

Suddenly, Nicky found it hard to breathe. 'So you actually like the fact I've… well, it's a bit of a mess?'

'Darling,' Jenny said, warming to the topic. 'I LOVE it. If I'm honest, it's one of the reasons I got amateurs like you involved. You know. Fabulous opportunity. But also Great TV.'

Nicky could hear her heartbeat loud in her ears. 'Jenny,' she said quietly.

'Yes?'

'Are you saying that you asked me to do the gig because I'm an amateur?'

'Well, not exactly,' Jenny said, her tone a little more guarded. 'More… I mean, of course I wanted you to succeed. But I knew it wasn't risk free too. Great for ratings if you do well, but if I'm honest, even better if you fail. Win, win. Or fail, win.' She laughed at her own joke.

'Fail, win? You said that you thought I'd nail it. That I'd be better than…'

'Well, you have done brilliantly! Much better than I'd expected, actually. It's been quite an eye-opener.'

'Oh.'

'But now,' Jenny said, still seemingly oblivious to the impact her words were having, 'well, I'll be honest, that paint spillage is the icing on the cake.'

'It is?'

'I can't believe,' her friend chuckled, 'you managed to smear it all over the tables and get it everywhere. And on a newly renovated floor too.'

'Oh.'

'It's fabulous!'

Nicky took a breath and tried to calm down. 'OK,' she said carefully. 'Can I just... clarify something?'

'Of course. Shoot.'

'Did you ask me to do this challenge because you thought I'd fail? Because you hoped I'd mess it up and it would make for an entertaining episode?' she said, working hard to keep her tone even.

'Well, not exactly. I didn't necessarily think you'd fail. I thought you might be... out of your depth a bit. And I was hoping... I suppose I was hoping we might hit a couple of roadblocks. You know. Keep the audience happy,' Jenny said, her tone reasoning.

'You told me you thought I was up to the job. That I'd maybe create a whole new career for myself.'

'Well, I like to be positive.'

'Positive! Jenny, you lied to me. You said that this was an opportunity for *me*. That I might get a whole new start out of it. You made it sound as if you...'

'As if what?' Jenny's tone was more serious now.

'As if you really believed in me!'

'Oh honey, of course I believe in you! This isn't about that.'

'Yet you gave me this role not only because you thought I'd fail, but because it sounds like you hoped I would. You actively wanted me to screw this up.'

'That's not what I...'

'So you don't believe in me at all. Do you?' Nicky said, feeling heat rush into her face and neck. 'You didn't think it was My Time.'

'I—'

'It was *your* time! Not mine! This was all about *you*!'

'I—'

'God, Jenny. I knew you were career orientated, but I never thought you'd sell your best friend down the river like this.'

'Honey, calm down. It wasn't that I didn't have faith in you. I knew you'd do the best job you could. I just... I thought it would be natural for someone... new to things to make the odd mistake or two. And I knew you'd rise to the challenge and make great TV in the process. What's not to like?' Jenny said.

'What's not to *like*? I don't like the fact that I've been forced to step away from all my responsibilities, from the life that I had built up. And yes, maybe it wasn't the most interesting or successful life. But it was *my* life. And I liked it.'

'Nicky...'

'And now you've made me want more! You made me believe I was capable of more. Made me believe *more* was an option that was open to me. And now I'm here and I thought I had this... bright future. Then you tell me that it was all in my head? You opened this kind of... of... locked box in me. And now I've got to shut the lid, to go back to ordinary life? To get laughed at on TV?'

'I'm sure nobody's going to laugh.'

'Maybe not. But you know, I'm pretty certain you'd be thrilled if they did!' Nicky said, pressing the 'end call' button before her 'friend' could respond.

As soon as she'd done that, she rolled over in bed and pressed her face into the pillow and screamed out her anger into its soft, muffling feathers. She was angry with Jenny, but more than anything, angry with herself.

What an idiot she'd been! Taking an opportunity to go to France, telling everyone about it. Her work would know when she got back. And then she'd have an agonising wait until the TV programme went out. And then what? She'd be some sort of figure of ridicule. The middle-aged woman who thought she could...

And it wouldn't help Robert at all, would it? If they were looking to highlight where she'd gone wrong rather than where they'd gone right? It wasn't just the paint job/floor disaster. Their episode would be forty-five minutes long. Plenty of time to talk about everything. But if the angle was to be 'project doomed to failure' rather than 'look at this transformation!' then he was going to look like an idiot too. He was going to lose his business. His livelihood. His dream.

She looked up, the air in the bedroom cold against her damp skin. Her new outfit hung on a hanger she'd hooked over the curtain rail. A long, pleated skirt in brushed satin, teamed with a silk top in a gorgeous sky blue. It had looked daring but flattering in the shop. Now, looking at it, it seemed to mock her. *Look who you thought you were!* it said, hanging there. *What an idiot!*

A text popped up on her phone. This time, from Tom. Her stomach dipped even more, but she felt compelled to open it.

Hi Nicky,
Sure it would be great to get a drink after filming. See you in a few days!

Followed by a thumbs-up.

A thumbs-up.

The emoji version of a polite rebuttal. And the way he'd worded the text. As if the drink was the main goal rather than spending time together. Not mentioning a date. Just being polite.

Oh God. She'd gone after a younger (albeit only slightly), good looking, successful man who no doubt knew exactly her 'role' in this reality TV set-up and was probably also laughing at her behind her back. She didn't even fancy him, not really. She'd just been convinced that he liked her and determined in the moment to make a change to her life. Now she'd embarrassed herself completely.

Well, no more. She might not be 'needed' at home by her daughters in the way she'd assumed, but at least she was loved, appreciated. Her job that she'd walked away from might not be particularly interesting, but at least it provided a steady income and wasn't too taxing. And while she might have realised during this 'break' that she needed to build a little more into her life, that didn't mean she had to take on every opportunity no matter the cost.

She was out.

The bonus was, if she walked out, she was confident that they'd have to cut Robert's whole B&B from the series. After all, they hardly had anything yet. A set of 'before' pictures just wouldn't cut it. So in walking out she'd not only save her reputation, her self-esteem, but rescue Robert from business-crushing ridicule.

Plus, getting on a plane and flying away would be a great way to avoid the embarrassment of seeing Tom again. 'See, Jenny,' she said. 'Fail, win. Just like you wanted.'

Yes, she'd probably cause more than a few headaches for Jenny by ducking out of the role. The thought made her feel guilty, but the guilt only went to fuel her determination. It annoyed her. Why was she worrying about the feelings of a woman who had set her up to fail?

It was the only way, she decided, getting out her phone and pulling up the webpage of the budget airline she'd flown out on, trying to see what flights were available. Only every time she pressed 'enter' on a flight route, the page would reset. She tried another, more expensive, airline and the same thing happened. She looked at her phone. There were only two bars here in the attic – and the Wi-Fi barely made it past the second floor. But the last thing she wanted to do was to go downstairs now, see Robert, have to explain her red face.

She needed help. But she'd resolved not to call Amy. To give her daughter a bit of space. Her other usual go-to person was Jenny, but she was hardly likely to speak to her ever again the way things had turned out. Instead, already feeling it was futile, she dialled Chloe.

As usual, her younger daughter didn't answer. 'Hi Chloe, it's Mum,' she said on the answerphone. 'Give us a ring when you get this.'

Then, slightly reluctantly, she dialled Amy.

'Hey Mum,' Amy said, in her usual cheerful phone voice.

'Hi love. Look sorry to call...'

'Don't be silly.'

'But... any chance you could do me a favour?'

'Oh, sure. Sure,' her daughter said.

'The internet connection's a bit crap here, but I need to book a plane ticket.'

'A plane ticket?' Amy's voice registered surprise. 'But haven't the TV company already arranged your travel home?'

'Yes,' she said. 'They did. But this is different.'

And she told her daughter how Jenny had let her down. How she'd failed in the task. How she'd be made into a laughing stock. 'I just want to get home as soon as I can,' she said. 'Any chance you could sort that out for me?'

'Oh, Mum. You know Jenny's completely wrong, don't you?'

'Amy, I just want to get home,' she said firmly.

'OK,' her daughter said. 'Leave it with me. I'll see what I can do.'

21

The next morning there was a gentle knock on her bedroom door as she zipped up her make-up bag after gathering her toiletries from the ensuite. 'Yes?' she said. Robert entered, his face downcast, an equally downcast Buster trailing in his wake.

'I still can't believe you're going to quit,' Robert said, with a shrug of his shoulders and a slight smile. 'Can't I do anything to convince you to stay?' His tone suggested he wasn't holding out much hope.

She shook her head.

Buster walked up to her and tilted his head, looking at her with deep, brown eyes. She held out her hand and touched his soft ears and he pushed his head gently against her hands. 'Sorry, Buster,' she said.

Robert walked over and pulled the voiles back a little to allow sunlight to stream more brightly into the room, then gazed over the tumbling views. 'It's going to be weird, you know. Not having you around,' he said. 'Does that sound strange?'

Yesterday, when she'd broken the news that Amy had booked her a ticket home and that she'd be leaving on the next available flight, he'd been horrified. 'But we've nearly done it!' he said. 'And I've got loads of ideas to sort out the... the spillage before the guests arrive. Please, don't go.'

She felt guilty, but for once had stuck to her guns. 'Robert, I honestly believe that this is best for both of us,' she said. 'The TV company aren't going to go after you for the budget money and we've really transformed this place, I think. You've got the new website, the pricing. In all the important ways it's all really complete. I just don't want to broadcast it to the world. It's not really the spillage – it's the fact that Jenny seems determined to paint this as a disaster story and I'm not going to let her.'

'Come on,' he said. 'I'm sure she didn't mean...'

'She told me I had an opportunity when all along she was just using me. Knowing that the worse it went for me the better it would bode for her.'

He was silent at this. Then, 'Look, I understand. She's really let you down. And it's a huge blow. But you know, we've been in this situation for almost a month... and I'd like to think that we're friends. You going now... it just doesn't seem right. For either of us.'

But he failed to convince her.

She'd hoped to catch a plane yesterday afternoon, but Amy had called to say the flights were booked – 'it's silly season, Mum: everyone's on holiday' – but she'd managed to get her a seven o'clock flight from Toulouse for today. As far as Nicky was concerned, the sooner she got back and pieced together the life she'd had before, the better. She wanted to put all of this – the dreaming, the ridiculous confidence she'd felt in herself, the fact she'd felt as if new doors were opening for her both in her work and romantic lives – behind her. She needed to accept reality. She had a good life, and there had been no reason to disrupt it.

She still wasn't sure how to feel about Chloe and Amy. But she'd put that on hold for now. All she had to do was get home. Where she was safe and she knew what she was doing and there were no awkward slip-ups because there were no risks.

'I'm sorry,' she said to Robert now, struggling to get her case zipped up with all the new outfits she'd bought. Annoyed, she opened the case and pulled out the more daring of her tops – the bright, vibrant colours seemed to belong to someone completely alien. She'd leave them here – perhaps Robert could take them to a charity shop or something. She laid them on the bed, then zipped her case up easily. 'I just can't... I mean. I'm going to miss you too,' she said, the words out of her mouth before she realised what she was saying. But it was true, she thought. She would miss his company, having someone there. And more than that. They'd really become friends over the past few weeks.

But leaving didn't mean she couldn't come back. She just had to get away now, before everyone turned up and there was momentum and the time for running away passed her by.

He nodded. He'd spent long enough trying to persuade her to stay yesterday to know that it was futile to try any more. 'Well, at least let me give you a lift to the airport,' he said. 'What time's your flight?'

'Seven o'clock. So I'll need to be there about five.'

'Right,' he said.

'Are you sure you don't mind?'

'Of course not.' He smiled, weakly. 'As long as you don't mind me spending the drive trying to change your mind.'

She laughed, but hoped he wasn't serious. 'I really am sorry,' she said.

'I know.'

'And I mean, it. I'll be back at some point... maybe soon. It's just the whole TV thing. It's not... it's not you.'

He checked his watch. 'Look, we won't have to leave here till about three. Do you want to grab a quick bite to eat out somewhere beforehand?'

'I'll need to print my boarding pass off,' she said, 'but Amy hasn't sent it yet. So sure. As long as I can use your printer when we get back?'

After he went back downstairs, she took a minute to freshen up, brushing her hair and pinning it back with a flower slide she'd bought from Michelle's shop. She glanced again at the colourful clothes on the bed and felt suddenly sad. Maybe she'd find a way to take them home after all. She'd have another go at fitting them in her case once they got back from the restaurant, she decided. Or perhaps she could borrow a backpack from Robert.

She began to make her way down the stairs to the upstairs corridor with Robert's *Privé* room, smiling to herself as she remembered how she'd let a pigeon in on the first day.

Memories of the weeks she'd spent here flashed through her mind. The ridiculous painting party. Their walks around Roussillon. The fact they'd connected in the way they had. Not just because they had something in common – being widowed – but because they were so at ease in each other's company. She felt a little pang of regret at what she was doing – a panicky moment of uncertainty. But it was too late in any case, she told herself. Amy had booked a ticket and she was going – that was that.

Then, as her foot touched the top step of the final flight of stairs that led to the corridor and front door, she heard a knock and paused. Robert answered the door and she could hear him talking. Someone – a woman – replied. Nicky couldn't work out what they were saying.

She wondered whether it was Michelle. She'd sent a message to her friend yesterday – unable to bring herself to meet her in person – explaining what had happened and while she'd received an understanding reply, Michelle had echoed Robert's belief that she ought to try to see it through. Nicky hoped her friend hadn't come to persuade her in person – she really wasn't sure she'd cope with another intervention.

The voices stopped and the front door closed. Had whoever it was left, or come in? She wondered. There was nothing to do but keep walking forward. She got to the bottom step and found herself in an empty hallway. Then, magically, Robert materialised by her side, an almost alarmingly large grin on his face.

'I've got a surprise for you,' he said. 'A visitor.'

Her heart sank. Michelle. She braced herself for another uncomfortable conversation.

'Who?' she asked.

'Ah, you'll see,' he said, as he guided her into the kitchen.

As she turned her rather jaded eyes to the table, expecting to see her new friend sitting there armed with reasons to stay and stick it out, she gasped. Because the person who had come to see her wasn't Michelle.

Instead, sitting at the kitchen table looking completely out of place in the room Nicky had sat and eaten in over the past three weeks was a person from a different world entirely. A young woman with a cream, floral summer dress, bright white trainers, her auburn hair tied in a neat ponytail.

'Chloe!' she gasped, rushing forward. 'Oh my goodness!' She threw her arms around her daughter, hugged her tight. Chloe's arms made their way around her back and returned the embrace.

'Surprise,' her daughter said.

'Just a bit.' Nicky pulled back and inspected her daughter at arm's length. 'What on earth are you doing here?'

Chloe laughed. 'Well, that's a lovely way to welcome your daughter!'

Nicky laughed. 'Sorry. Of course I am delighted to see you. But...

it's a shock that's all. And I'm really, really sorry. But didn't Amy tell you that I'm flying back this afternoon?'

Chloe looked down at the table then back up at her mum. 'No, you're not,' she said.

'I'm... what?'

'Look, sit down,' Chloe said.

Nicky obediently slid into a chair realising that Robert had already slipped unnoticed out of the room.

'What do you mean, I'm not going back?' she said, cautiously.

'Amy rang me after you spoke to her. And we agreed.'

'What?'

'She didn't book a ticket for you, Mum. She booked one for me. Or rather, I booked my own. Look, the point is, we are not going to let you quit!'

Nicky felt panic in her chest. 'But I'm not quitting, not really,' she said, feeling rather desperate. 'The thing I thought I was doing... it was never really real – don't you see? Jenny didn't think I was capable of it. And that's why she gave me the job. She thought I'd mess up. And now I'll be a laughing stock. Robert will be a laughing stock. He'll lose his business... he'll...'

'But,' her daughter said slowly, 'Mum, you haven't messed up.'

'I have, I...'

'What, a bit of paint?'

'It's not that. I mean, that was just the... the trigger. The thing that made me call Jenny. Then I found out. Then I realised what a fool I'd been making of myself. It all sort of fell apart for me.'

'A fool?'

'Yes. Thinking of myself as this TV star or whatever. Transforming someone's business. I even bought—' She pulled at her top as if to emphasise to Chloe that it wasn't her usual style.

'And you look great, Mum.'

'Well, thank you. But you know. Everything just seemed to fall apart at once and I just realised that this isn't me. That I can't be this person.'

'*Who* isn't you?'

'This person who can come in and see what businesses need to do to succeed. You know, change people's lives. Dress... well, more glamorously. It's not me.'

Chloe reached a hand over and covered Nicky's. 'Mum,' she said. 'If it isn't you, then who is it? Because from my perspective you've described the woman I see in front of me.'

'I...'

'No, listen. You've done it. You've transformed this place. You've changed this guy's life already. Amy's been filling me in on all you've achieved. We've been so, so impressed.'

'Surprised?'

'No. Impressed.'

'Oh.'

'And we are not going to let you quit. Mum, it's not the role that isn't you. It's *quitting* the role that isn't you.'

'But I...'

'No buts! The older I get, the more I... well, marvel at how you held us all together. You. Completely. And you inspired me, Mum. I knew that I could go out there and take a risk starting the business and that I had it in me to be strong even if things went wrong – just like you were.'

'Oh.'

'And you're going to let a misunderstanding with a friend mess this up for you?'

'It's hardly a misunderstanding... it's...'

'Look,' Chloe said. 'I'm not sure what motivated Jenny to offer you this. And maybe she did pick you for the wrong reasons. But the point is if she doubted your capability: She Is Wrong. You are more than capable of doing this. You've already done it, practically.'

'But...'

'So show her, Mum. Show her the person you are. The person we all see whenever we look at you. This strong, independent woman who doesn't quit even when the odds are stacked against her.'

'I'm not sure if I...'

'Yes. You can, Mum. And you don't have a choice. Because there is no ticket, and Amy said those guests arrive in a few days.'

'I... but...' Nicky faltered.

'And Mum,' Chloe added, reaching forward and grabbing Nicky's hand. 'I know you're mad at Jenny right now. But you guys have been friends for a long time. I want you to do this, for you. But I think, when you... well, when things aren't so raw, you might be glad you stuck it out for her too.'

'But she...'

'I know, Mum. She did a bad thing. But Jenny, well, she's been a pretty great friend over the years. You know, after Dad. And well, she's almost like family. So... I'm mad at her too, but I think you guys will probably make it up eventually.'

Nicky looked at her daughter and shook her head, mutely.

'What?'

'Just wondering when you became so... well, grown up, I suppose!' she said.

'Meaning, I'm right? Making sense?'

Nicky shrugged. 'A little. I suppose I have been a bit clouded by... well, how insulting it is to find out Jenny thinks so little of me.'

'Ah, she doesn't, Mum. Not really. She knows how brilliant you are – how could she not? She just messed up. We all do it.'

Nicky nodded. 'I suppose,' she said, like a reluctant daughter coming around to her mother's wise words.

'Anyway, I'm certainly not going to give up a week in the sun now I've booked it because you've had a sudden wobble. You're staying and that's that.'

'A week?' Nicky said.

'Well, the spa order's in, and I worked my fingers to the bone for that one. But it's paid well. And if I've come to Provence, I'm planning on making the most of it!'

Nicky smiled. 'Wow, you're here for the week?'

'I am. But Mum, I'm not here because I *want* you to do the show no matter what – I wouldn't do that to you. I'm here because I *know* you can. I know that Jenny is wrong and that you're not going to make a fool of yourself – far from it. You're making yourself proud. All of us proud.'

'Oh Chloe...'

'It's all true. In fact, there's only one thing that you need to do that you seem incapable of.'

Nicky's chest lurched. 'What's that?' she asked, a little fearfully.

'Asking for help. Asking for support,' said her daughter. 'Amy said you were upset the other day when she told you she didn't need you as much as... you thought. That we worried about you. But we only worry because we know that your whole life could *fall apart* before you let on or asked us for any help. You'd never let us see any cracks in your armour before it was too late so we have to keep an eye on you.'

'But I...'

'And it comes from a good place. For so many years you had to bear it all for us. Be the strong, stoic one. But we're grown up now. We can carry some of it with you. And we want to. We want to help. And you deserve it, Mum.'

'I...' she said weakly, sensing she'd lost the argument.

'You're brilliant. And now I'm here to help you prove that. And I'm not going to let you fall at the final hurdle.' Chloe's hand tightened on Nicky's. 'Mum, you're not going anywhere.'

22

'Are you sure you won't come with us?' Nicky asked later that evening as she and Robert made their way out of the front door. Chloe had persuaded her that the outfits she'd bought from Michelle's shop made her look 'peng' which, after a little interrogation, she'd found was A Good Thing. She'd dutifully donned a blue silk blouse with the cream linen trousers. Chloe had persuaded her to team the outfit with her bright, white trainers and although she'd felt the two styles would clash, she had to admit the combination worked.

Robert had dressed up for the occasion too, donning a new crisp white shirt, well-fitted jeans and a belt that Théo had described as 'bijou'.

'Mum,' Chloe had whispered when he'd left the kitchen, 'I thought you told Amy he wasn't attractive? That man is hot! I mean,' she'd clarified, 'you know. For someone of *your* age.' And Nicky had felt weirdly proud of Robert as she'd agreed he was looking pretty attractive these days.

'Seriously, I'm shattered,' Chloe said now. 'And I've got a few emails to answer. I'll just hang out here, if that's OK? You kids go have fun.'

'Sure,' Nicky replied. She fought the urge to offer to stay home with her daughter. Clearly Chloe needed some 'me' time, and that was OK. She didn't need to read anything into it or worry about her grown-up, eminently capable girl.

'And don't do anything I wouldn't do!' Chloe trilled after them, making Nicky blush.

After the surprise of Chloe's arrival and a light lunch – this time quiche and salad – whipped up by Robert, who had repeatedly assured Nicky he'd had no idea Chloe had been coming, they'd spent the afternoon discussing what could be done about the paint disaster. In the end they decided that, for the imminent guests at least, they could simply hide away the paint-splattered chairs (after all, there were only two guests, and sixteen chairs between them was excessive to say the least) and give the floor a go with some chemical treatment tomorrow. Then if that didn't work, Nicky and Chloe would go out and buy a rug to cover the whole thing up until they had more time to get it sanded off properly.

'We've got so little time,' Nicky said, regretting the fact that she'd wasted so much time packing her case, then unpacking it again. 'Do you think we'll get it all sorted?'

'It'll be fine.' Chloe smiled. 'I'm pretty good at covering up marks on the floor. Remember my sixteenth?'

Nicky snorted, remembering the red-wine, beige-carpet combination and how Chloe had tried to hide the enormous spillage by dragging the sofa into the centre of the room and hoping nobody would question it.

'That doesn't exactly fill me with confidence...' she said, unable to stop herself from smiling, nonetheless.

'What, you mean you noticed?' Her daughter laughed.

Robert looked at them as they dissolved into giggles. 'Is this how it's going to be from now on,' he said, with a raised eyebrow.

''fraid so.' Nicky smiled.

Even if it was a disaster, she'd told herself, they were in it together now – and that made a lot of difference.

Now as she walked at Robert's side along the sun-baked roads on the way to the brasserie, she thought about what her daughter had said about asking for help, letting other people know when you needed something, acknowledging it, even to yourself.

When Steve had died, she'd had help initially, from both sets of parents, and several friends. But as time had gone on the full hands-on help had naturally fallen away as life had moved on and she'd got her strength back. Mum had aged, Dad had grown sick then passed away four years after Steve. Her sister had moved to Scotland, other friends had moved on. Life hadn't waited for her to be ready.

Raising the two girls, she'd got used to being the place where the buck stopped. And for the last decade, hadn't felt able to fail or mess up or ask anyone to rescue her. Perhaps that was why she had kept her horizons so small, she thought.

But being self-sufficient for so long had made her forget how lovely it was when someone did step up to help. She'd been so paranoid that people would think she wasn't coping that she'd put up walls and forgotten that it was OK to reach out sometimes.

'People like to be needed, Mum,' Chloe had told her. 'You of all people must know that.'

Maybe Chloe was right – maybe she'd forgotten that it was OK to actually ask, that needing support didn't mean you weren't coping.

'Penny for them?' Robert asked now.

'What?'

'Sorry,' he said. 'You just looked deep in thought.'

'Oh,' she said, grinning. 'Sorry. I was actually thinking about Jenny.'

'Ah.' He made an awkward face.

'Just... I know I've given her a bad rap while I've been here. And I suppose that's what happens when a friend becomes your... well, boss, I guess. I can honestly say I'm not going to be queuing up to work with her again.'

'I can understand that.'

'But as a friend... you know. She's... Well, she's pretty special. And I know I'm angry with her. But maybe I've been a bit harsh in some ways.'

'I'd say, she's lucky to have a friend like you.'

'But I'm lucky to have her too... really I am. At least most of the time.'

They settled into the same table they'd chosen last time they'd been to the brasserie. For the evening sitting, the courtyard tables were decked out with wine glasses, cutlery, napkins and menus in leather-bound folders. It was still light, but the rattan overhead took the heat and intensity out of the sun, and shades had been raised over each table to provide additional comfort. A soft, classical soundtrack played quietly.

Other diners were scattered on about half of the twenty tables, most of them were in pairs and there was a gentle murmur of conversation.

'This is lovely,' she said slipping into the seat he pulled out for her.

'Yeah, I always come here,' he said. 'Force of habit. Plus they do a great vegetable quiche.'

'Didn't we have quiche for lunch?'

'Good point!' He picked up a menu pointedly. 'Maybe I should choose something that I don't tend to heat up in the microwave on a regular basis.'

'About that,' she said more carefully now. 'You said you used to cook sometimes. Before... you know? I just wondered whether you wanted me to help you try again. Not just for the guests, but for you. I mean, pizza is great obviously. And quiche.'

'And I do a mean pie and chips.'

'Frozen?'

'Frozen.'

She smiled. 'I'm no cordon bleu chef, but I could show you a few recipes if you like, get you back into the swing of things? You were pretty good with the curry the other day.'

He returned her grin. 'Thank you. I doubt I'll be expected to cook anything for the show though... I mean, will I?' He looked suddenly panicked.

'No! No. I mean, I'd like to do it. But not for the show. For you.'

'Oh.' He flushed a little. 'Well, if you get time... I mean, it'd be a help. Definitely.'

They fell into silence and she looked around the courtyard again.

When the waitress arrived, they ordered a pitcher of white wine and a bottle of water.

'I'm glad you're staying,' he said.

'Me too,' she said. 'Sorry about all that. You know. Dramatic flouncing.'

'Don't be silly. You only flounced a little bit.'

'Ha.'

'No, honestly. I completely understand. It must have been a shock, finding out...'

'It was. Although looking back... well, what she said wasn't so terrible, I don't think. It was more... I suppose it sort of confirmed all my worst fears about myself,' she said. 'It just took my confidence away.'

'But it was still a bit cruel. I mean, you say Jenny is your best friend, but it doesn't sound like she knows you very well.'

Despite the fact she was angry with Jenny, Nicky felt herself bristle slightly when Robert criticised her. 'I suppose, maybe she doesn't know the 'work' me?' she suggested. 'Just the coffee-shop and babysitting and drinking white wine version.'

'Perhaps that's it.'

'Anyway, Chloe being here really helps.'

'I can imagine.'

'It's just, doing this on my own... you know? It was tough.'

Their wine arrived and Robert served a little into each of their glasses. 'Oh yes,' he said. 'I am familiar with that feeling.'

She felt a stab of guilt. Robert was in a similar situation to her. But without an Amy or a Chloe for moral support. 'Sorry,' she said.

'No, don't be. Sometimes I think I'd got so used to doing things by myself, I forgot that life doesn't have to be like that. If that makes sense.'

'More sense than you know.' She smiled at him and their eyes met for a second before she turned away and reached for the menu.

'Anyway, I'm glad Chloe stopped me before I went home and ditched the whole thing,' she said as her eyes scanned the selection of starters. 'I think I was focused on me, and I should have thought a bit more about you.'

'It's OK,' he said. 'Even if you had gone, even if the programme had fallen through, at least you'd kind of woken me up from the state I'd got myself into. You know, ever since you arrived I've felt more... motivated. As if I've been shocked back into life.'

She smiled. 'I think the shock part might have been the pigeon.'

They both grinned.

'Seriously though,' he added. 'When you said you were leaving, I was gutted. And it wasn't just the programme. It's been nice having someone here. Someone who's well, not a guest, but a friend. At least I think that's what we are.'

She nodded. 'Yeah, I think I'd use that word.'

'It's been a long time since I've felt part of a team,' he added. 'And it's been nice.'

'Well, I think you've done really well, all things considered,' she added. 'You know, after Marie. Just keeping something going like this. Here on your own. Lots of people would have gone under completely.'

Robert's eyes were on his menu too, but she noticed they seemed to catch the light more than before as if he was holding back tears. 'Well, I'm lucky to have some great friends out here,' he said. 'I mean, people really came through for me. The place kind of... I felt almost as if everyone was holding me up.'

'That's so nice,' she said, thinking about Jenny again. How she'd taken time off after Steve's accident. Helped her to arrange everything. Stood beside her, even, at the crematorium. 'Jenny, she's been there for me like that too. Your friends kind of become your family don't they, when things go wrong.'

'Amen to that,' he said, raising his glass for a clink. 'To friends old and new.'

'Friends old and new,' she echoed. She realised as she took a sip of her wine that Robert and Michelle were probably the first 'new' friends she'd made in the last decade. She was friendly with work colleagues, had a couple of people she sometimes talked to at the end of a yoga class. But she'd never really got close to anyone. In all that time.

They made their order and she decided to try to move the conversation on. 'So,' she said. 'Floor cleaning and possible rug shopping tomorrow.'

'Yes, and I need to make sure we've got enough fresh fruit.'

'And that the shower is pristine!' she said, remembering the look of distaste on one of the guests' face last time.

'You know, I'm still sure they planted it for effect,' he said.

'Wouldn't put it past them,' she said, thinking of Jenny and the stunts she'd pulled before. Hopefully there wouldn't be any subterfuge this time.

'We've still got €50 or so left in the kitty by the way,' he said. 'And I thought maybe if we get time we could get some sort of cake made. You know, to celebrate the grand reopening.'

'Sounds nice,' she said. 'I'm sure the crew would gobble it up.' Mentioning the crew reminded her of Tom and his friendly but dismissive text. She felt her cheeks get warm at the memory. It would be awkward seeing him again. She wondered why she'd felt motivated to send him a text. Just because he'd seemed to like her? 'Can I ask you a question?' she said, deciding to distract herself by asking something she'd promised herself she wouldn't.

'Of course.'

'Where did you get that stack of notes anyway? What did you do? Sell your grandmother's jewellery or something?' she joked.

He looked down, picking up his fork and beginning to turn it over between his fingers. 'Actually,' he said. 'You're not far off the mark.'

'Really?'

He sighed and looked over her shoulder for a moment. She turned her head to see what he was staring at before realising he was simply looking beyond her at something intangible. 'It was a necklace,' he said. 'It was a diamond necklace.'

'Oh,' she said.

'Marie's. I actually,' he cleared his throat, 'I gave it to her on our wedding day, you know. And... well, I suppose I was holding onto it because I felt it meant something.'

'Oh, Robert.'

He shook his head. 'But you know, this place. It meant something too. And I think if she could... if I'd been able to ask her she'd have said to sell it. Even though the jeweller only gave me about two thirds of what it was worth.'

'Oh Robert,' she said, feeling guilty and wishing she hadn't asked. So when she'd splashed out on paint or new duvets, she'd been spending money raised from selling something far more precious than she'd realised. 'I feel awful about that. If only they hadn't cut the budget... if only.'

He held a hand up. 'It's OK,' he said. 'It's only a necklace, when all's said and done. It's not... it's not *her*.' He wiped the back of his hand hurriedly across his eyes. 'And I've realised, hanging on to 'things' doesn't really help, does it? Because it's not as if I need anything to remind me about her. She'll always be... you know... I'll never...'

'I know,' she said, reaching a hand out and touching his arm. 'You don't have to explain.'

By the time their main course arrived, both of them were slightly red-eyed. The server looked at them nervously. 'Was everything all right messieurs-dames?' he asked them. 'Perhaps the escargots, they were too spicy, non? You get some of these in your eyes, it is not good.'

Robert looked at Nicky and as their eyes met, they began to laugh. And as she laughed, Nicky felt as if something had lifted. 'Don't worry,' she told the server. 'Everything's fine.'

23

'You know what, it looks pretty good,' Chloe said as the three of them stood in the newly decorated dining room. They'd worked tirelessly the previous day bringing the room up to scratch and finally everything seemed to be coming together.

They'd eventually settled on a large, woven rug to cover up the centre of the room, and squirrelled the ruined chairs away to be dealt with later. One of the tables had been taken out too, and the rest had been put at different angles. The cream walls still had splashes and touches of other colours left to make sense of the 'design choices' they'd claimed to have made last time; but Michelle's penis mural had been painted over and the space covered with one of Victor's tasteful watercolours.

The curtains had been removed and replaced with light voiles to soften the edges of the windows and light now flooded in, taking the room from rather sombre to bright and uplifting. They'd placed menus in the new holders they'd bought from a local artisan and added extra options to the breakfast menu. Robert had arranged for the patisserie to deliver pastries in the morning ready for their guests.

'It does,' Nicky said, smiling. Now that everything had come together, she wondered what she'd been panicking about. The mess and the feeling of being overwhelmed, teamed with finding out Jenny's low opinion of her acumen had come together in a perfect storm of anxiety making her want to run. She was glad Chloe had stopped her. Because however the next bit went, she knew she'd achieved something special here. They all had.

She glanced back at Robert, who was looking at the room too, a small smile on his face. 'All right?' she asked.

'Yeah. Yeah, just thinking,' he said. 'It's kind of how I always imagined it might look one day. I just didn't know how to get it from A to B.'

'Oh, I'm sure you could have,' said Nicky. 'Sometimes you just need a deadline or an extra reason to get off the starting blocks.' She thought again of the push that Jenny's request had given her. Perhaps it hadn't been well meant. But the end result was still the same. She'd discovered more about herself in the past weeks than she had over the last ten years. As if she'd stepped away from her old life and looked back on it, able to see more clearly both the positive and negative aspects. Whatever happened next, she'd go home a slightly different person. A person who knew more about herself, understood more what the people in her life needed or wanted. A person who was determined to make a few changes.

She imagined herself back home. Back in her familiar two-bed semi and felt a sudden pang. It was going to be strange getting back to her old life. Being alone in a house again.

'Have you thought...' Robert began.

But before he could complete the question, there was a heavy knock on the door. They all jumped, although they'd been expecting the guests to arrive at any minute. Robert smoothed down the front of his shirt. 'I guess this is it,' he said.

'Right, we'll make ourselves scarce,' said Chloe, 'so you can do the hosting bit.'

A tiny frown crossed his features then cleared almost instantly. 'Yes,' he said. 'I sort of forgot I'm the... the only host here.'

'You'll be fine,' Nicky said. 'Just remember, they're going to nitpick a bit. But that's their job.'

He nodded.

Nicky and Chloe walked through to the kitchen area and listened as Robert opened the door with a cheery 'Bonjour!' and welcomed in their guests.

'Do they really not realise we know exactly who they are?' Chloe mused. 'I mean it's pretty obvious, isn't it?'

'I suppose,' Nicky said, 'most B&Bs have more than one lot of guests. Especially around this time of year. But Robert... well, he's sort of wound things down recently. So...'

'Ah, OK,' Chloe said. 'I suppose that's good in a way. At least we know we have to bring our A-game for these two.' She'd seemed to get quite into the idea of the B&B and had baked mouth-watering cookies yesterday afternoon when they'd come back from the shops laden with the rug as well as new towels and various other last-minute accessory impulse buys.

'You can put some in the rooms,' she'd told Robert as he'd bitten into a crumbling morsel.

'Wow. Shame to waste them on guests,' he'd said, his eyes widening at the taste. Then he'd caught her eye. 'But yes,' he'd said. 'Absolutely.'

'I can always leave you the recipe,' she'd offered. 'It's one of my own.'

'Thanks,' he'd replied.

They sat at the kitchen table, barely breathing, as they listened to the footsteps go upstairs. A door creaked and clicked shut. Then one set of footsteps came back down the stairs and the kitchen door opened. Robert was there, flushed but smiling.

'Think that went OK,' he said. 'So far so good!'

Then they were all there in the kitchen, quietly wondering what they were meant to do next.

'So,' said Chloe at last. 'Mum, you said you wanted me to look over those spreadsheets, your presentation, that sort of thing.'

'Oh, yes, if you don't mind. Just… you know, with your business brain you might well pick up on some extra things to tweak.'

'Sure. Do you want me to do it now?'

'No, let's get these guests out of the way first,' she said. 'Why don't we go for a walk instead? If that's OK?' she asked Robert.

'No problem,' he said with a stoic smile.

They disappeared out into the early afternoon sunshine and onto the narrow road that led to the centre of Roussillon. The streets radiated heat from below and the sky above was clear, with no clouds to break the relentless glare of the afternoon sun.

'Blimey,' said Chloe, 'it's scorchio!'

'Yep.' Nicky smiled. 'But you get used to it after a while.' She was wearing a pair of linen shorts borrowed from Chloe with a patterned, fitted T-shirt, and had teamed the outfit with the white trainers Chloe had convinced her to sport the other night. It had never occurred to her in the past to pair something well-tailored with shoes she'd usually see as casual. But the comfort she'd felt when walking on the cobbled street the other night had convinced her they'd been a great choice.

'Yes,' said Chloe, 'so I see.' She looked sideways at her mother as they walked up the slight incline at the side of the red stone wall, with its breathtaking views over the countryside.

'What's that supposed to mean?'

'Well, you seem… and don't get me wrong… very *at home* here.'

'Well, it is beautiful. So…'

'And the company's not bad either?' Chloe prompted.

'Oh!' Nicky wasn't quite sure how to take that. 'Are you saying you think there's something going on?' she asked. 'Because honestly, nothing's happened.'

'Actually,' said Chloe, 'I was going to say how relaxed you two seem together. You could do worse you know, Mum.'

Nicky felt her cheeks get hot. 'Chloe!' she said. 'I doubt Robert's in the least bit interested in me.'

'I wouldn't be so sure,' Chloe said. 'I've seen the way he looks at you.'

'Don't be silly.'

'I'm not! And you know, he's not wrong, Mum. I mean you've always been amazing, but here you've kind of. It seems like you've blossomed!'

'Blossomed!' Nicky laughed. 'I thought that was something young girls do when they become women. Can people actually blossom in their forties?'

'OK, how about you've grown some new shoots?' Chloe grinned.

'Chopped off the deadheads?'

'Ha, yeah. Weeded around your roots.'

Nicky laughed. 'I suppose if I'm honest, just stepping away from life back home has made me realise a few things. You know, about myself and about... what I want. What I mean to other people.'

'This isn't about what Amy said?' Chloe's brow furrowed.

'No. Well, not really. I mean, it was a bit of a shock. It made me feel about a thousand years old when I heard her say "mum duties".'

'Oh, we didn't mean...'

'Don't worry. I know,' Nicky said. 'It's actually quite sweet that you girls want to look out for me. But the whole conversation made me realise that I've been underestimating you.'

'Underestimating?'

'Yes. I mean look at you. You're a successful businesswoman.'

'Oh, I wouldn't go that far...'

'Well, you should. Because it's true. And Amy, I mean she's a wonderful mum, and she's got great prospects ahead for her career when she's ready.'

'Definitely.'

'I suppose what I'm trying to say is that when your dad... you know, had his accident. Well, you were so young. So vulnerable.'

Chloe nodded. 'Looking at it now,' she said, 'as an adult. It must have been terrifying for you.'

'It was. I mean, I had my own grief of course. But protecting you became my whole purpose.'

'Oh, Mum.'

'But I think what it did too was make me see you as fragile and vulnerable. And you're not any more, are you?'

Chloe flexed a bicep. 'We're pretty tough cookies, I admit.'

Nicky laughed. 'Anyway, it was good for me to realise that. Because the last thing I'd have wanted at your age is a mum who hovered over me all the time watching my every move.'

'You hardly...'

'You know what I mean. I'm proud of you. You're capable. And I need to acknowledge that. And it's good. It's brilliant in fact.'

They were silent for a moment and, as they walked, Chloe wrapped her arm around her mother's back. Nicky returned the favour and they made their way into the square with the brasserie's now familiar maroon awning quietly enjoying their closeness.

This time, Nicky chose a table outside the front of the brasserie and they ordered two iced teas which arrived promptly, complete with paper straws and tiny umbrellas.

'Gosh, I didn't know they still made these,' Nicky said, twisting hers. 'Do you remember you always wanted me to buy those for your birthday parties.'

'Yes! And those funny bendy straws,' Chloe said.

'And those awful party hooter things,' Nicky said. 'The worst invention for parents since... since...'

'Candy floss?' Chloe suggested.

'Yes!' Nicky said, laughing at the shared memory Chloe had been referring to. When she'd bought the girls candy floss and they'd managed to stain every item of clothing they had pink. 'God, that stuff is awful.'

'Can I ask,' Chloe said a moment later, after sipping deeply from her cool drink, 'if Robert *is* into you, whether you'd... well, be interested?'

'I'm not sure.'

Chloe looked at her quizzically.

'What?'

'Feeling hot, Mother?' she said. 'Because you've gone an awful shade of pink.'

* * *

When they returned to the B&B, the two 'secret' guests were sitting in the garden, drinking coffee that Robert had made in the cafetière.

'How's it going?' Chloe asked, with a smile.

'Well, I think,' he said. 'It's so hard to tell what they're thinking. I wish I had some sort of surveillance equipment to hear what they're talking about.'

'You do!' Chloe said. 'They've no idea who I am. How about I pop out and have a chat with my fellow guests?'

'Would you mind?' Robert asked.

'Make me a coffee and we're on,' she said.

As she watched her daughter walking out and introducing herself to the couple, Nicky felt a shiver of pride at how confident she seemed, how quickly she'd thrown herself into the task here; how she'd somehow helped them to pull it all together.

Robert was looking too, as the kettle boiled on the stove. 'She's great,' he said. 'You must be really proud.'

'Yes. I am.'

'Good walk?'

'Lovely,' she said. 'Although she gave me the third degree about us.' As soon as she'd said it, she regretted it.

'Us?'

'Yes, she had some idea that we were... well, you know.'

Now it was Robert's turn to go red. 'Oh,' he said.

'Don't worry. I put her straight.'

'Oh, right. Good,' he said, his shade darkening.

There was a silence as he got out another, smaller cafetière and measured out some fresh coffee. 'Out of interest,' he said. 'When you... put her straight. What did you tell her?'

The shade of his face, particularly his ears, was beginning to concern her. With so much blood rushing to his cheeks and ears, could he possibly have enough circulating in his body to sustain life? 'Oh,' she said. And was about to follow up with, 'I told her we were just friends,' but somehow found herself saying instead, 'Well, I said we get on well, but that nothing's happened...'

He nodded, his back still to her. 'And if it did?' he said. He turned around and their eyes locked. 'It's just...' he said, moving closer to her. 'Since you've been here, everything's seemed...'

He was right in front of her now, looking down. She felt a shiver running through her as if something inside was waking up. She tilted her head, almost on autopilot, inviting him to kiss her. He smiled. 'It's just been,' he said...

Before he could finish the sentence Chloe suddenly burst into the room and he jumped back, turning abruptly to the kitchen counter. 'Just grabbing my sunglasses,' she announced. 'And,' she added in a more hushed tone, 'word on the street is you're quite the hit so far.' She winked at Robert. 'And no hairs in the shower… yet.'

'So far so good,' he said. 'Coffee will be out in a minute.'

'I'll just,' Nicky said, before her daughter had the chance to leave the room and she had to respond to his unanswered question. 'I must just…' Then she left the sentence hanging as she rushed out of the room, into the corridor and up to her bedroom, her heart racing.

Once there, she closed the door and leaned against it, feeling a surge of anxiety. And a strange sort of guilt. Because although she'd had a couple of dates, chatted to a couple of people online since Steve – even kissed one, albeit politely rather than passionately – this was the first time she'd felt a real sense of longing.

Felt that in that moment if he'd kissed her, she'd have kissed him right back.

24

The next morning, she was up early, knowing that the secret guests would be packing up and leaving, verdict intact, shortly. Yesterday Jenny had emailed to say the next filming would take place on the fifteenth, leaving them a day to ready themselves.

She'd started to feel nervous around Robert. Because something had shifted between them. Thoughts rushed in her head: the way he'd smiled at her, his brown eyes crinkling; that dimple she'd noticed in his cheek; how it might have felt to kiss him.

Annoyed with herself, she pushed the thoughts away and tried to focus. It had just been a moment. Besides, the more she thought about it the more she wondered whether it had all been in her head. He'd probably never intended to kiss her at all.

She was itching to find out what the guests had thought. Chloe's conversation with them yesterday in the garden had suggested a positive first impression, but she knew all too well how nitpicky guests could be – especially in the interests of good TV.

She wondered whether other designers – famous and amateur – were waking up with similar thoughts today. Was Laurence Llewelyn-Bowen nervous about the verdict? Was Rochelle Humes confident she'd impress both the viewers and the judges with her changes? And what about the amateurs like her? That guy who'd just graduated from college? Or the older woman who'd spent her life making curtains for the rich and famous?

One thing she was sure of was that the job that she'd done was now the best she was capable of on a limited budget and within a limited timescale. She was lucky, in some ways. The problem she'd been handed was fixable. Robert's location in Roussillon was a tourist trap, and although before he'd struggled to fill the B&B out of season, and had received some poor reviews for aspects of the accommodation, with the exposure of the TV programme and the professional slickness of his new website, he could probably now guarantee being full in and out of season no matter how many hairs were discovered in showers, no matter how brusque he appeared as a host.

The place had everything going for it. There was no noisy road to block out, no anti-social behaviour on the streets outside. Mismatched bedding, slightly sub-par cleaning standards, the prospect of pigeon attacks; they were all things that could be remedied. His accounts, too, had been well-kept. He'd simply been too depressed over the last few years to update his calculation of expenditure vs. his price, meaning he'd been barely making anything even when he did get bookings.

'Do you realise,' she'd told him when she'd gone through the books, 'if you factor in washing, electricity, cleaning and the price of croissants, etc, you're probably making about fifty cents an hour while you have guests. And that's before tax?'

He'd flushed with embarrassment, as she'd explained how he could quadruple his hourly rate, yet only raise the overall price by around €15 a night – looking at lower-energy washing solutions, coming to a deal with the patisserie, taking breakfast orders the night before to minimise waste. There was so much he hadn't thought of and she'd been grateful that she could actually make a difference.

For the first hour of the day, she stayed in her bedroom, sipping coffee and drinking in the view across the countryside and waiting for the guests to finish breakfast before making an appearance. It didn't seem right, somehow, to interrupt their stay; they might be aware she was here and her purpose and she wanted them to be able to do their job without feeling spied upon. Even though she longed to do exactly that.

There was a rap on the door, then before she had time to speak, Chloe appeared wearing a pair of shorts and a vest top. She flung herself down on Nicky's bed, almost causing a coffee disaster, and cupped her head in her hands the way she'd always used to as a child when she'd come in to talk with Nicky first thing in the morning before school. And suddenly she didn't seem like a twenty-two-year-old entrepreneur but a ten-year-old girl again.

'Hi love,' Nicky said, 'Sleep OK?'

'Yeah, great thanks,' Chloe said. 'It's so quiet here.'

'I know. Gorgeous isn't it.'

'Yeah.'

They were silent for a moment.

'So, filming on Tuesday. The Final Verdict.'

'Yes.'

'Are you nervous?'

Nicky turned to look at her daughter. 'Just a bit,' she admitted.

'Not surprised. I think I'd be shitting myself.'

'Chloe!' Nicky admonished on autopilot; despite the fact she'd probably have used that expression herself.

'Sorry, but I mean. And Ryan – I can't believe you've met him already. What's he like in real life?'

'Exactly as you'd expect.' Nicky smiled.

'Insane?'

'I'd say eccentric. Nice though. Kind. Funny.'

'Good looking?'

'Not really my type. But yes – even under the layer of make-up they trowel on for the cameras.'

They grinned at each other.

'Anyway, at least we have a few days to relax after the filming tomorrow,' said Nicky. 'Maybe get to know the area a bit more. I have to take you to meet Michelle, she's great. And maybe you can help me get my wardrobe sorted for the last bit.'

Chloe nodded. 'Love to.'

Outside, they could hear a rumble of voices. A car engine started. Then the front door of the B&B slammed.

There was a thunder of footsteps up the stairs and they only just had time to glance at each other as the door was flung open. 'They're GONE!' Robert announced, loudly with an enormous smile. He was wearing an outfit Nicky had helped him to select – short-sleeved shirt, tailored trousers – and sported an apron around his middle. Buster raced in behind him, obviously wondering what the urgency was about, and slipped on the polished floor, skidding into the bed.

'Do you celebrate all your guests' departures like this?' Chloe asked quizzically, reaching down and patting Buster on the head.

'Ha. Only the very worst ones,' Robert said. He ran his fingers through his hair. 'God, but that was tense.'

'Did it go OK, though?' Nicky asked.

'Yeah. I mean, I spilled a bit of their tea in the saucer. And not sure whether I overdid trying to be gregarious,' he said, his brow furrowed.

'In what way?'

'Well, I tried to stay and chat at the table a bit more. Made a few jokes... but, well, nobody laughed.'

'Oh dear.'

'Perhaps they're just not the joking kind?' suggested Chloe, kindly. 'I'm sure you were hilarious.'

'Ah, ignore me,' he said. 'It's just... once you're accused of not seeming friendly enough, you're obviously going to try to be friendly, aren't you? But then you worry if you're coming across *too* friendly, or whether you seem natural or whatever. In the end you forget where normal is. God, I hope I've done OK.' He blew upwards, lifting some of his hair briefly.

'I guess we'll find out tomorrow,' Nicky said. 'But you know, don't worry. All the B&B owners will be in the same boat. On the programme, I mean. Nobody will be that used to the cameras.'

He nodded. 'Well, anyway, it's done,' he said. 'And the good news is they hardly touched any pastries, so we have a PILE of them downstairs in the kitchen to work our way through.'

'Good news indeed,' said Chloe, sitting up.

'Brilliant, we'll be down in a bit,' said Nicky.

'Great.' He turned to leave. 'Oh, and I hope it's OK but I invited Michelle over a bit later to celebrate. You know, a bit of bubbly. Early afternoon.'

'Sounds like a plan.'

He paused, as if slightly reluctant to say something. 'And she's bringing Pierre.'

'OK?'

'And.' He reddened. 'I suppose I got a bit carried away and said she should invite some of the other people who helped out.'

'Oh.'

'And she's put something on Facebook,' he said with a grimace.

'Robert...' Nicky said. 'Are you telling me you've somehow arranged a party?'

'Yeah,' he said, colouring.

'You do remember the last party?' She looked at him, half joking, half panicking.

'Yeah. It kind of got out of hand,' he said with a grimace. 'But look, we can set everything up in the garden. It might be nice, you know, get our mind off things... thank the people that have got us this far.'

Nicky nodded. It would be nice to do something to celebrate, even if at this stage the only thing they were celebrating was a hair-free plughole. 'OK, but no paint.'

'No paint.'

'No punch?'

'Definitely no punch.'

'And no enormous blue penises.'

'Well, I can't guarantee...' he began, smiling. 'But I'll see what I can do.'

As he left, pulling the door closed behind him with a gentle click, Chloe looked at her mum with raised eyebrows. 'Enormous blue penises?' she queried. 'You are going to have to tell me what *that* was about.'

The more she thought about it, the more the party seemed like a good idea. She'd been so buried in her work that she hadn't had the time to relax. And Robert was right, so many people had pitched in to help, and while the painting party hadn't exactly finished as expected, the point was that people had turned up to try... whatever the result. It was right to celebrate that.

It would be nice to kick back – after all they'd made the changes they needed in readiness for tomorrow and would have ample time to clear up the garden before the filming took place. Plus she was mindful too of how Chloe had given up a week of her time to come out and help – the least she could do was give the girl a bit of a holiday along the way.

Late morning, Nicky and Chloe drove to the large supermarket twenty kilometres from Roussillon to stock up on drinks and snacks and wheeled the enormous clinking and rattling trolley back to Robert's car. Nicky had driven there, but Chloe insisted on driving them home, so Nicky handed over the keys.

Nicky hadn't been in a car with Chloe for a while and was surprised how careful a driver her daughter was. Almost ridiculously careful. Was it something to do with the accident? With Steve? She wondered. Because although she knew Robert's car wasn't the most powerful, she'd definitely expected they'd go faster than this.

A Citroen came up right behind them, a red-faced driver clearly keen to force them to put their foot down, but Chloe simply slowed down. 'Nobody intimidates me,' she said. 'And besides,' she added. 'We have precious cargo on board.'

'The vodka?' Nicky asked.

'The vodka.'

But as more and more cars began trailing in their wake, Nicky leaned over and checked the speedometer which read 40 kph. 'It is a 60 though,' she said to her daughter. 'I mean, maybe a little more speed wouldn't hurt.'

'Nah, I'm good,' her daughter replied.

Nicky wondered whether it was driving in a foreign country that was bothering her. 'Do you want me to drive?'

'Seriously, Mum!'

'It's just.' Nicky gestured to the rear-view mirror and Chloe, taking a glance, acknowledged the problem.

'I'm not making any friends here, am I?' she said.

'Not really.'

'OK.' Chloe put her foot down and suddenly they were cruising along just below the speed limit. Then, to Nicky's surprise, just as the Sat-Nav was preparing her for an upcoming left-hand turn,

Chloe signalled right and turned into an unfamiliar street, parking the car jerkily against the pavement.

Nicky turned to her, feeling suddenly alarmed. 'Chloe,' she said. 'What's wrong?'

Chloe's neck turned red, a classic sign that she was panicking about something; she'd been unable to hide much growing up due to the tell-tale patches that would appear above her collarbone. She turned to her mum. 'Look, Mum, I don't want to arrive back at the B&B too soon. That's all.'

'But why ever not?'

Her daughter looked down, seemingly unable to make eye contact. 'Don't worry,' she said at last. 'It's just... I could do with a break from the place, I suppose.'

'OK,' Nicky said slowly. 'But why?'

'Can I tell you later?' Chloe said. 'It's nothing bad, not really. I can't really explain.'

'Oh.' Nicky wondered whether Chloe realised that telling a mum not to worry about an unspecified thing was probably one of the cruellest things she could do. But at the same time, she knew she'd have to be brave about whatever it was. Perhaps Chloe just needed a break. Perhaps Robert had upset her in some way. 'Are you sure you can't...'

'Honestly, It's nothing. I promise. Just... well, I thought maybe we could just take a bit more time,' her daughter repeated.

'OK,' Nicky said. 'Well... how about we park up and take a walk. Maybe go to Michelle's boutique or something? You could buy something for the party? Or maybe help me pick out something to wear for the final filming? We were going to go later anyway.'

'That,' said Chloe, starting the engine to move the car into a more sensible parking position, 'sounds amazing.'

Still, as Nicky stepped out of the car into the morning heat, and linked arms with her daughter for the walk into town, she couldn't shake a feeling of unease. It was unlike Chloe not to be completely open about things. Unlike her to try to avoid certain situations. She was always someone who went in guns blazing and asked questions later.

Come to think of it, it had been Chloe who'd suggested they go to the supermarket twenty kilometres away instead of the local one ('it's apparently cheaper, Mum') and who'd spent ages choosing the drinks ('how different can vodkas actually taste?'). Had Chloe simply wanted to get away?

Something was up. And until she was sure what it was, she wouldn't be able to fully relax.

But she did what she always did. Put on a brave face and pushed the worry to the back of her mind as much as she could.

She was an expert, after all, at keeping calm and carrying on.

25

Nicky felt slightly sick as they finally made their way back to the B&B after a shopping session and a quick bite to eat at the brasserie. Chloe had seemed normal in the shop and had thrown herself in to trying on some summer dresses, chatting and laughing with Michelle as if they were old friends. But during lunch her manner had changed and she'd seemed distracted, checking her mobile phone continuously and muttering things about 'work stuff'. Now, as they approached the accommodation, she wondered whether Chloe was finally going to tell her what was up.

Suddenly, a text message pinged on Chloe's phone and her daughter picked it out of a pocket and had a quick glance.

'Chloe! Not while you're driving!' Nicky exclaimed.

'Sorry, Mum. I wouldn't usually,' she said. She was smiling now, having read whatever it was. Nicky wondered whether Chloe had a boyfriend she hadn't told her about. It might explain some of the erratic behaviour – but not all of it.

As the B&B came into view, Chloe pulled up against the kerb and jerked the handbrake into place, then turned to Nicky, now fully grinning. 'OK,' she said. 'I realise I've been acting a bit weird. But you'll see why in a sec.'

'And you can't tell me now?' Nicky asked, feeling more churned up than reassured.

'Not just yet.' Her daughter smiled.

They got out of the car and lifted some of their shopping from the back seat. There were three bags, too, from the boutique and Nicky felt a little sick suddenly at the amount they'd spent. She wasn't a TV star yet, after all, and certainly wasn't drawing a TV star's salary. Worse, none of the clothes she'd bought would really work properly in England – she couldn't imagine striding into her high street office in orange silk.

But it was done now, she thought, picking up as many bags as she could manage, kicking the door shut with her foot and lumbering towards the front door. Chloe, ahead of her, and carrying just one of the bags, seemed ridiculously light on her feet.

Chloe knocked on the door and as it swung open, she dropped the bag and practically leaped into the hall, squealing with delight.

And then, finally, Nicky saw why. Standing, looking completely incongruous in the middle of her new life, her new adventure, was Amy, clutching a chubby baby in her arms.

'Amy!' she said, placing her bags down and stepping into the hall. 'What on earth are you doing here?'

'That's a nice way to greet someone who's flown for two hours just to give you a hug,' said her daughter, stepping forward and slipping an arm around Nicky's waist. She leaned into Nicky, her cheek pressed against her mum's and Nicky breathed in the scent of shampoo and, underneath it, the scent of Amy – the girl whose head she'd been sniffing for over two decades.

'Now you know why I was taking my time on the way back,' Chloe said. 'I didn't want to ruin the surprise.'

Rose reached up, grabbed a handful of Nicky's hair and giggled delightedly.

'It's amazing to see you,' Nicky said. 'Absolutely amazing. But you didn't...'

'I know, I didn't have to,' said Amy. 'I wanted to.'

'You know Amy, never one to miss a party,' quipped Chloe.

'There's a party?'

'It's a long story.'

They made their way through to the kitchen where Robert was already setting out his largest cafetière and a plate of madeleines.

'I'm so sorry; I seem to be taking over your entire house,' Nicky said to him.

'Don't be silly. It's a B&B, it's meant to be full,' he said. 'It's good practice for me, if anything.'

'Well, it's really nice of you not to mind,' said Nicky, looking at her three girls proudly. She was glad that Robert had got to see them all, and almost overwhelmed that they were there at all.

* * *

Once they'd settled Amy and her two enormous suitcases into a room and emptied the car of party treats, they spent an hour putting everything together ready for their guests. According to Robert the potential number would be about twenty but 'you never know' who else might turn up. They'd kept as much as they could outdoors, and set out covered bowls of snacks on little tables, and glasses and drinks on a little wall at the edge of the patio.

Nicky offered to put Rose to bed for her afternoon nap and give Amy a break – an offer that was gratefully accepted. Their journey had been difficult, and apparently Rose had grizzled in the back of the taxi from the airport continuously.

Settling Rose took longer than she'd imagined, meaning by the time Nicky emerged from the attic room, wireless baby monitor in hand, the garden seemed to be full of people dressed in shorts and T-shirts and summer dresses, some in sunglasses with hats and others seeking the shade under tree branches and sunshades. It looked more like the party after a wedding than a casual drink. It was the venue that did it – the sun shining gloriously on the newly mown grass, the overhanging trees rich with cherries, walnut casings and apples, and the wisteria which stretched around the edges of the garden, alive with the hum of bees.

She saw Michelle almost straight away, standing with Pierre and sipping sparkling wine. 'Hi Michelle,' she said, walking up to her. 'Pierre.'

'Hi,' her friend replied, with a wide smile. 'I thought you said there wasn't going to be punch.'

'There... there isn't...' Nicky said, before noticing the enormous orange bowl of liquid, already half empty, at the centre of one of the garden tables. 'I mean, there wasn't.'

'Think our host might have had a bit of it, already,' Michelle said, nodding towards the end of the garden, where Robert appeared to be dancing to the music emitted by a wireless speaker.

'Oh, bloody hell,' said Nicky, then remembered that of course everything was ready inside. And nobody had any paint. She'd get up early to make sure the finishing touches were in place. It wouldn't be like last time. If Robert had a headache, well, it was his problem.

'Mum, there you are!' A grinning Chloe appeared at her side. 'Have you tasted the punch? I found Robert's punch bowl and wanted to try one of the recipes I've seen on Instagram. It's great, don't you think?'

'I haven't had a chance yet,' said Nicky cautiously. 'Is it strong?'

Chloe snorted with laughter. 'Mum, it's punch. The whole point is that nobody knows! You pour as much stuff as you can in the bowl, then make it just about drinkable with fruit juice. It's meant to pack a punch – see. Punch! Get it?'

'I thought you said there was a recipe?' said Nicky, wondering whether that was in fact where the name punch came from. It didn't sound quite right.

'Oh recipe smessapee,' Chloe said with an elaborate wink. 'I may, just may, have gone a little off-piste.'

Amy arrived at her side then and shoved a glass into her hand. 'Try the punsch...' she said, slurring her words slightly.

'Piste indeed,' Chloe said, putting an arm around her sister.

'Oh Amy – how much have you had?' Nicky asked.

'Itsch delicious,' her daughter told her solemnly. 'Chloe made it and sche's a scheefff.'

'Mm, thank you,' Nicky said, allowing just a millilitre to brush her lips and feeling them sting with the chemical hit. She'd better stay sober, she decided, if just to keep an eye on the baby when she woke up. 'How much has she had?' she asked Chloe quietly as Amy wobbled off.

'Don't worry; I'll keep an eye on her,' said Chloe. 'Think she maybe just hasn't drunk anything for a while.'

People milled around. One man introduced himself as 'Cabbage' and told her he was living off-grid and had only heard about the party when a few revellers had walked past his front gate and cheerily invited him along. Robert's neighbours, a French couple in their sixties, briefly said hello then wandered off in search of snacks.

Someone turned the music up and – as if the tune was being played by some sort of modern pied piper – people gradually began to dance along, until Nicky found herself the only seemingly sober and rhythm-free reveller in a crowd of mainly middle-aged dancers.

She stood at the edge of the mêlée and set her punch down, replacing it with a small glass of white wine she knew she could handle and watched the party from the sidelines. It was nice to see Chloe and Amy together – they both had such busy lives that seeing each other was a relatively rare treat now. They danced together, hand in hand, making over-the-top and exaggerated dance moves and dissolving into giggles, Amy noticeably wobblier than her sister.

Part of her wanted to throw caution to the wind, knock back a glass or two and join in. But she knew she wanted to do her best tomorrow – for Robert, for Jenny, for herself – she couldn't risk being in a state for filming.

A few couples danced together and others stood in groups and sort of danced and gossiped all in one. Robert, apparently several glasses of punch down, was performing some sort of elaborate dance move that involved him waving his hands in the air and once doing some sort of attempt at some breakdancing. (Either that, or he'd tripped over. It was hard to tell.) She held in a giggle as she watched. He was definitely no dancer but it was nice to see him letting go and enjoying himself.

As the party went on, Nicky stood and wandered around, smiling at people and sipping her wine, and was just about to approach a group of friendly-looking guests in an attempt to break into their conversation when her phone went off.

She checked it; the screen was flashing, Jenny.

Of course. Of course it was.

She walked quickly towards the back door and slipped into the comparatively quiet kitchen to take the call.

'Hello?'

'Hi,' Jenny said, her voice sounding more cautious than usual. 'You OK?'

'Yes. Fine thanks.' She still felt herself stiffen when talking to her old friend. She'd been so angry at Jenny's words and it wouldn't be easy to simply shake them off again. At the same time, she had a sense that one day they'd be able to get past it all. Just not yet. And definitely not now. 'Can I help you?' she asked.

'Just wanted to make sure you're all ready.'

'For the filming? Yes, definitely. We'll be all sorted in time, don't worry!'

Nicky leaned on the countertop and looked out of the window over the sun-drenched garden. In the distance, she could just make out the top of Robert's head, bopping away. She smiled, in spite of herself.

'You're all sorted now, you mean.'

'Well, almost.'

'Oh.'

'What? We're just having a little drink now. A celebration. Did I tell you the girls came over? No probably not.' She realised they hadn't really spoken since their argument. 'Well, anyway. The girls are here. And they can help me clear up later or tomorrow if necessary…'

'Oh, that's great the girls are there. Although, the clearing up… um, about that…'

'Not that it's going to be too messy. Nothing a few binbags won't fix!'

'Nicky…' Jenny's tone made her heart turn over slightly.

'What? You're not changing the schedule again?'

'No. But look. I know we said tomorrow, and it's all still on for then, don't worry.'

'OK?'

'Um, but I've just had a call saying they've decided to do an impromptu 'night before' visit. Just to take a few shots and get a feel of everything before tomorrow.'

'This evening?' Nicky looked at the revellers in the garden, at Robert's formerly cute elaborate dancing, with new eyes.

'Look, really they're only going to get a few shots of the place, and a quick interview with you and Robert. Nothing you can't handle, honestly. No looking through the books or anything like that. Then it's watching the guest footage tomorrow and...'

'Jenny!' Nicky interrupted, looking again in the garden and seeing that Robert had now grabbed the hand of some unfortunate woman and was spinning her around on the makeshift dance floor. 'It really isn't a good time...'

There was a silence.

'I'm so sorry,' Jenny said. 'You probably won't believe me when I say this time there's nothing I could do. But you're there, they're there and... there isn't anything I can...'

Nicky cut her off, looking frantically into the garden.

Amy stepped into the kitchen, swaying a little.

'Amy,' Nicky said. 'I'm going to need your help.'

She explained the situation to her usually sympathetic and helpful eldest child only to have that child burst into uncontrollable giggles. 'Oh Mum,' she said. 'What are we going to do? We're all pissed! Everyone. Have you *seen* Robert?'

'Yes. Yes I have seen Robert. And that's the problem,' she said. 'We can't have the crew show up now. We just...'

Amy nodded, her face clearly trying to look serious but failing. 'What we need,' she said, 'is coffee. And lots of it.'

She went to the cupboard where Robert kept the guest coffee, opened it and pulled down the enormous bag, grabbing it by the bottom seam and somehow sending ground grains raining onto the countertop and floor. 'Oh shit,' she said. 'Too much coffee.'

This was no use at all. Nicky left her daughter attempting to clear up the grains with a teaspoon and put them back into the bag and raced across the garden, practically knocking people out of her way. She came across Chloe but saw the same, semi-glassiness to her eyes as she'd seen in Amy's. 'Never mind,' she said, racing on, until she was at Robert's side.

'Nicky!' he exclaimed, joyful that she was there. 'Where did you spring from! Have you tried the punch?'

'Listen... Robert,' she said. 'You have to sober up.'

'Dance to the MUSIC,' he sang. 'Move to the muuuuSIC!' He grabbed her hand.

'Robert!' she said, trying to get her balance as he performed what was clearly in his head an elaborate dance routine but to anyone not several shots down looked more like a drunken man stumbling on a grassy area. 'I need to talk to you.'

'What?' He attempted to put her into a twirl. She wrenched her hand free, her heart thundering with near-panic.

'Robert. You need to LISTEN. I have something to say.'

'Oh!' he said. 'Say no more.' He grabbed a fork from one of the tables and clinked it against his glass. 'Everyone!' he called. 'Everyone! Nicky wants to make a speech!'

Someone turned down the music. Everyone turned, swaying like an army of half-mobile zombies. All eyes were suddenly on her.

'No,' she said. 'What I need to say, Robert, I just need to say this to you.'

'Oh.' His eyes widened as if he had just caught her gist. 'Oh, sorry everyone. Apparently it's *private,*' he said with a wink. Then, 'Actually, though, now I've got your attention, I'd like to say something if you all don't mind?'

As if, she thought, anyone could stop you...

He turned to the crowd. 'Thank you all for coming,' he said. 'And helping. Since Marie died, you've all... well, I suppose it's true what they say. Until something like that happens, you just don't know who your friends are.' Perhaps the gravity of his words calmed him down as he seemed, suddenly, sober. 'You have all come through in so many different ways. And I can honestly say I wouldn't have made it without you.'

Everyone began to clap. Robert wiped a tear from his eye.

Even Nicky felt a bit emotional at his words.

'And you,' he said, turning to her. 'Nicky. I want to thank you. It's not too much to say that you've changed my life. In more ways than you realise.'

'Thank you,' she said, hoping to make him stop. 'But I need to talk about...'

There was the unmistakable sound of a van pulling up outside.

'Friends,' Robert said, suddenly giving into the alcohol whizzing through his veins again. 'You gotta have friends...' He broke into song, just as outside she heard the van door slam and the sound of loud voices on the street outside.

26

'Hi, great to see you!' Nicky lied as she opened the front door to the familiar ensemble. She avoided Tom's eye and tried to concentrate on the mammoth task she already had on her hands. 'What a surprise! Look, we're having a few drinks in the garden.' She could feel a line of sweat forming on her brow and couldn't for the life of her have said whether this was due to the summer heat or the barefaced terror she was experiencing. She laughed and stepped back as the five of them came into the hallway. Ryan, smelling strongly of a floral aftershave, leaned in and kissed her on each cheek.

'When in France!' he said, with a laugh. 'Ooh, get me, I'm becoming all European!'

The others tittered politely.

'Shall I take you through to the dining room, maybe you can set up some of your equipment there?' she suggested.

'Where's Robert?' Fern asked.

'He's just... well, he had a bit of a headache to be honest. He's having a rest. I was hoping we could go ahead and film a few bits without him?' she lied. In fact, Robert was in his room where she'd dragged him just before she'd opened the door.

'Stay there,' she'd hissed into his bemused face.

'But...' he'd said. 'My party!' He'd sat down miserably on the bed. 'I was having fun.'

'Robert,' she'd said, putting her hands on his shoulders and staring into his eyes, hoping to find the remnants of sober Robert still lingering within this intoxicated version. 'The crew are here. Trust me. You need to stay here. Just for a bit, OK?'

He'd seemed to accept his fate at that point and had nodded mutely.

Now, as the camera crew began dragging equipment into the dining room where she'd cleared a corner for them to stack their various mysterious boxes of 'kit', she made an excuse and managed to make it into the garden. Chloe was there, serving punch into a crystal glass for Cabbage, whose arm was swaying rather alarmingly.

'Chloe,' she said, hoping her daughter was still in a state approaching sober. 'I need your help.'

Chloe looked up, dripped some punch into the glass and gave it to Cabbage. 'Sure,' she said. 'Snacks?'

'No, Chloe,' she said soberly, shaking her head. 'No. Not snacks.'

Luckily Chloe had, despite earlier appearances, remained relatively unscathed by alcohol in order to keep an eye on Amy as she'd promised, and on hearing about the imminent disaster became deadly serious. 'Leave it with me, Mum,' she said. 'I'll get rid of this lot. Don't worry.'

'Are you sure?' Nicky looked dubiously around at the twenty or so guests who looked well and truly settled in for the evening.

'Don't worry,' Chloe said confidently. 'I have my ways.'

Nicky decided to take her word for it. She had her own disasters to avert. 'Well, good luck,' she said. 'Come and find me if you have any problems.' Although if she was honest with herself she had no idea what she'd do if her daughter did come asking for help.

She made her way back through the kitchen area, and was just about to push open the door into the dining room when someone walked through, nearly bumping into her. Tom. 'Oh. Hi,' she said, feeling her cheeks get hot.

He was looking rather dishevelled, presumably from a few weeks on the road, staying at various hotels and a car journey today. His face sported a thin layer of stubble and his hair, which had been styled with product last time they met, was soft and unkempt in a way that made him look younger than he had before.

'Hi,' he said, with a small smile. 'Good to see you.'

'Yes,' she said. 'Look, I'm sorry about the message.'

'Not at all,' he said, smiling. 'I'd love to go for a drink...'

'...to wrap up filming?' she finished for him. 'Yes, we could all go...'

'No,' he said, stopping her and putting a hand on her arm. 'If I'm totally honest, I'd like to go for a drink just with *you*.'

'Oh.' She looked at him, taking in the kind hazel eyes, the tanned complexion, noticing how his T-shirt seemed to fit in all the right places. 'Oh.'

'Is that "Oh... no"?' he prompted, with a slight smile.

'No! I mean, no it's not an "oh no",' she said, not entirely sure whether her answer had made any sense. 'I was just surprised, that's all.'

'Surprised? But I mean, your text...'

'I know. It's just...' She couldn't tell him that she'd spent the days after sending the message feeling embarrassed to have sent it. That she'd done it on a whim, because he'd called her attractive and she'd decided to take a chance. 'Oh, I don't know,' she said. 'I suppose I'd sort of thought you weren't interested.'

He nodded. 'Sorry,' he said. 'I'm crap at text messages. It's the emojis. I always forget to put emojis, according to Ryan. People think I'm being sarcastic when I'm being serious, or that I'm being dismissive when I'm actually... Not.'

'Oh,' she said again.

'So?'

She felt an almost overwhelming urge to run. To race to the front door, fling it open, leap into Robert's car, start the engine and roar off into the early evening air. To put as much distance between herself and this man as humanly possible. There was no time to analyse why. Perhaps her own fears, perhaps something to do with Steve. Perhaps the fact she hadn't been on a date for a decade. But she suspected deep down that it was because she'd now felt something spark between her and Robert. And remembered how things were supposed to feel. How things had once felt with Steve. Tom was objectively handsome but she felt stiff and awkward in his presence.

Then she remembered what Jenny had said. That she should take any opportunity – that *love*, or in this case, at least *like* was infinite. Maybe she'd been cautious for too long. Besides, Robert hadn't mentioned their near-kiss since, and she was pretty sure he was trying to forget about it.

And after all, it was only a drink. And now she'd been silent for what was becoming an embarrassingly awkward amount of time. 'Yes,' she said. 'Yes, let's go for a drink.' After all, she hadn't felt instantly attracted to Robert either. Perhaps getting to know Tom a bit more would help.

His smile widened. 'Well,' he said, 'thank God for that. I thought I was about to get shot down.'

'Yeah, sorry.' She crinkled her nose. She wanted to say something about being indecisive (but surely that would be insulting), or something about Steve or being afraid or ten years away from the dating scene. But none of it painted her in a very attractive light.

Instead, she said, 'Right, well, I'd better...' and nodded towards the door behind him.

'Oh!' he said. 'Sure!' And stepped aside to let her through.

The four others looked up when she appeared again in the room. Fern was sitting in one of the chairs, a guy she didn't recognise was rummaging through a bag and Mo was at a table lining up make-up brushes. Ryan was looking at the painting on the wall, chin in hand, like an art critic sizing up a masterpiece. Tom reappeared behind her from the kitchen and gave her a smile as she turned to look at him.

'So,' she said, about to suggest they interviewed her about the room or something to deflect from Robert's absence, despite the fact the whole idea made her sick with nerves, when she heard a stumbling tread on the stairs.

'Hello?' called a voice. 'Anyone home?' And the door swung open so violently that the handle hit the wall, making a dent in the plaster. Robert stood there, T-shirt on back to front, one sock up and one down, slightly red-eyed and looking as unkempt and worse for wear as she'd ever seen him.

'Headache, eh,' Tom murmured. 'That looks more like a headache in the making.'

'Oh, bloody hell,' she said softly.

'Hang on,' Robert said, peering at Ryan in drunken confusion. 'It's Ryan Camberwell? Off the telly?'

'The very one, my man. The very one,' said Ryan, smiling widely, patting him on the shoulder and winking elaborately at everyone else in the room.

Robert's face broke into a smile. 'You're famous!' he said.

Then his eyes fixed on Nicky.

'Nicky,' he said. 'Look, I'm sorry I didn't stay in my room. But I heard all the noise and...' He gestured around. 'Did you *know* that Ryan Camberwell was HERE? In my B&B?'

Now everyone was looking at Nicky. She gave a shrug. 'Well, at least he can't say I didn't try,' she said quietly.

'Don't be daft, this is brilliant,' Ryan said, coming over and slinging his arm around Nicky's shoulders. 'I can just see it now. The celebration after the success. Miserable B&B owner finds happiness.' He used his right hand to paint an arc in the air as if creating his vision in front of her. 'Plus,' he continued, nodding at Fern. 'When people are pissed they make GREAT TV.'

'That,' said Nicky, 'is what I was afraid of.'

Five minutes later, she managed to drag Robert upstairs and encourage him into some of his new clothing. 'Look,' she said. 'Splash some water on your face. And drink some coffee.'

He obeyed, wobbling slightly. 'They're here to film us?' He was suddenly seeming to realise how important this was.

'Yes, they are,' she said.

'But the people? The party?'

'Chloe's sorting it,' she said, sitting next to him on the bed, then getting up abruptly when it felt a little too intimate, especially as he was still buttoning his shirt so was practically half-naked.

Robert nodded, his fingers struggling a little with the buttons.

'Look,' she said. 'Let me.' She reached forward and grabbed the little plastic circles, pressing them gently through the buttonholes. She felt a tingle in her touch as her hand brushed his bare skin and tried to think about something else. Anything else. He looked up at her, his eyes studying her face.

'What?' she asked as she stepped back to admire her work.

'Just. Thank you,' he said. 'You're amazing. You know that?'

'That's the punch talking.'

'No,' he said. 'You are.'

'Right. Well, you're definitely looking better.' She took in his neat hair, the well-fitted tailoring. 'Guess we'll have to go down and face the music.'

'OK, I'll just finish this coffee,' he nodded at the mug of instant she'd made him, 'then I'll be down.'

'OK,' she said, smiling and slipping out of the door.

The noise from the garden seemed to have died down at last, and, once she returned downstairs, she tugged her own dress into place and allowed Mo to 'work her magic' on her under-eye bags and get her 'camera ready'.

Twenty minutes on, when they heard Robert's tread on the stairs, everyone paused slightly and she could feel the question in the air: what state was he going to be in? After his earlier performance, expectations were low. Which was probably why, when he actually did walk in, there was a collective gasp.

'Robert, my man!' Ryan said. 'You look blummin' amazing! Where did you get that new gear?'

'Thanks.' Robert blushed slightly. 'It's all thanks to Nicky though.' He tugged slightly at his shirt as if it was tucked in too tightly. But it remained in place, neatly, accentuating the fact that he had been hiding a pretty decent body underneath all the baggy trousers and band T-shirts.

'Well, whatever she's got up there, I want some of it!' Ryan said, shaking his head. 'I think you're on the wrong makeover show, love.'

Nicky grinned. 'Ah, it was all there. I just had to uncover it.' Then she realised how pervy that sounded. 'You know what I mean,' she finished weakly.

Then there was nothing for it but to go through the motions. Tom went outside with Ryan and they made a great pretence of knocking on the door and having Robert open it. 'Oh!' he said, in a rather exaggerated attempt at acting. 'What a surprise! Come in! Come in!'

'We'll be finding out properly about everything you've done tomorrow,' said Ryan, 'but we thought we'd come and have a little sneak peek!'

Robert led them obediently up to the two empty bedrooms, and Nicky could hear the rumble of voices and exclamations from upstairs. She crossed her fingers and hoped beyond hope that Robert wasn't going to say anything ridiculous, or trip up, or puke onto the camera. Ryan's claim that it was a 'sneak peek' suggested it was a casual visit. But the cameras were rolling and she was pretty sure the judges would be reviewing all the footage, sneaky or otherwise, when they made their final decision.

Several weeks of preparation, hard work, worry and stress. If it ended in disaster (or as Jenny might call it 'Good TV') then it would be all for nothing.

Finally, they heard footsteps on the stairs and the three of them appeared in the dining room. 'And this is the *pièce de résistance*,' Robert said, gesturing around the room.

'Ooh, I love it,' Ryan said, as if he'd not spent the last hour or so getting ready in the very same room. 'You've toned down the recluttering vibe a little, but added so much French charm. I love the paintings and is this a new floor?' he said, gesturing to the parquet, its paint stains thankfully still covered by the rug.

'It was there all the time,' Robert said proudly. 'But Nicky encouraged me to get it sanded down and revarnished.'

'Well, it's certainly a great space for guests to relax in,' Ryan said. 'But what did our mystery customers think when they came to stay a few days ago? Stay tuned to find out!'

Tom lifted the camera from his shoulder and everyone visibly relaxed. 'You have actually done a great job, my man,' Ryan told Robert. 'This place looks fab. We might even stay here next time we're passing.'

'Thanks,' Robert said, grinning, his features still a little loose and lopsided from drink. 'And you know, was that thing I said upstairs OK?'

'Man, it was brilliant, straight from the heart.' Ryan patted his chest. 'Got me in the feels.'

'Right. Thank you.' Some of Robert's habitual awkwardness was reappearing.

'What did he say, out of interest?' Nicky asked, her heart pounding.

'Ahh.' Ryan patted the side of his nose. 'You'll see!' Which didn't help to calm her nerves at all.

After agreeing that they'd be back in the morning to show the footage from the guests, the crew packed their things up and started heading out of the door. Nicky checked her watch; it was only eight o'clock, but she was exhausted. She walked through to the kitchen and looked at the garden out of the window. It was a mess of scattered food and discarded glasses. The last thing she wanted was to have to clear up, but it looked as if they had their work cut out for the evening.

Chloe and Amy, having heard the front door slam, appeared in the kitchen, Amy clutching a wide-eyed Rose in her arms. 'How did it go?' Chloe said.

'OK, I think.'

'It went brilliantly,' said another voice, making them all jump. It was Tom, who hadn't yet disappeared into the crew's MPV.

'Oh!' Nicky's heart was either leaping or sinking. It was hard to tell.

'Just wanted to check that it's OK to pick you up in say, an hour?' He checked his watch. 'Thought we could grab a bite along with that drink, if that's OK with you?'

'Oh,' she said, looking at the garden. And suddenly she realised she had a perfect excuse to get out of the date. 'Actually, I think I might have to...'

'Don't be silly!' Amy said, catching on more quickly than a

slightly tipsy person might ordinarily. 'We can do that, can't we, Chloe?' She gave her sister a nudge.

'Oh?' said Chloe. Then, looking from Tom to Nicky, added, 'Ohhhh. Yes. Definitely.' She nodded, a smile spreading across her face.

Robert, the last one to cotton on, looked rather confused. 'Tonight?' he said. 'I thought it was tomorr... Oh.'

And with that, Tom kissed Nicky lightly on the cheek, winked to the rest of them and made his way jauntily out of the room to join his waiting colleagues.

'Oh Muuummm,' Amy said, with a wicked grin. 'Looks like you've pulled.'

27

In the end, she'd chosen a different bar. She'd been going to take Tom to the brasserie – more or less the only place she actually knew in Roussillon – but had a last-minute change of heart and googled local eateries to see what else was available. Somehow it hadn't seemed right to take Tom to Robert's favourite place. Although she wasn't quite sure why.

La Sirmonde was located a ten-minute walk from Robert's B&B. As they set off, the sun was still high in the sky, but seemed to have slipped into its evening wear – turning it from a forceful white light to something more mellow and orange as day began to morph into night.

Tom had turned up in the MPV and had seemed surprised when she'd told him they'd better walk. 'The streets are so narrow,' she'd said. 'It's only ten minutes. We might as well make the most of the evening.'

'Fair enough,' he'd said, with a nod.

He'd gone to some effort to smarten himself up – he was wearing a powder-blue short-sleeved shirt which accentuated his hazel eyes, navy washed jeans and a pair of brown leather shoes.

When he'd arrived at the door, he'd whistled approvingly at the ensemble she'd put together – a smart-casual mix of cropped jeans with one of her silk tops and a pair of Chloe's sandals. 'Looking good,' he'd said.

'Thank you.'

'Isn't it beautiful,' she said now as they walked up the slight incline towards the town centre. The orangey glow of the evening sun set off the red in the stone buildings, giving the whole place a warm glow. Little signs outside small buildings informed her they were passing tiny galleries, or tucked-in eateries, tourist shops, a small, organic grocery store.

'You think?' he said, looking around as if for the first time. 'I think after a while,' he confided, 'I don't really notice that sort of stuff. I travel a lot, you know? And most of the time I'd rather be back in London.'

She nodded. 'I know what you mean,' she said, although this was only half true. She missed the familiarity of home, the routine of it. But she didn't think she'd ever stop noticing her surroundings.

After walking a bit further in silence, the road curved to the right and she could see the signage for La Sirmonde – written in carefully moulded metal letters above the gate to a pretty court-yard. Inside the yard itself, several tables were scattered about. Simple, with glass tops and rattan chairs, paper menus and napkins. Several of the tables were already occupied – two with couples and another with a man on his own. A larger family had pushed two tables together to create a bigger surface and crowded around plates of what looked like burgers, chips and pizza.

'This is it,' she said, gesturing unnecessarily towards the gate.

'Thank fuck for that,' he said. 'Excuse my language. Just my feet are fucking killing me.'

'Well, let's get a table.' She went up to a wooden lectern behind which a man in jeans and a white T-shirt was writing in a diary. '*Table pour deux, s'il vous plaît*,' she said in her best, faltering French.

The man looked up. 'But of course.' He smiled. 'You are lucky, we have had a cancellation.' He showed them to a table in the corner of the courtyard, where they could see over a wall that revealed views across rolling countryside, topped by the blue and orange of the early evening sky.

'This is perfect, thank you.' Nicky slid into one of the seats. Tom sat down opposite her and nodded at the waiter who left them to look at the drinks menu.

'Wow, well, this is beautiful,' said Nicky.

Tom, deep into the menu by this point, made a grunting noise. She turned her attention to her own menu – Tom was no doubt hungry after a day's travelling and filming. Perhaps they ought to order sooner rather than later.

The waiter reappeared a few minutes later and took their order and they sat in silence for a moment. Nicky found herself almost tongue-tied, trying to think of something to say. 'So,' she said at last. 'Have you always wanted to be a cameraman?'

He nodded. 'Well, for a long time, yeah. It's a good gig.'

Silence again.

'What about you?' he followed up. 'Designer?'

She shrugged. 'Yeah, kind of. I mean, life doesn't always take you in the direction you think it will, does it? So I suppose it's... well, it hasn't been straightforward.'

The problem with being widowed, of having had this enormous, life-changing thing happen to you, is that it's always there, lingering in your back story. There always comes a point when you have to share that information, talk about what happened. Meaning you have to relive it all, often during social occasions or when meeting new people, when small talk is called for rather than deep-and-meaningful discussion. But for any of her story to make sense, she had to talk about what had shifted her life out of focus for so many years.

So she did. She told him about her and Steve, about receiving the phone call. The rush to the hospital. The aftermath. Bringing up the girls on her own. How her own life, her own plans had gone on hold ever since. Until now. Until this opportunity had woken her up.

Tom listened, his eyes sympathetic, and nodded his head now and then. 'Bloody hell,' he said, when she finished.

'Yep.'

'Sorry you went through all that.'

'Thanks.'

Then. 'It was a bit like that with my divorce,' he said.

'Really?'

'Yeah.' He shrugged. 'I mean it took me months to get over it.' He seemed to check himself, as if he realised how insensitive he was being. 'Obviously, your story is worse,' he said, making a face.

You think? she wanted to say.

'It's fine,' she said, on autopilot. Obviously it was anything but fine. But that was what you had to say, wasn't it? Especially with new people. You couldn't dump a load of trauma on the head of someone new. You had to feed it to them in bitesize portions, so as not to drive them away. She couldn't tell Tom that part of her would always be married to Steve. She couldn't tell him that she was afraid of making a step forward. She definitely couldn't tell him that she hadn't slept with anyone else and probably had cobwebs 'down there'. So she told him it was fine so they could move the conversation on.

That had been one of the nice things about talking to Robert over the past couple of weeks, she'd realised. That Robert understood intrinsically what she meant – how much to talk, when to change the subject. He understood the burden of pain that she carried and the things that made it feel lighter. They'd connected.

It was more than that though. More than the connection of both being bereaved. He was easy to talk to; he understood her, her humour. There was an ease when she was with him that she definitely didn't feel now.

But that wasn't fair, she told herself. She knew Robert better. It was always awkward at first with someone new.

Tom talked about his own past – the tour of a TV studio that had ignited his ambition, a brief marriage in his late thirties that had been a mistake. The fact that, at forty-six, he still felt he had plenty of 'gas in the tank'.

Their meal arrived and they tucked in, her to a *steak haché*, chips and salad and him into an enormous, thin crust pizza. The fare was basic, but delicious, and sitting in the courtyard with the rumble of conversation around them, Nicky felt relaxed and began finally to let go and enjoy herself.

Once they'd finished dessert – a chocolate torte with Chantilly cream – they split the bill, then began the walk back to the B&B. Tom's arm tucked itself around her back and supported her a little as she stumbled on the unfamiliar heels, her muscles slightly loosened by the wine, her balance slightly thrown off by the uneven road. It was nice to feel the support. Nice to have someone at her side.

As they neared the B&B she began to wonder how the date might end. What would Tom be expecting? Might he invite himself up? The prospect of even a kiss to end the date felt overwhelming. But maybe if she was dipping her toe back into life again, she should just go with the flow? She looked at Tom and he glanced back and smiled. 'Nearly there,' he said.

'Yes,' she agreed, and they lapsed into silence again.

At the front door she felt a little like a teenager – awkward and wondering and not really knowing what she wanted to happen. Nothing felt natural, everything felt staged, almost as if she was playing a part in a movie rather than actually, really there. She was living in her head too much, unable to let her heart – or body – override her thoughts. Maybe she did have actual cobwebs.

In the end, the decision was taken out of her hands. Tom leaned forward, and she automatically closed her eyes and did the same. Only his lips landed on her cheek, just left of her mouth. 'It's been lovely,' he said. 'Thanks.'

'Thank you,' she said. 'I really enjoyed myself.'

'I hope you don't mind my not coming in,' he said. 'It's just…' His cheeks reddened. 'It's always awkward, isn't it?' he said. 'But you know. I had a great time. We're just not…' He gave a shrug in place of a word.

She knew, instantly, what he meant. The slightly stilted conversation, the perfectly pleasant walk together, the sharing of histories. They didn't have anything in common. They didn't have that spark.

Oddly, even though she felt the same, she felt a pang of hurt at being rejected. But as she wished him goodnight and turned the key Robert had given her in the lock, she felt relieved too.

It would take time, she thought, stepping into the hallway which still held a ghost of the smell of fresh paint, to get to know herself again. To recognise different feelings within her own body that she'd repressed for so long.

Perhaps she ought to go on a lot more dates.

Perhaps she should never go on a date again.

Either way, this one was over. And it hadn't been too bad.

'Tom not with you?'

Nicky jumped. Robert was standing in the kitchen doorway, framed by the glow of yellow light which spilled into the darkened hall.

'No, he had to head off,' she said.

'Good date?'

She shrugged a 'no big deal' shrug. 'It was OK,' she said. Then, 'Didn't really click though,' she added.

'Tea?'

'Go on then.' She followed him through to the kitchen and leaned against the counter as he plopped teabags into mugs and filled the kettle. 'Have you been on many dates?' she asked. 'You know, since Marie.'

He shook his head, back still turned to her. 'No. Not yet,' he said. 'One. A set-up. Bit of a disaster really. It was too soon.'

'It's hard, isn't it?' she said. 'That was my first... well, my first proper date.'

Robert looked at her. 'Proper date?' he said.

'Yeah, I mean Jenny and I... well, we made a Tinder profile a while back. And I did get chatting to a couple of guys. Two 'dates'. But so ghastly I've kind of blanked them out.'

'They don't count?'

'They definitely don't count. Believe me, if you want dating disaster stories, you've come to the right place.'

Robert laughed. 'I'll bear that in mind.'

'And don't get me started on dick pics,' she added, regretting it almost instantly.

Luckily he laughed. 'I'll make a note of it,' he said.

He turned to her, his head tilted slightly, eyes glittering in the lamp's glow. 'But yeah, it's hard. And even harder for people... like us,' he said with a small smile. 'I mean, there are all these rules for dating, aren't there. But when you're in my... our position things are a little more complicated. Not that dating isn't complicated in the first place.'

'Definitely,' she said, as he added milk, removed the teabags, placing them on a small saucer, and handed her a mug. She sat on one of the pine chairs and he perched himself on a stool. 'I mean, I know that Steve... well, I'm pretty sure he'd want me to be, you know. Out there. Especially after so long. He wouldn't... I know if the situation were reversed I wouldn't want him to be alone,' she said. Robert nodded. 'But at the same time, it still feels like cheating in an odd way. And also... I don't know. I wonder whether the idea of dating a widow – whether it isn't too much for some people.'

'Maybe,' said Robert. 'I mean, all that... those memories. The fact that if a tragedy hadn't happened, you probably wouldn't be single. It's a lot to take.'

'Much easier to date someone divorced who can slag off their ex and regale you with his faults,' she said, smiling.

'Exactly.'

'So how do we do it?' she asked, looking at him.

'I have absolutely no idea,' he answered, with a shrug.

They sat in silence, sipping their tea.

'I suppose,' he said into the silence. 'I suppose maybe it takes time... I don't mean getting over everything. I mean, learning how to do it again takes time. How to do it in this new way, with this new you.'

'That's it. Because you know how your old self dated. What they wanted. The sort of thing they'd say. But this is like being a brand-new person and starting all over again.'

'Exactly. Brand new, but broken. Which makes it...'

'Bloody exhausting.'

'Definitely.'

They grinned at each other.

'Although maybe,' he said. 'Maybe when you meet the right person... maybe it feels more natural.'

'Yes,' she said, catching his eye. 'Maybe that's what it is.'

He nodded thoughtfully.

'You know,' she added. 'Jenny said to me that moving on... it didn't mean betraying Steve or anything. That I could still love him. But that I could love someone else as well.'

'Oh,' he said.

'That love is infinite.'

Their eyes locked for a second.

'It's nice,' she said after a moment.

'What's nice?'

'Talking to you. Talking to someone who really *gets* it.'

He nodded. 'Agreed. You don't have to... well, explain anything.'

'No. And I suppose I don't feel... it's weird, but when I told Tom about Steve, about the accident, I felt as if I was dumping a load of trauma onto him. I felt guilty that I'd had this horrible past.'

Robert laughed softly. 'Yes. I can understand that. Like *sorry I had to go through bereavement and ruin your dinner with my tragic life story.*'

She snorted. 'Yes. I'm really sorry if my ten years of grief put you off your green beans.'

And they laughed quietly together in the way that you only can when you really truly understand another person.

Later, when she looked back on what she'd done next, she could see why she'd misinterpreted the signs. Sitting together, laughing. Her failed date and the fact he seemed to have waited up for her. The way things felt easy, natural with Robert in a way they hadn't with Tom.

The conversation had paused, and their eyes had met again. And she'd moved towards him and lifted her mouth, tentatively touching her lips to his.

For a moment, he'd leaned towards her, sinking into a soft, gentle kiss. Until abruptly he'd pulled away, stood up and said, 'I'm sorry.'

28

It was hard to sleep, after making her way to bed, feeling embarrassed and rejected. Hard knowing that they had a day's filming tomorrow. Knowing that she'd have to face Robert no matter what. The more she tried to doze, the more her body seemed to rebel against it; her mind filled with thoughts of things she had to do and worst-case scenarios she needed to avoid. Her body refused to settle into the mattress. In the end, she flung off the covers and got out of bed at half past five.

Once showered, she dried her hair and pulled on a clean pair of leggings and a T-shirt. She'd change later when the TV crew turned up, but for now this would do. Making her way down the now familiar stairs, she paused by the window to take in the view. The sun had risen, but remnants of the sunrise still scattered the clouds with golds and pinks. The trees and bushes were alive with chattering birds and in the corner of the garden she saw a couple of red squirrels scurrying into the bushes.

She turned and made her way down the second staircase and into the kitchen, where she found debris from what must have been a difficult night for Amy. Two baby bottles sat on the edge of the sink, one half-filled, the other empty. Next door, a little Babygro was soaking in the laundry room sink.

Nicky filled the kettle and turned it on, then went to the laundry room, emptied the sink of water, ran the hot tap and, adding a little detergent, washed the tiny Babygro clean, squeezing out the water and setting it on the side for a moment. Then she returned to the kitchen and cleaned out the bottles, drying them carefully with a tea towel then putting them in a bowl with a sterilising tablet ready to be used again. She made an instant coffee – she preferred her coffee fresh, but this morning couldn't be bothered– and took it and the tiny damp Babygro out into the garden to benefit from the fresh, morning air. Robert's washing line was curled up into its casing and it didn't seem worth running it across the garden for one item. So she laid the little Babygro on the back of a chair where it would catch the first of the morning sun. Then, she pulled out another chair and sank into it, gratefully.

She blew on the top of the coffee and inhaled its rich scent before taking a sip, feeling it slip hotly down her throat. There were only four days left, she realised. Today's filming, then some sort of judge looking over the footage. Tying up loose ends. Her plane was booked for Friday and by Monday she would be back at her usual desk. The thought was strangely unsettling. But it always felt like that, she reasoned, when you thought about coming home from a holiday. When real life came and interrupted your little slice of paradise.

After all, life couldn't be a holiday all the time, could it?

It sort of was though, she thought, for Michelle and Robert. They'd chosen to make a life in a place where others dreamed of going for a fortnight a year. But at what point did a beautiful holiday location become ordinary? Robert said he had stopped seeing the beauty of his surroundings. So really, was it any different from living anywhere else in the world?

Before she could speculate any more there was a noise behind her and Amy appeared, looking rather dishevelled in her dressing gown. 'Hello, love,' Nicky said, turning to look at her. 'Difficult night?'

'Pretty much par for the course.' Amy shrugged. 'She's sleeping now and I suppose I should be too. But I just couldn't.'

Nicky smiled, sympathetically. 'Join the club,' she said. 'Something's in the air today. Would you like a coffee?'

'No thanks. Not yet,' her daughter said, removing the Babygro from the back of the chair and laying it instead across the edge of the table, then sitting down in its stead. 'Thanks for doing that,' she said. 'It's endless, isn't it?'

'It seems that way,' Nicky said. 'Then suddenly it does end. And you sort of want it all to come back again.'

Amy smiled. 'The motherhood conundrum,' she said. 'The minute you give birth you're always wishing you could be in a different place on the timeline.'

'It's worth it though,' Nicky reassured her.

'Thank you. I'll bear that in mind tomorrow at 3 a.m.'

The two women smiled at each other. 'So, how was the date last night?' Amy asked, raising an eyebrow.

'Ah, it was OK.' Nicky shrugged. 'Nice to have done it, you know? But I don't think we're going to see each other again.'

'Oh, why?'

Nicky shook her head. 'No chemistry.'

'Well, then the man's a fool,' said Amy.

Nicky smiled. 'He seems like a good guy. And you know, he's a few years younger, so it was flattering that he wanted to go out with me at all I suppose. It's just...'

'Just...?' Amy prompted.

'The whole dating thing. God, it feels so exhausting just considering it again.'

Amy laughed. 'I can imagine. But you know, it could be fun, too.'

'Let's hope so.'

'Can I ask something?'

'Sure?'

'What about Robert?'

'What do you mean?'

'Well, he's pretty handsome, for an old guy.'

Nicky snorted. 'Don't you start. That's what your sister said!'

'Well, he is. Objectively. He seems nice. And you have... well, you guys kind of understand each other. Because of Dad, you know. And Marie.'

'Yes. It's been nice to talk to someone who's been through, well... similar,' Nicky admitted. 'But we're just friends.' She thought about the night before and felt herself redden.

'Sure about that?' Amy cocked an eyebrow.

'Amy!'

'Well, let's just say I've seen the way he looks at you,' her daughter said with a grin.

'What do you—'

But before she could finish her sentence there was a loud 'Good morning!' from behind her and both of them jumped.

'Oh,' Nicky said, turning to see Robert himself standing there with a glass of orange juice. 'Hi.' She felt herself get hot, hoping that he hadn't heard anything. And really, what could he have heard? She reassured herself. Amy could have been talking about Tom, or someone else entirely.

'Hi,' he said. 'You two are up early.'

'Yeah, couldn't sleep,' they said in unison, then laughed.

'Ready for today?' Robert asked Nicky, perching a buttock on the edge of the table, then thinking better of it.

'As ready as I'll ever be,' she said. 'It'll be nice to get it over and done with.'

'Yes. I know what you mean. You... you must be looking forward to getting home?'

'Well, kind of. I guess.' She shrugged. 'Everything will seem a bit ordinary, though, I think after this.'

'Perhaps you'll be handing in your notice at work anyway,' Amy said. 'Once the job offers come flooding in.'

'Ha, well, I won't hold my breath,' Nicky said. 'But I suppose you never know.'

'What about you?' Amy asked Robert.

'Me?'

'Yeah, I mean you said you weren't a natural host. Do you think you'll be sticking it out once the cameras stop rolling?'

Robert looked thoughtful. 'You know what,' he said. 'If you'd asked me that three weeks ago... well, I'm not sure what I would have said. But things seem more... possible now. I feel... I guess I feel ready to make a go of it again. I can kind of feel things coming together.'

'That's great,' Amy said. 'And it's all thanks to Mum!'

'Don't be silly,' Nicky said.

'But it is,' Robert said. 'Seriously. It's more than just the paint and the furnishings and stuff. I... things seem different now.'

They sat in silence for a couple of minutes, before Amy got up. 'Well, better see whether Rose is stirring!' She disappeared into the house and the silence returned.

'Look,' Robert started, after a minute or two, clearing his throat. 'About last night...'

'Oh, please. Don't,' she said. 'It was a mistake. And I shouldn't have...'

'It's just...' he tried again.

'Honestly, please don't explain. I get it. I do,' she said, standing up decisively. 'And we'd better get on. They'll be here soon.'

Forty minutes later, Nicky's phone beeped to tell her that the crew were en route. In her room, she ran a brush through her hair and sprayed it with a conditioning balm. Then she carefully applied tinted moisturiser to her skin, a touch of blusher to her cheeks and a slick of lip balm to her lips. She leaned into the mirror to apply some mascara then stood back to inspect the damage. No doubt Mo would touch her face up even more, but she looked as camera ready as she was going to get.

She made her way downstairs, just as Robert was helping to move an enormous box into the dining room for Tom. Ryan was already inside, exclaiming over the tableware they'd laid out in readiness. Tom, en route back to the van, caught her eye. 'All right?' he asked.

'Yeah, good, thanks.' She smiled.

It was slightly awkward, but nothing she couldn't handle.

Shortly afterwards, she was perched on the same chair as before, watching the laptop with Robert, and hoping beyond hope that the mystery guests had been less scathing in their commentary this time.

It started off well, with the couple exchanging first impressions of their host. 'He seems friendly enough,' the man remarked. 'Not sure about the dog though.'

'Yes. I did think he ought to have offered to carry my bag upstairs,' the woman sniffed. 'But otherwise satisfactory.'

The tour continued with video vlog tours of the room and the dining room, the view over the garden. The woman, of course, found a rogue, missed dropping from the pigeon encounter on the floor by the banister. 'What's this?' she exclaimed loudly, scratching at the white stain with her finger. 'Some sort of paint mark?' She sniffed her finger. 'Stanley,' she said. 'That is *not* a paint mark.'

Seeing as they'd been finding and scrubbing away various undiscovered droppings from the pigeon's visit for the past three weeks, it was annoying that the woman had managed to find the only one that had evaded their notice. But as they watched, Nicky felt Robert twitching slightly at her side. Looking at him briefly, she realised that he was barely holding in laughter. Which set her off. They wobbled away, trying to keep straight faces against the odds.

The shower passed muster, and the breakfast was even given a 'good' grade. All in all, they'd raised their 'secret guest' score from 2.5 the first time to a healthy 4.0 – with 0.5 taken off for the 'mystery faeces' incident.

After watching and 'live reacting' to the footage, they were each interviewed individually about the project. When it was Nicky's turn, she was asked to stand by the fireplace to showcase the painting above the mantle. She was glad that they'd taken measures to de-penis the area.

'So,' Ryan said, all smiles and wicked glances, 'you've made quite the transformation here. What advice would you give to other B&B owners?'

She stumbled out an answer about careful budgeting and ambience, then he continued.

'And you've consciously recluttered the space, is that right?'

'Yes,' she said, trying to remember what they'd actually said the day after the painting party. 'B&Bs shouldn't try to compete with hotels. Rather they're a home from home. And life, especially family life, can be messy. We don't want our holidays to feel messy, but it is nice to feel comfortable. Hence the ornaments, some of the paint splashes, the – um – mismatched furniture. These old stone houses aren't going to have the modern fixtures of a Holiday Inn, so we've tried to do something different. No clean lines. But more interest. More heart.'

Ryan nodded as if she'd just said something wise. In all honesty, she hadn't a clue what had just come out of her mouth. She only hoped that when they watched it back it would sound OK.

Robert's turn came and they chose to have him standing in the kitchen in his half-apron, looking as if he was catering for guests. 'Yes,' he said. 'Bookings are up,' (which was true) 'and I'm looking forward to next year.' (Which might not have been true.)

Then finally, with an 'it's a wrap!' from Fern, the camera was placed down. Ryan flung himself into a chair, legs ensconced in his trademark skinny jeans and topped with pointed shoes, taking up what seemed like half the room. 'Ah, thank fuck for that,' he said. 'No offence. But all this property stuff does my head in. Anyone fancy a drink?'

They dutifully popped some champagne in the garden and Nicky was given the lowdown on what would happen next. The footage would be judged, a decision would be made and the 'lucky winner' would be revealed. All within the next few days.

She'd expected to feel relieved. Elated even. But as she sipped and nodded and made the right noises to Fern, she was grappling instead with an overwhelming feeling of sadness.

29

'If anything, it feels a bit of an anti-climax,' said Nicky, cutting into her *filet du porc* the following lunchtime. 'Do you know what I mean?'

They'd spent yesterday resting after the previous day's filming, but Nicky had earmarked today to teach Robert her failsafe Chinese chicken recipe. Then they'd all woken so tired and washed out, they'd decided to treat themselves to a meal instead. The brasserie was yet again their destination; and Nicky hadn't known whether to be flattered or embarrassed when the owner had greeted her by name.

'Ah, Madame Nicky!' he'd greeted her.

'Come here often?' Chloe had said quietly in her ear.

'Maybe once or twice,' she'd admitted.

'I get that,' Chloe said now, 'kind of like, what happens next?'

'But I guess it's not over, is it?' Amy added. 'I mean, you might win! And even if you don't, I reckon Jenny will have other gigs up her sleeve after this one.'

Nicky snorted. 'I doubt it,' she said. 'She wanted me to mess up, remember?' She still felt a flash of anger whenever she thought about her friend, the betrayal that had felt so personal, so cruel.

'Come on, Mum,' Amy said. 'We all know that wasn't what she meant. Not really.'

'I know,' Nicky admitted. 'But still...'

'Would you though?' Robert asked. 'I mean, if something similar came your way? Would you want to do it again?'

She thought about the ups and downs of the past four weeks. Discovering a new place. The stress of budget cuts and painting parties and secret filming and deadlines. 'Maybe,' she said. 'I suppose it's got variety if nothing else.'

'You can say that again,' said Robert. 'Not sure I'd want to revisit much of that. Although,' he added hurriedly, 'it's been a great experience, obviously.'

'What about you then?' Amy asked. 'What's next for your lovely B&B?'

'Well, with the number of enquiries I'm getting already just on the back of the new website it looks like it's really going to work out,' he said.

'It's lovely,' Chloe said, 'that you're able to fulfil Marie's dream for her.'

'Yes,' he said, looking sad for a moment. 'But also, moving forward. It's like, I've done her proud and I can kind of start thinking what *I* want a little bit more too.'

'Makes sense,' Chloe said, forking an enormous lettuce leaf into her mouth.

'And great you've got so many enquiries,' Amy said. 'It'll only get better once the TV show airs.'

'Unless they include the pigeon dropping incident,' said Nicky.

'Yes,' he grinned, 'unless I'm thwarted by pigeon poo.'

'Happens to the best of us.'

They silently contemplated their meal for a moment. It was

lunchtime, and the brasserie was buzzing with life; a low rumble of conversation almost drowned out the piped music played into the small courtyard. The air was cooler than usual and grey clouds on the far horizon confirmed the weather forecast – it was due to rain and thunder this afternoon. For now though, it was warm enough, bright enough to enjoy their lunch al fresco and they were making the most of it.

Rose gurgled in her pram and Amy automatically reached out an arm to rock her back and forth, before returning to her meal.

'Blimey,' said Chloe, 'you've got this motherhood thing nailed.'

'Ppfft,' her sister scoffed. 'You should see me at around midnight before you say that.'

After they'd finished their meal, Chloe and Amy went for a walk with the pram and Robert and Nicky were left to return to the B&B alone. Nicky found herself babbling on about the show, about the trip home, about her girls – anything to prevent him bringing up the other night again. Then, as they turned the corner of the street about half a kilometre from the B&B, the first drop of rain hit Nicky on the shoulder.

'Looks like it's starting,' she said, as bigger drops began to plop down sporadically, gaining momentum. There was a rumble of thunder, although she'd yet to see any lightning.

'Nearly home,' Robert said as they picked up their pace.

'I hope the girls are OK.'

'They'll be fine. There are plenty of shops to shelter in.'

'Look, when we get back,' Robert said, now jogging as the rain started to fall in earnest, 'I really do need to talk to you.'

They ran the last few metres with their heads down against the now driving rain, so she didn't see the woman sitting on the doorstep until she almost stumbled over her. A woman in black skinny jeans and a cap. With an enormous umbrella protecting her and an overnight bag resting by her feet. A woman who, when she looked up, Nicky recognised instantly.

'Jenny! What are you doing here?'

Her friend got up, smoothing her trousers down, and handed her the bunch of flowers she'd had next to her on the step. 'Well, that's a nice way to welcome your best friend,' she said, folding up her umbrella with an awkward smile.

Robert stood back and let the pair of them into the hall. Nicky reminded herself, as she took Jenny's coat and placed the flowers on the hall table, that she was angry with Jenny. It was hard to remember when she was so pleased to see her.

'Why are you here?' she asked, trying not to show how much she was feeling; a mixture of delight at seeing her friend and hurt remembering how she'd been set up to fail by the person she'd thought of as a best friend.

'I'm here,' Jenny said, turning towards her, eyes earnest, 'because I'm a bloody idiot.'

Nicky wondered suddenly whether this might be yet another TV curveball. There was a new task? There was another challenge? They'd have to do some sort of last-minute event as a final test? Part of her fizzed with excitement at the possibility. *I've enjoyed this*, she thought.

'I was so wrapped up in my own shit, my own career, that I didn't think about you. Or yours. Or,' she sighed, 'or how all of this would make you feel. I just saw a problem, thought of a solution and put it into place. As if you were... well, just a normal person. Not my best friend.'

'To be fair, it's not a great thing to do to a normal person either.'

'Touché. Although I do work in reality TV. Morals can't always get in the way of good footage,' Jenny said, raising an eyebrow.

'Yes, so I've realised.'

'Well, anyway. I thought about calling. Then I thought, you'll probably be sick of my calls. And I wanted you to know that I'm apologising properly. Not just because I have to, or because you're upset. But because I really, really mean it.'

Nicky looked at her friend, her earnest eyes, the rain dripping from her lower legs where the umbrella's protection had ended. She thought about Jenny – how she'd been there for her, making her laugh, holding her up, helping with the girls. And their argument, her lack of faith, seemed to pale into insignificance.

She finally allowed a smile to spread on her face. 'You know what,' she said. 'I think we're all allowed to slip up now and then.'

'I'm forgiven?' Jenny asked, hopefully.

'Just about,' Nicky said, slipping her arm through her friend's.

'I suppose it'll help when you find out that not only was I officially a crap friend, but I was also officially completely and utterly wrong,' Jenny added as she followed Nicky into the kitchen. The kettle had been recently boiled, but Robert was nowhere to be seen. Evidently, he was giving them room.

'Wrong?'

'Well, yeah. Obviously. You did a beautiful job. I've seen some early footage.'

'You say that,' Nicky said. 'But we really only pulled things together at the last minute. I mean... God. It was a close call at times!'

'No, *I* don't say it.'

'What?'

'Sorry, I'm not making any sense,' Jenny said, walking up to her and putting out a hand, touching her arm lightly. 'What I'm trying to say is, it's not just me saying that. Ryan and the team. You guys have been quite the hit!'

'We have?'

'Yes. They loved the concept, the sensible way you went about things. They also said that the spark between you and Robert on screen is evident. You did good, kid.'

'Oh!' She'd been so focused on getting over the line without embarrassing herself, she'd forgotten that she was in a competition at times. 'You mean better than... than,' she searched for a name of one of the more famous designers, 'Claude McVee?'

'To be honest,' said Jenny. 'That was a bit of a disaster, all told. Let's just say, leopard print, zebra stripes and some sort of naked sculpture were featured.'

'So great TV?' Nicky teased.

'Fabulous TV. And I'm sorry. You know, that I underestimated you. I just get so wrapped up in my own shit sometimes. I've been in this game too long, I reckon. I've forgotten the difference between making popular TV, creating memorable moments or scandals or disasters, and actually making good TV. TV that means something.'

'Oh, don't be too hard on yourself,' Nicky said, pouring water from the kettle into two mugs. 'You've done so well. I mean, I've watched you in awe, how you've managed to get where you are.'

'Thank you,' Jenny said, taking the tea from Nicky. 'And thanks for this too, obviously.' She raised her mug slightly. 'But I think this whole thing's been a wake-up call for me. You, calling me out like you did. Well, it got me thinking. And I'm not sure I'm in the right job.'

'Oh, don't say that!' Nicky said, setting her tea down on the table. 'Jenny, you are a brilliant producer, you have fabulous ideas. You won an award for that dog training series last year. You're nailing it.'

As if to prove she wasn't actually nailing it when it came to *all* dogs, Buster bounded in from the garden. He hovered at the kitchen door, sussing out the new person then, having decided Jenny had the right aura or smell or whatever it was he was using to measure her up, rushed to her side and put his paws in her lap, his tongue reaching for her cheek.

'Buster!' Nicky said sharply. 'Down!'

'Hmm,' said Jenny, rubbing Buster's head absent-mindedly as he dutifully set his paws back on the tiled floor. 'Looks like I might have a gig for you if they ask me to do a second series. That was text-book dog-trainer behaviour.'

Nicky laughed. 'He was trained long before I came here.'

'Anyway,' Jenny said, her hand still rubbing away at one of Buster's soft, black ears. 'Thank you. For saying all that. It's... well, it's nice to know you think of me that way. But I suppose what I mean was that I've been sucked into this reality TV production gig. And it's great and it pays well. And I know loads of people would give their right arm to be where I am.'

'Definitely.'

'But it's not where I wanted to be, you know, at this age.'

'I thought you were twenty-one!'

'Ha ha. Well, the mirror is telling me otherwise.' Jenny grinned.

'So,' prompted Nicky gently. 'What do you think you do want to do?'

'Still TV,' Jenny said. 'Only maybe something more meaningful. Covering, you know, proper topics.'

Nicky nodded. 'Sounds cool.'

'Well,' said Jenny, sipping from her tea. 'Whether I can truly reinvent myself is another matter.'

'Of course you can. Jenny, the longer I've known you the more I've realised you are pretty much capable of anything you set your mind to.'

'Including potentially screwing over my best friend you mean?'

'Well, yes... But imagine if you took all those persuasive and... well... sneaky powers and used them for good? You'll be producing serious documentaries in no time!'

'Thank you,' Jenny said, as Nicky slipped into the chair opposite.

'You're great at what you do.' Nicky shrugged.

'Manipulating people.'

'Well, yes. But making great TV was what I really meant.'

'Thanks.'

'No need to thank me. It's true.'

'No, I mean... what I'm really saying is thanks for... well, all the rest of it. For forgiving me for being an arse. For being there for me despite my... well, little ways. You're a good friend you know.'

'Thank you. And you too. I mean, apart from the "setting me up to fail" bit... although that's worked out OK,' Nicky said. 'Thank you for being there. I've... getting a bit of distance, a bit of perspective from it all, has been good for me. I've been thinking about the last decade, since Steve... And I wouldn't have got through it without you. Meeting me, talking to me, always there to support me.'

'Is that how you see it?' Jenny asked.

'Yes! I mean who else would take time out of their busy schedule to meet me in a café week in, week, out? To cheer me up with anecdotes about Jacob's toilet habits. To force me to eat chocolate fudge cake on a regular basis. You've supported me from the word go and I really am grateful.' Nicky smiled.

Jenny shook her head. 'You daft cow,' she said.

'What?'

'Yes, I guess I have tried to support you when I can over the years. But if you think all the meet-ups and the phone calls and the coffees and all of it. If you think that was me supporting you, then you've got it all wrong.'

'What do you mean?'

'Nicky, you've been my rock for all those years too. Without you, I'd be a quivering mess. Well...' Jenny corrected. 'Even more of a quivering mess than I am already.'

'Oh!'

'Yep. It wasn't just me helping you. A lot of it was because I needed you. Not the other way around.'

'Well, we needed each other,' Nicky said.

'Darling,' Jenny said. 'You are the wind beneath my frickin' wings.'

As they began to sing the Bette Midler classic in exaggerated, quivering voices, Robert stepped into the room. He took one look at the pair of them, and stepped out again.

After which, they descended into the kind of giggles that are always best enjoyed with a friend.

30

'Are you sure you ladies wouldn't rather go out by yourselves?' Robert said doubtfully two days later, after Jenny had told him her plan for that evening.

They'd spent her first day relaxing in the garden and most of yesterday wandering the streets of Roussillon shopping for souvenirs and saying hello to strangers some of whom even in this short time, had started to feel familiar. Now, on the penultimate day they were sitting in the garden sipping orange juice when Jenny had announced that she was taking them out for what she termed a 'slap-up meal to end all slap-up meals'.

'Nope. You're coming and that's final,' she said. 'I've already booked the table – there's a little restaurant out of town – La Cave – do you know it?'

'What, the Michelin starred one?' Robert asked, his eyes widening. 'You managed to book that at short notice?'

Jenny gave them a wink. 'It's amazing what you can get when you have a few strings to pull,' she said.

'Isn't it a bit pricey?' Robert asked.

Jenny shook her head. 'It's not on me, in any case,' she said, 'before you say anything, I've got the company credit card. And after they slashed your budget and messed you around, the least they can do is shout you a plate of escargots and a glass of Pinot Grigio.'

Amy and Chloe opted out of the evening. 'I'm knackered,' Chloe admitted, 'and it's back to 100 miles an hour tomorrow. Plus it'll be nice to spend a bit more time with Rose.'

'And your lovely sister of course?!' Amy prompted.

'Well, that goes without saying.'

Nicky had been surprised that they hadn't taken up the offer of a fancy meal, especially one that was on expenses; and even more surprised when Jenny didn't put up a fight as she had with Robert. But they all seemed happy so she left them to it. Perhaps the last thing the girls fancied was spending time with three mid-lifers talking property shows and business advice, however good the food might be. And despite Jenny's claims about company credit cards, perhaps she'd be glad not to completely max it out.

'When did you book all this anyway?' Nicky said later, as she checked her hair in the mirror. At Jenny's insistence, she'd got a little more glammed up than she might ordinarily have for a meal with friends.

'It's a posh restaurant, darling,' her friend had said. 'We might as well make the most of it.'

'Oh, a few days ago,' Jenny admitted.

'So you were pretty sure you'd be forgiven?' Nicky said, an eyebrow arched.

'Not at all,' Jenny admitted. 'If you'd blown me off, I'd have offered the booking for you and the girls, or you and Robert and slunk home on a budget airline.'

'OK,' Nicky said, still not convinced. Something about Jenny's manner, the odd furtive look, seemed off. As if something was on her friend's mind. But perhaps it was just the strangeness of having so many people from her life at home here in France with her – the two lives colliding – that made her feel disorientated.

Robert appeared. After having been given his own set of fashion hints from Jenny, he'd opted for a pair of his new smart navy trousers and a short-sleeved white shirt. He'd made some attempt to style his hair with gel; the product had made his tresses brilliantly shiny.

'Ready?' Jenny asked them both, and, as if on cue, a taxi pulled up outside. It was a black car and looked sleek and expensive, its back windows darkened to protect the identity of the passengers.

'See you decided against booking Jean-Paul at the local taxi firm,' Robert quipped. 'Slightly upgraded transport from his ancient Citroen.'

'Well,' said Jenny, 'I like to shop local when I can. But didn't fancy a near-death experience on the back roads.'

The driver – a rotund man in a white shirt and black trousers – got out and opened the door and they climbed into the car, noting the plush leather, the spotless interior. 'Maybe I should get annoyed with you more often,' Nicky said, 'if this is the result.'

Jenny grinned. 'Much as I love you, my darling, this is a once in a lifetime. Or at least once a decade, experience.'

The word decade somehow pierced through Nicky's good mood – thinking back ten years always did. She wondered what Steve would have made of the new direction her life was going in. It was hard to imagine him as he might have been now, in his forties – a man in midlife rather than the younger man he'd been when his car had veered off the road. Stepping outside her bubble had brought back to her how much time had passed.

She looked out of the window and watched the familiar shops and cafés fall away as they turned out of Roussillon and made their way along an unfamiliar road. It was eight o'clock but the sun was still shining. They continued along narrow roads, trees with sun-yellowed leaves creating a tunnel for the black car to drive through, then suddenly they noticed a stone wall, to the left of the car, which ran several hundred metres alongside the road. As they turned a corner, above it, they could just see the turret of a chateau.

'Nearly there,' Jenny said, squeezing Nicky's hand. 'Are you excited?'

'This isn't La Cave,' Robert said, noticing the sign for the chateau.

'Sorry, darling. But it's a change of plan,' Jenny said. 'Can't give it all away at once, or where would the surprise be?'

'Is this even a restaurant though?' Nicky asked as the taxi began bumping up the slightly uneven drive towards a gravelled forecourt. The chateau was small by castle standards, and clearly recently renovated. The pointing between the slightly reddish stone was bright and clean, and everything looked solid and well cared for.

'It's sort of an events venue,' Jenny said. 'But let's just say I called in a favour or two.'

A man in a smart suit came and opened the car door and Jenny stepped out followed by a rather bemused Robert and Nicky. They were led into a stone hallway, with an enormous staircase peeling off to their right.

She wanted to say that to be honest, a bit of pizza or a burger would have done, but didn't want to upset Jenny who'd obviously gone to a lot of trouble. Something about the chateau made her feel nervous and she was glad that her friend had persuaded her to put on her best dress for the evening – at least she wasn't visiting a castle in a pair of jeans.

Finally, they were shown to a dining room with four, linen adorned tables set out in its spacious interior. The ceiling was white and moulded and hung with four enormous chandeliers. All but one of the tables was full and Jenny led them confidently to it.

Nicky looked around. It felt more like a family wedding than a restaurant. The people at the tables chatted companionably and sipped at wine and champagne. A couple of the other guests looked over at her and exchanged glances. 'Jenny,' she said, when the feeling of strangeness became too much. 'What exactly is going on?'

'I've no idea what you mean?' Jenny said, with an odd little smile which could indicate that she was confused by the question, or – more likely – she was hiding something.

Robert met Nicky's eye briefly as they sat at the table and helped themselves to bread from an enormous basket at its centre.

Nicky tried to relax. It was all so beautiful and decadent; she'd make the best of a quiet evening with her two friends. She bit into a piece of bread, the crust cracking under her teeth, the soft interior fresh and floury against the roof of her mouth.

And then it happened. The double doors burst open once more and suddenly two cameramen rushed up towards her and Robert, with Ryan at the helm. 'Good evening, you lovely pair,' he said, his teeth shining almost fluorescently in the yellow light. 'Surprise!'

What was he doing here? Nicky looked at Jenny who simply smiled, nodded and gave her a little wink but revealed absolutely nothing. She tried to chew the bread as quickly as possible, her mouth moving rapidly. It remained gluey and doughy and reso-lutely enormous in her mouth.

'Sorry to interrupt your evening,' Ryan said. 'But a little birdie told me you were flying home tomorrow. And we couldn't let you go without a proper goodbye!'

'Hom,' Nicky began, the doughy mound in her mouth restricting her tongue.

'Do you mind popping over here so we can talk properly?' He expertly guided Nicky and Robert towards the far wall, where there was enough space to talk to them properly, the cameras still rolling.

'So, four weeks ago you two hadn't met. Robert was running a disaster of a B&B – all grumpy welcomes and faded wallpaper,' Ryan began.

Nicky, finally able to swallow, felt the lump of bread make itself craggily down her throat.

'I...' Robert started to object, but realised he wasn't going to win this one.

'And then designer and business guru extraordinaire, Nicky Green, swooped in and transformed your B&B into a place even *I* might consider staying at,' continued Ryan, smiling wildly and winking elaborately at the camera.

'But that's not all,' he continued. 'We have a very special guest with us tonight, ladies and gentlemen.'

The cameramen moved slightly to let a man step forward. He was wearing leather trousers and a leopard print shirt, one pointed shoe and an enormous plastic hospital boot. 'Is that...?' Robert asked.

'Yes,' Nicky said. 'Yes, I think it is.'

'It's Haaamisssshhhh Clark-Robertson!' Ryan cried, almost unable to contain himself.

'Hi guys.' Hamish smiled, reaching out a hand for a shake with each of them.

Nicky, shakily, reached out and shook Hamish's soft, well-manicured hand. Her own, she realised, was probably a little worse for wear from the work they'd been doing. She hoped the cameras didn't zoom in and hand-shame her (if that was even a thing).

'Hamish here was part of the team who judged the final business transformation. And I'm pleased to tell you that... you have officially won!' Ryan said.

'We've... what?' Nicky asked, feeling a bit faint.

'You've won!' Ryan said, suddenly producing a bouquet of enormous flowers seemingly from nowhere and thrusting them at her. 'You are this year's *The Great B&B Rescue* winners. How do you feel?'

'Um... um... I mean, brilliant. I think,' Nicky stumbled into the mic, feeling a little as if she might throw up.

'And you, Robert. How does it feel to have your business transformed, for Marie's wishes to have finally been fulfilled?' Ryan said, grinning.

'Well, I mean it's great,' said Robert, rather uncertainly. 'Although, obviously I wish that Marie was here to see it. She would be...' He was overcome briefly with emotion. 'She'd be thrilled. And she'd have loved everything we've done,' he said. 'And, you know, I love it. I love it too. The whole experience has been eye-opening.'

'Nice one, mate,' Ryan said, patting him on the shoulder.

In the background, Jenny was grinning and nodding and clapping along. Nicky shot her a 'YOU COULD HAVE WARNED ME' look which she hoped wasn't caught by the camera.

Once they'd answered a few more questions, the crew relaxed and joined them at the table. Waiters brought out bowls of thin soup and some more bread and they could finally relax. Nicky, sitting next to Tom, felt slightly awkward on top of the strange sense of surrealness that she'd already developed since arriving. It was a heady mix and it took several glasses of champagne to shift.

Ryan, who seemed to have forgotten about his soup altogether, was getting through wine at an alarming rate. 'Can't knock the French,' he said. 'Champers for starters. I love it.'

'There's soup, too,' Jenny pointed out.

'And you guys,' Ryan said, clearly feeling at one with the world. 'You must be so chuffed with it all.'

'Well, just kind of getting my head around it,' Robert admitted. 'I mean, I knew Nicky had done a good job. But this sort of thing... winning, I guess. It doesn't happen to blokes like me. Not usually.'

'Me too,' said Nicky. 'Not that I'm a bloke but...'

'Well, get used to it,' Ryan said to her with a wink. 'Looks like we're going to need you in series two.'

'Ryan!' Jenny hissed. 'I was going to be the one to tell her that.'

Nicky took a deep gulp of champagne and tried to smile. Winning the competition, the surprise filming, the chateau, bubbles and now a potential new career. She'd been thinking of today as the end of something, when actually it seemed it was only the beginning.

She looked at the people who'd been part of this adventure for the past few weeks. Tom, who smiled and nodded at her and hadn't made her feel awkward at all after their slightly stilted date. Ryan, who seemed over the top on TV, but was actually really personable and approachable once the cameras stopped rolling. Fern, who was efficient and focused, but always had time for questions and support. Jenny, who'd made the whole thing happen – perhaps with a different outcome in mind – but who'd been there for her for years to boost her confidence and make her laugh. And then there was Robert – who'd seemed a bit awkward at first, but who'd thawed over their time together and had emerged as a sweet man, a man who understood how she felt in a way nobody else fully could. Maybe he didn't find her attractive; didn't want anything more. But she was sure they'd remain firm friends.

She found herself grinning. If someone had told her a month ago she'd be in this situation she'd think they were having a nervous breakdown. Yet here she was. No longer stuck. No longer in a rut. No longer needed in the same way. And somehow released from a prison of her own making.

Opposite, Hamish Clark-Robertson leaned in and asked her, 'I have to say,' he said. 'I love this whole conscious recluttering theory. You'll have to tell me all about it.'

31

Nicky folded the dress carefully, tucked it into her suitcase and reached for the next, carefully draping it over her arm and laying it on the bed before creating a small square from the bright material and slipping it onto the bulging pile of clothes she was determined to take home. Remembering her packing struggles last time, she'd invested in an additional suitcase, and although this had meant paying a fortune for extra luggage allowance, she figured it was worth it.

It felt odd to be packing. The B&B, for all its pigeon-catastrophes and DIY mishaps, had become her home over the past month. Part of her was looking forward to walking back into her house, getting back to some sort of normality. But another was yearning to make the experience of being here last a little longer.

She was going to have to get used to moving around, she supposed, if this offer of a series two spot did come to something. Jenny wasn't going to be working on the next series – but it was looking like her place in the line-up was secure, no matter what.

She thought about the little business advice office that she'd worked in for the last decade – the people who'd become to feel almost like family. The desk that had become a home from home. She'd miss that, too, she realised. Perhaps every time your life changed significantly you left a little of your heart behind.

But perhaps it didn't matter. Perhaps the more places and people you loved, the more love there was to go around. You didn't leave part of yourself that you needed. You stepped into a new version of yourself. Like Jenny had said, you didn't move your affections from one thing to another – love was infinite.

She glanced out of the window at the sky, a cloudless blue and the view that stretched forward across the town wall and over fields and copses and houses and little roads to the horizon. Back home in St Albans, the weather was 22 degrees and cloudy. Not too bad for this time of year. But hardly Roussillon standards.

She would no doubt be back, as she'd promised Michelle. Perhaps for a holiday in the spring. Or maybe before. But she wondered whether any visit would capture the magic of this one. This had been far more than a holiday; far more than a job. It had been an experience that had changed her world both inside and out. Had woken her up.

She finished folding the last of her dresses and began to push down on the suitcase lid, hoping to get the zip closed. She'd gone to town a little in Michelle's shop, buying new clothes, reinventing herself. But as Chloe had said herself, it had been 'about time'. 'You've got an image to keep up now, Mum,' she'd said when they'd visited the shop the other day.

Nicky had snorted. 'Hardly!' she'd said.

'Well, even if you don't,' Chloe had said, 'what does it matter? Wear what makes you happy. I think you've earned it.' And she'd wrapped an arm around her mum. 'After all, you must have a bit more spare cash now Amy and I aren't eating you out of house and home. Plus you're on a TV star's salary now.'

'Hardly millions though.'

'Still a pretty good chunk of change though.'

Nicky lifted the two cases from the bed to the floor, testing their weight, and realising that if she didn't want to clatter down the stairs and break an arm, she probably ought to ask for some help to get them to ground level. After that, they could be wheeled so she'd be OK.

Almost as if she'd conjured it, there was a knock on the bedroom door.

'Come in,' she said, knowing it would be Robert on the other side. He opened the door and smiled at her.

'Seems odd to see you leaving,' he said. 'Got used to having you around the place.'

She smiled. 'I've got used to being here.'

'Look,' he began. 'I never managed to...' Before he could continue, Buster lolloped in and looked at them both, his head on one side, left ear cocked.

'Oh Buster,' Nicky said, stepping forward and giving his head a rub. 'I've got used to you too.'

Robert reached for her case. 'Do you need a hand with that?'

'Do you mind?' she said. 'I hate to ask for help.'

'Yes,' he said. 'I've noticed.'

She smiled. 'Well, seeing as I've more or less maxed out my credit card in Michelle's shop over the last week, I think I'd better accept. Thank you!'

'Time for a drink?' he said. 'It's two o'clock – taxi's booked for four, right?'

'Yes,' she said, looking at her watch. The girls and Jenny had gone for one last wander around, but she'd opted to stay back, be the one to print out their boarding passes and make sure everything was in order. They had time.

This morning, she'd been to see Michelle. She'd told her about the win, said her goodbyes and been surprised to see her new friend tear up a little as she spoke. 'Are you OK?' she'd asked, feeling reciprocal tears in her own eyes.

'Yes, fine,' Michelle had said. 'It's just... It's just quite rare, isn't it, to find someone that you really click with. I'll miss you.'

'I'll miss you too,' Nicky had said, realising it was true. 'But look, I'll be back. I'm sure.'

'You think?'

'Yes, and you know I might even stay at the B&B if Robert's got any room!' She had grinned.

'I bet you will,' Michelle had said, with a wink.

'What?'

'Well, you could do worse than our Rob,' she said. 'You two have really hit it off, haven't you?'

Nicky had smiled. 'Why does everyone keep saying that?' she'd protested. 'We're friends, is all. Good friends.'

'If you say so.'

She wondered if Robert had said anything, or whether Michelle was just speculating. It was hard to know. And after so long away from the dating scene, she had no idea how to read the signs any more. Once or twice she'd sensed he was going to say something about the kiss, but in the end neither of them had brought it up; besides, he'd made it clear then by backing away that he simply wasn't into her.

What would she have done if he'd reciprocated, she wondered. Would it have been a one-time thing? Or something more? There was definitely a something there, at least on her side. A connection. Not only because of their mutual bereavement, but in their humour, their conversation, the fact they could be silent around each other and still comfortable.

But he either wasn't interested or wasn't ready. There wasn't a happy ending to this particular story.

Anyway, maybe she'd had enough endings in her life, she'd

decided – happy or otherwise. The accident, changing her job, the fact that everything around her had seemed to be evolving recently with the girls and even her friendship with Jenny. Those endings had made way for new beginnings, and she should be grateful rather than always looking for more.

Over the weeks, she'd come to know herself differently, to see her position in the world differently, her life and her future differently. And here she was now, halfway down the second set of stairs, but metaphorically on the cusp of something brand new. Not an ending at all.

In the kitchen, Robert pulled the cork from a bottle and filled half a glass for them each. They sat down at the table, a table that had become so familiar to her over the past few weeks.

'Well,' he said, 'here's to an amazing experience.'

'Cheers to that,' she said. 'And thank you, for everything.'

'Thank me? Thank *you!*' he insisted.

'Thank *us*,' she said and they lifted their glasses and clinked them together.

'You know,' he said. 'Before you came, I wasn't sure if I'd done the right thing applying for the programme. I thought I might have bitten off more than I could chew.'

'I know the feeling,' she joked.

'But seriously,' he said. 'I was hardly the ideal B&B host, was I? And then that footage, saying I was rude...'

'Just ignore it,' she said. 'People get the wrong impression all the time.'

'That's just it,' he said. 'I think I *was* rude. Or I came across that way. I mean, I held myself back – even with you when you first came...'

She grinned. 'I did wonder whether you actually wanted me here,' she admitted. 'But I've got to know you now. And you know what? You're almost likeable.'

He laughed. 'Compliments indeed! But seriously,' he continued. 'It was almost like a last-ditch attempt to get things sorted here, before I gave up entirely. I was kind of... lost, I guess. I didn't know what to do first. I was kind of lonely, I suppose I almost resented guests when they came because I'd got used to my own company. I stopped knowing how to react to people... you know?'

She nodded. 'I get that, completely.'

'Anyway, so the whole experience. I suppose it unlocked part of me.'

'The new, dynamic B&B host?' she said.

'Well, maybe not quite. But you know. Someone who is looking outward again; looking forward.'

She sipped her wine. 'That,' she said, 'I can completely relate to.'

There was a silence that might have become awkward, but it was broken by the front door opening loudly and banging against the wall. 'Sorry!' Jenny called. 'Don't know my own strength.'

Amy rushed in and began to put powdered milk into one of the bottles she'd sterilised that morning. 'Rose is just about to wake up,' she said. 'She'll be starving when she does. We lost track of time.'

'We've got a good hour before the taxi, don't worry.'

'Good.' Amy gently stirred the milk then put the bottle into a bowl of boiled water to warm. 'Don't let me forget this, whatever you do,' she said to them.

Chloe and Jenny entered, placing a large bag of meringues on the table between them.

'Jenny!' Nicky said. 'Didn't we decide yesterday that we're going to eat healthily from now on?'

'No,' her friend said. 'We said we'd be good once we got home. This is our last supper.'

'Go on then,' Nicky said, reaching for the bag. 'If you insist.'

What seemed like minutes later, they were standing outside the

B&B, brushing off meringue dust, as a taxi driver loaded bags into the people carrier they'd booked.

Nicky looked up at the B&B, the three-storey building with its red stone and white, shuttered windows. When she'd arrived she'd no idea how much this building would come to mean to her. And she'd definitely miss it, she thought.

'Bye then,' she said to Robert, feeling a little shy but forcing herself to lean in for a hug. He wrapped his arms around her and gave her a tight squeeze, his arms steady and strong behind her back. She felt a shiver run through her; a feeling of recognition. Like she'd known him for much longer than a month. She returned his hug, then he nodded and stepped away before saying goodbye to Jenny and the girls.

Nicky slipped into the back seat of the car and moved over to allow room for the others to clamber into the other seats. She clipped on her seatbelt feeling a little bit teary.

'Been good to meet you, Robert!' Jenny called. 'Congrats again on the win. Will let you know when it's going to air as soon as we're scheduled.'

'Yes, bye Robert!' Chloe called.

'And Buster!' said Amy, almost indignantly.

'Oh yes, of course. And Buster.'

Hearing his name, the dog lunged forward, with Robert grabbing his collar just in time. 'Not this time, boy,' he said. 'I'm afraid you've got to stay here with me.'

'Sorry,' said Chloe. 'I've activated the hound.'

'Bye,' Nicky called softly. Robert looked in and caught her eye, holding it for a couple of seconds.

'Or au revoir,' he said. 'If that's not too cheesy. Until we meet again.'

'It is quite cheesy,' she said. 'But then again, we are in France.' They smiled at each other, despite the terrible pun.

'Anyway, in the words of the Terminator, we will be back,' Jenny said. 'Although we'd better get a discount on this place if we do.'

'For you lot?' Robert said. 'I reckon I could knock off... ooh, 5 per cent?'

They laughed and Chloe pulled the door closed. As the taxi turned and began to make its way down the slope away from Roussillon, Nicky looked out of the window at the views flashing by. She felt sick in the pit of her stomach, possibly because of the imminent flight, or the meringue and wine combination. But possibly, too, because part of her wasn't yet ready to leave.

32

'This is so frickin' exciting!' Chloe said, patting Nicky's knee enthusiastically.

'Chloe!'

'What? Frickin' isn't even a swear word.'

'No, I mean, that actually hurts.'

'Oh, sorry.' Chloe withdrew her hand and gave a sheepish grin. 'I'm just so excited.'

November had come around and the series had started. They'd sat through two episodes of *The Great B&B Rescue* so far over the past two weeks, but this was 'her' night. Jenny had put on a spread and invited them all to enjoy the programme in her living room, champagne and all. They had all come along for the occasion – even Ryan, in a pair of drainpipe jeans so skinny it looked like his legs might snap at any moment; Fern looking more relaxed than usual in casual trousers and a hoodie, her hair loose; Tom had joined them, sporting his usual jeans and band T-shirt combo and Mo had come along too, for once not wielding a make-up brush in Nicky's direction.

Jenny's living room was large, but with eight of them there, or nine if you included Rose, dozing for now in her pushchair, it felt a little on the cramped side. Luckily she had an enormous TV over the fireplace so they would all enjoy an uninterrupted view of the programme.

'Are you excited?' Jenny asked now, filling up Nicky's empty flute.

'Excited is one word for it,' said Nicky. Watching herself on TV, especially an enormous ultra HD TV, would be the equivalent of looking at herself in the mirror for an hour. And while she was feeling more confident about herself these days, she wasn't sure whether she was ready to cope with the 'reality' of herself writ large on the screen. 'Bricking it fits too.'

'Ah, don't be daft,' Ryan said. 'Look, I'll let you into a secret – I've already seen a lot of the footage and trust me, darling, you are fab-u-luuus!'

She smiled. She'd grown used to Ryan and his over-the-top enthusiasm. It was exhausting, but also a little bit infectious. Yesterday, when she'd signed the contract for the second series – after a train journey to London – he'd taken her and a few others to lunch at The Ivy and had had them in stitches for most of the meal.

Last week, she'd finally said goodbye to Business Friends after working her notice; enjoying a celebratory drink in the pub after work and hugging the people she'd shared her working life with for a decade goodbye. Despite being ready to leave, it was always a pull walking away from the familiar. She'd even shed a little tear when she'd got home, and resolved to pop in to visit everyone again as she'd promised.

That was the problem with starting over. It meant a series of endings as well.

The room fell silent as the continuity announcer began. 'Now on Channel 8, we journey to the south of France for the latest edition of *The Great B&B Rescue*. Robert's B&B is failing, but can

Design and Business Guru, Nicky Green, help to change his fortunes?'

'There you go!' Jenny said. 'Design and Business Guru. Write that on your CV!'

The theme tune, which had become familiar to Nicky over the past couple of weeks started, flooding her with anticipatory anxiety. The last two makeovers they'd watched had been of a chalet near the Pyrenees, and a small hotel in Nice. Both 'business advisors' had seemed so professional, slick and impressive. She was finding it hard to believe that she'd genuinely won. She wondered whether she, too, would come across as 'slick' to viewers.

It didn't seem likely.

'Oh slick, schrick,' Jenny had said when she'd mentioned it earlier. 'Anyone can fake that for the cameras. You have something they could never have. Genuine talent and... you know, you're *real*. Relatable.'

The credits faded and the programme opened with an aerial shot of Roussillon. Nicky's stomach clenched.

Clips from moments in the show were shown on the screen. Ryan entering a room and gasping. A visitor holding a hair. Nicky mid-sentence saying, 'It's been a case of bringing it back to life.' And a clip of Robert, his face earnest saying, 'She's amazing. She hasn't just changed my business; she's changed my life.'

Nicky felt her heart lurch at his words. She recognised the outfit, his expression; it was the interview he'd done after the revellers had been sent home, when punch had loosened his tongue. Suddenly she felt desperate to hear the whole thing. What else had he said? She leaned forward as the programme began in earnest.

Then, as often happens at the most inconvenient times, the doorbell rang.

'Oh bloody hell,' Fern said. 'Tell them to bugger off.'

'Just leave it!' Jenny said. 'It'll only be leaflet droppers or something.'

But Chloe, seemingly unable to ignore the bell, got up and slipped out of the room.

On the TV, Robert was being interviewed. Talking about his back story – how he'd come to live in Roussillon, his original plans and how they were thwarted. The camera zoomed in to pick up a bit of moisture in his eye as he talked about Marie. 'Someone once said that you never lose grief. Grief never gets any less. You just learn to grow around it. To hold the grief and love you had for one person in your heart, but grow more capacity to love new people, to love yourself again. To embrace something new without feeling as if you'd betrayed someone from your past.'

Nicky felt a tear well in her eye, recognising the truth in his words. But it was more than that, she realised. She missed him. Viscerally.

Over the three months since she'd come home, she'd kept in touch via email – even the odd FaceTime. But seeing him on the TV made her feel desperately sad that he wasn't here in real life. Should she have tried harder to talk to him?

Then, there *she* was, grinning on screen, looking both nothing like herself and exactly like herself at the same time. And she was talking about her plans for the business. She sounded... professional, like someone who had everything together. Almost an Alex Polizzi in the making. Where had all that come from?

The crew were chatting a little about this and that, pointing out angles and nodding along as she was seen touring the B&B, inspecting little patches of dirt or mould, looking into plugholes. *I actually look* she thought *as if I pored over everything with a fine-tooth comb* when in reality she'd simply done as she was told – the shots of her close inspection, her apparent disgust at finding crumbs on the dining room floor, had all been shots taken as directed by Fern.

They certainly made her look thorough, but also a bit on the critical side. She hoped Robert, watching back in Roussillon, would know that she hadn't been as horrified by his housekeeping as she'd appeared to be.

The crew and even Ryan fell into silence, presumably taken in by the spectacle of her on her hands and knees looking at a floorboard, then rising up to check the windowsill for cobwebs.

'God, he's going to hate me,' she said, as the camera zoomed in on her finger, which was covered in dust after being run along a radiator.

'Oh, he could never do that,' a voice said.

A familiar voice.

She whipped her head around, mouth open, and there, standing in Jenny's living room with a smiling Chloe at his side, was Robert, wrapped up in a huge coat – worlds away from the T-shirt and shorts she was accustomed to seeing him in – and smiling broadly.

Robert was here. In England.

'Robert!' she said, her heart leaping with a combination of shock and pleasure. 'What are you doing here?'

'Well,' he said, taking off his coat and hanging it over the arm of the sofa then stepping forward to sit next to her as Chloe pointed out her vacant space, 'clearly I'm here to ruin your viewing! Sorry I'm late, I wanted to get here earlier. But traffic. I'm not used to allowing the time for hold-ups.'

'But... here in the UK?' she reiterated, her focus completely taken from the TV.

'Well,' he said, glancing up and making eye contact with Jenny for a second. 'I got in touch with Jenny last week and she invited me to join you all. I hope that's OK?'

'In England?'

'Well, yes.'

'But...'

'I'll be honest,' he said, holding her gaze for a minute. 'I'd been meaning to come over for a while.'

She opened her mouth, TV forgotten. 'You have?'

Jenny reached for the remote and pressed pause. The hotel guests froze on the screen, their faces wrinkled with distaste.

All eyes were now on the live show happening in the living room.

'Yes,' he said. 'But I wasn't sure, after everything, whether I'd blown it?'

'Blown it?'

'Because you know,' he said. 'I never did get to tell you what I wanted to say. And... Well, I realised when the series started, seeing everyone on the programme taking risks. That I was fed up of being afraid.'

'Oh,' she said, feeling an understanding pass between them.

She wanted to ask him how long he was staying. Where he was staying. Whether he had time to see her again while he was here. She wanted to catch up properly with him – know what he'd been up to for the past three months while she'd been busy working her notice and signing contracts and looking forward with trepidation and excitement to a new sort of future.

Had he, like her, experienced more of a shift? Found that his grief had become a bit easier to bear now that his life had moved on? She wondered whether finishing the B&B had helped him to focus more on the future, just as her new role had helped her?

And more than anything, she wondered what he meant by being afraid, and what exactly it was he'd come to say.

'Come on,' said Ryan. 'Be quiet, mate. I want to see this thing live, if I can!'

Jenny pressed play and people's attention returned to the screen.

Sitting next to Robert, her senses on high alert, Nicky looked around the room and took in anew the people she was with. Some she'd loved from the day they were born, others she'd come to love over the years. But the new friends as well – the recent friends – she loved them too, she realised. Not to the same depth; not in the same way. But her life was richer for having these new people in it.

She felt Robert's fingers graze her own, and suddenly, subtly they were holding hands. And she felt a surge of unfamiliar hope.

It was like Jenny had said: you didn't have to put a limit on love, be scared of feeling affection or attraction or warmth towards new people. There was always more capacity to connect and develop feelings for people. Whether it was love for family, friends – old and new – or the more romantic, all-consuming type of love.

She looked at Robert, his face preoccupied now by the television. He was a wonderful man. And someone who, in a short time, she'd become close to.

And she realised she knew what she wanted. And that, like him, she was no longer afraid.

She looked at Jenny and caught her friend's eye. Jenny gave her a wink. And she thought again of her friend's words all those weeks ago. 'You'll still have all of that love for Steve; you'll just find more. You can have more.'

'Darling, it's infinite.'

33

Robert drained the last of his coffee and stood up as the words on the departure screen changed to 'boarding'. 'I really do have to go,' he said, sadly.

Nicky stood and picked up her handbag. 'I know,' she said. 'I wish you didn't.'

'That's what happens when you run a successful B&B, I suppose,' he said with a grin. 'No more extended holidays. Even in November.'

She smiled. 'I've created a monster,' she said.

'I'll miss you,' he said, then, simply, standing forward and wrapping his arms around her tightly. 'It's been...'

'I know,' she said.

'And I wish.'

'I know,' she said, squeezing him tightly before letting go and stepping back.

It had been ten days since the programme aired. Ten days spent showing Robert the sights and sounds of her own hometown. Admittedly, not quite as picturesque as his, but with its own quirks and charms and beautiful views. But his email inbox had been full of enquiries since and the B&B was fully booked from next week until well into the new year.

Tomorrow she had a meeting in London with Lou, Jenny's replacement on *The Great B&B Rescue* and would be talking through details and timings and dates. She was nervous, but as Jenny had said, 'At least this time you'll have time to plan properly.' This time she wouldn't be thrown in at the deep end. She wasn't yet fully confident, but she could definitely keep herself afloat.

'This is harder than I'd thought,' he said, walking towards the queue for passport control. 'I could cancel them, the bookings, I mean.'

'Don't be silly,' she said firmly. 'This is your livelihood. It's important.'

'I know.'

'Plus it's going to rain here for the next week. At least Roussillon will be dry – milder too.' She tried to smile, but felt her lips wobble slightly.

'Good point.'

'And Buster's probably driving Victor mad by now.'

'I think that's a given,' he said, reluctantly stepping a little further from her as the queue moved.

'Time to go home,' she said, thinking how sad she'd felt when she herself had had to go home, to watch Roussillon grow smaller in the back window of the taxi until it and her hopes had disappeared.

She looked at this man who over a short period of time had come to mean so much to her. He returned her gaze, his expression soft, a little sad.

Suddenly she found herself walking forward, apologising to the few people who'd joined the queue after Robert. 'I'm not pushing in, promise,' she said as one man gave her a stare.

Robert laughed as she walked towards him. 'I don't think they'll let you fly without a ticket or passport,' he said.

'Oh, I know that,' she said. 'I just wanted to give you this.'

And she stood on tiptoes and pulled him to her, pressing her lips to his for one last kiss to add to the hundreds they'd shared over the past ten days. She felt him respond, pulling her in closely to him.

And something deep inside her relaxed. They weren't going home. They were already there. Home wasn't England any more. And it wasn't France. It was him. He was her home.

Someone coughed behind them and she realised the queue had moved on and a large gap had formed between Robert and the next person. 'Sorry,' she said, breaking away and trying to avoid the disapproving gaze of the impatient man behind.

'Don't you rush, love,' a woman said. 'You say your goodbye properly.'

She walked back to the end of the queue and looked back at Robert, whose eyes were still fixed on hers as he stepped forward to reclaim his place in the queue. He was nearly at passport control now. After that, he'd be swallowed up into the interior of the airport and disappear altogether.

'Bye,' he mouthed at her, smiling.

'See you,' she said. 'See you soon!'

After all, it would only be a few days before she saw him again. Back home, her bags were packed and once the meeting was out of the way, she'd be boarding a plane too, travelling to Roussillon, back to a future that was uncertain, but exciting.

Two nights ago, she and Robert had snuggled together on her sofa, watching the next episode of *The Great B&B Rescue* and marvelling at the mishaps they now knew were most likely staged or at least stage-managed. And they'd talked about their future, and what might happen next.

'Thank you,' she'd said.

'For what?'

'For coming over and well, rescuing me,' she'd said.

And he'd laughed.

'What?'

'I think it was more the other way around,' he'd said. 'You rescuing me.'

'Well maybe we rescued each other,' she had said.

It was strange, she thought. She'd gone to France to rescue a business, but in the end, she'd been rescued herself. Rescued from the rut she'd got herself into. Rescued by the change in her life, by being forced out of her comfort zone. Rescued by Jenny – whatever her motivation. Rescued by her daughters, who'd shown her how capable they were and gently helped her to let go a little. Rescued by Robert who'd flown over to tell her he'd made a mistake when he'd pulled back before. Who'd asked her to give him another chance. And she'd rescued herself, too, she realised – because she'd finally given herself permission to move on.

Steve would always be part of her life, just as Marie would be part of Robert's. But for the first time in years she could look back with fondness, but forward with a smile.

ACKNOWLEDGMENTS

Thanks to all the people who have supported me throughout my writing journey. My husband, Ray, who is patience itself and never afraid to point out an error in a manuscript (despite the inevitable fallout). Thanks to my children for understanding when I disappear to my office rather than play Snakes and Ladders (it's almost always for a legitimate reason, I promise).

Thanks to my wonderful new editor, Isobel Akenhead, for her insight and support. And to all at Team Boldwood, my fabulous publishers. You have made me feel so welcome and valued and that means a lot.

Thanks to the authors and reviewers who have supported and continue to support my writing. The D20 authors who are brilliant cheerleaders, the SquadPod Collective – a brilliant set of reviewers, and 'The Fiction Café Book Club', 'The Motherload Book Club', 'The Friendly Book Community' and Anita Faulkner's 'Chic Lit and Prosecco' groups on Facebook.

Thanks to authors Nicola Gill, Isabelle Broom, Heidi Swain, Veronica Henry, Alex Brown and Tim Ewins, who have all read and reviewed books for me even when I know they have enormous TBRs to work through.

Thanks to my friends in France who have been there for me and shown me a different way of looking at life. And to those in England whom I don't get to see as much as I would like.

But most of all, thanks to tea. Without tea, none of this would have been possible…

MORE FROM GILLIAN HARVEY

We hope you enjoyed reading *A Month in Provence*. If you did, please leave a review.

If you'd like to gift a copy, this book is also available as an ebook, large print, hardback, digital audio download and audiobook CD.

Sign up to Gillian Harvey's mailing list for news, competitions and updates on future books.

https://bit.ly/GillianHarveyNews

Explore feel-good escapist reads from Gillian Harvey:

ABOUT THE AUTHOR

Gillian Harvey is a freelance journalist and the author of two well-reviewed women's fiction novels published by Orion. She has lived in Limousin, France for the past twelve years, from where she derives the inspiration and settings for her books.

Visit Gillian's Website:

https://www.gillianharvey.com/

Follow Gillian on social media:

twitter.com/GillPlusFive

facebook.com/gharveyauthor

instagram.com/gillplusfive

bookbub.com/profile/gillian-harvey

tiktok.com/@gillianharveyauthor

Boldw**oo**d

Boldwood Books is an award-winning fiction publishing company seeking out the best stories from around the world.

Find out more at www.boldwoodbooks.com

Join our reader community for brilliant books, competitions and offers!

Follow us
@BoldwoodBooks
@BookandTonic

Sign up to our weekly deals newsletter

https://bit.ly/BoldwoodBNewsletter

Printed in Great Britain
by Amazon